D0919801

Love in the Land of Barefoot Soldiers

Yucca Publishing books may be purchased in bulk at special discounts for sales promotion, corporate gifts, fund-raising, or educational purposes. Special editions can also be created to specifications. For details, contact the Special Sales Department, Yucca Publishing, 307 West 36th Street, 11th Floor, New York, NY 10018 or yucca@skyhorsepublishing.com.

Yucca Publishing® is an imprint of Skyhorse Publishing, Inc.®, a Delaware corporation.

Visit our website at www.yuccapub.com.

10 9 8 7 6 5 4 3 2 1

Library of Congress Cataloging-in-Publication Data is available on file.

Cover design by Yucca Publishing

Print ISBN: 978-1-63158-013-0
Ebook ISBN: 978-1-63158-030-7

Printed in the United States of America

Love in the Land of Barefoot Soldiers

A Novel

Frances Vieta

Horn of Africa - 1935

INTRODUCTION

Love in the Land of Barefoot Soldiers is a work of fiction. The names, characters, places, events and incidents are either the products of the author's imagination, or historical fact used in a fictitious manner. Except for well-known historical figures, any resemblance to actual persons, living or dead, or actual events is entirely coincidental.

Some people will wonder what the difference is between Ethiopia and Abyssinia. There is none. The confusion is historical: Ethiopia of classical times became Abyssinia in the Middle Ages and remained thus until the end of World War II. I have chosen to use Ethiopia, in almost all instances, because Haile Sellassie did the same. There are also many variations of the Ethiopian spellings of names and places. I used the ones Haile Sellassie used in his autobiography.

In 1935, Ethiopia, eight times as large as Italy and twice the size of France, was, save Liberia, the only independent country in Africa. Under Emperor Menilek II, she successfully withstood an Italian attempt to colonize in 1896 by annihilating an Italian army at the Battle of Adowa. The Italians never forgot that blow to their honor.

In 1935, there were fifty-two members of the League of Nations including both Ethiopia and Italy. The League had been created after World War I to prevent another major war. The U.S. never joined the League and by the time of this book, both Japan and Germany had withdrawn.

In November 1934, both Italians and Ethiopians died in a border clash at WalWal in the undemarcated no man's land between Ethiopia and Italian Somaliland. Despite the fact that WalWal was more than sixty miles inside Ethiopia, Italy demanded heavy retribution. Ethiopia requested arbitration through the League. Italy stalled, but continued to send armaments to her colonies, Eritrea and Italian Somaliland to the northeast and southeast of Ethiopia. The WalWal incident was to become Mussolini's pretext for conquest. His mind was long set.

CHAPTER 1

THE CLANGING OF THE anchor against the chains signaled the docking of the Royal Italian ship *Cesarea.* This was Djibouti in French Somaliland, an important port on the Red Sea along the Horn of Africa. It was May 30, 1935.

Ceseli Larson braced herself against the swaying deck as she focused her binoculars. Up on the hill a French flag jumped in the sea breeze above the governor's residence. *I have come so far*, she thought, as she saw for the first time a mere suggestion of tawny desert and the purplish mountains, her gateway to Ethiopia.

Crossing to the other side of the ship, she saw naked young boys diving for coins. She searched in her satchel for an Austrian silver *Thaler,* threw it high into the air and watched as one boy jumped up out of the water catching it in his outstretched hand as the sea green water fell away from his young body. He smiled his thanks, pantomiming with laughter and waving at her excitedly.

She waved back, while with considerable difficulty holding on to her wide-brimmed straw hat and felt tiny drops of sweat begin to drip from her hairline. She could feel the heat through the soles of her shoes as she watched the gangplank as it was put in place.

Going back to the dockside, she looked anxiously at the scene below searching for someone to signal her. She knew she had the habit of biting her lower lip when she was nervous and she wasn't surprised to be doing so now. *I'm not very hard to find*, she thought, *I'm the only woman disembarking.*

In fact, Ceseli Larson was not the kind of passenger one would expect to be disembarking from an Italian ship at a port on the Horn of Africa in 1935, but typical was hardly a way of describing this keen, intelligent and headstrong twenty-five year old. As the only child of the acclaimed international lawyer, Hamilton Larson, she was very much like him. Growing up without a mother, Ceseli had traveled extensively with her father from an early age and was equally at home in New York, London, Paris, and Geneva, speaking the languages of the fashionable salons in all of them.

She was raised to participate in a man's world with the same aspirations usually reserved for sons.

She had the brains to match her beauty. Educated at the best American schools, she majored in the classics and had chosen the University of Pennsylvania's well-respected school of archaeology for her graduate work. This choice was the result of her love of history and her many trips with her father to Greek and Roman ruins. Her motive for coming to the Horn of Africa was clear: despite the recent death of her father, she fully intended to pursue their carefully made plans to write her doctoral dissertation on the obelisks of Ethiopia's royal city of Axum.

She felt increasingly worried until she finally saw her name on a chalk board with a little bell waved in her direction. The man was jostling through the crowds that waited for the ship's passengers. Waving at him, she started down the swaying gangplank. At the bottom, he called out over the general shouts and yells of the porters and attendants.

"Mademoiselle Larson? I'm the Thomas Cooke travel agent, Henri. I have your ticket for the express train to Addis Ababa," he said, patting his vest pocket. "We can go straight to the station; it's not far. I'll carry that for the mademoiselle," he said, politely reaching for her satchel.

"Thank you, Henri, but I'll carry it myself. These are my cameras and I never let them out of my hands." He was quite stout, she saw, with a small dark goatee and ruddy complexion and he was wearing a sweat stained French kepi hat. She tried not to notice his tobacco stained teeth.

"As you wish, mademoiselle. I have arranged for your luggage to be brought directly to the train. Now, this way please," he said, cheerfully leading her off through the crowd.

She hitched her canvas camera satchel onto her shoulder and followed him. "Henri, is it always this hot?" she yelled above the din in the streets.

"At times, the sand fleas, the flies and the heat are unbearable. I'd like to say you get used to it, mademoiselle," he called back, shrugging, "but you never do. That's the price for living in the 'Queen of the Sands'."

"That's what you call this place?" Ceseli asked, as she passed the towering cones of sea salt that lined the dock entrance, the only product of this tiny French enclave. She followed him through the hundreds of hustling ebony-skinned stevedores who were now unloading the ship. They stared at her and made her feel uncomfortable and she was aware of the fact that she would soon be all alone, a stranger in a foreign land.

The street narrowed abruptly as they left the dock area as she followed him through a shortcut that was dark after the blaring light of the port. It was cooler here, but smelly, and flies seemed to land on her face with great regularity. She brushed them aside with one hand while she held tightly to her camera bag with the other.

As she hastened to keep up with him, she was jostled to and fro by the men and women in the crowded street. The women, wearing brightly colored head scarves, were laughing and bumping each other while the men in blue, tan, and black *jellabiya* seemed to be walking hurriedly ahead. There were small children everywhere and they were pointing at her. She felt increasingly uneasy in these unfamiliar surroundings.

She saw the whitewashed stone and mud buildings squeezed between formal Ottoman style ones with their okra walls and green trim. On the other side of the street were shops brightly painted in light blue, yellow, green, and pink. There was a long line of people outside a small shop and she wondered what they were selling. *Bread*, she thought, noticing how peacefully the shoppers waited.

At a shop on the left, a man was sitting on a three-legged wooden stool which he had pushed back at a precarious angle, but it didn't seem like he was going to fall. From the minaret of a tall white mosque, the lilting voice of a muezzin was calling the faithful Muslims to prayer. His sing-song voice was new to her inquisitive ears.

"We're almost there, mademoiselle," Henri yelled back over his shoulder as they neared a long rectangular shed made of cement blocks and corrugated iron that served as a train station. Inside there was such confusion that she found it difficult to keep up with him. The high ceiling gave some relief from the heat, but not from the smell that she would come to know as the smell of East Africa. It tickled her nose as she tried to decipher it: a pungent mix of disinfectant, sweat, garbage, animal fur, urine, and sewage combined.

After the extensive studies she had made on dress and physical characteristics, Ceseli found that she was easily able to distinguish among the indigenous peoples: the slender Danakil, almost naked in their short desert loincloths, the Amara and Galla tribes intermixed with Arabs. A few wore leopard skins. One tall imposing man, with his lion's mane headdress and long cape, she recognized as being a *Fitaurari,* or provincial governor. A young boy held his leather shield and ceremonial fly-whisk which served as a symbol of rank. Another man dressed in a simple khaki uniform carried the governor's broad-brimmed sun hat. The Fitaurari was boarding a train car with a large entourage of well-armed men. Most of them scampered up onto the roof using toe holds that were imperceptible to her untrained eye.

"Over here, mademoiselle," Henri beckoned. "*Icí* is the waiting area for the first class!"

Large wooden crosses identified two Catholic missionaries with their ankle length white cotton robes. Several of the other men looked Mediterranean, Greek or perhaps Turkish. A few were Arabs with their flowing white jellabiya, and several were well-dressed Africans in British tailored slacks and office jackets. One man stood out from all the other Africans, not only because of his white linen suit, but also for his strikingly blue eyes and honey complexion. *He is extremely good looking,* she thought. She also noticed, with some apprehension, that among these first class passengers, she was again the only woman traveler.

The conductor's shrill whistle blow signaled that the first class passengers should board. Ceseli followed Henri out to the train and the travel agent led her to a compartment at the very end of the first class car and waited for the porter in his starched khaki uniform and perky red fez. Around his waist was a wide red sash and hanging from that a large key ring that held several huge keys that seemed to be relics dating back to King Arthur. As the porter opened the compartment door, she noticed his holster and revolver. He had a wide scar running from his right ear to his chin. None of the stubbly dark hair of his beard grew along the scar line.

"Thank you, Abdullah," Henri said pleasantly to the porter. "This is Mademoiselle Larson; she is going to Addis," he said as he handed over the tickets. "When you exchange places with your Ethiopian colleague, please urge him to take special care of her, *n'est pas*?"

"Mademoiselle Larson," Abdullah said in his heavily accented, but understandable French. "*Bienvenue.*"

"*Mercí,*" Ceseli smiled at him.

Turning back to Ceseli, Henri changed his tone to one of concern. "We put you in the last car because you don't get the stench of the engine. I hope that was right," he said, looking around. "Someone is meeting you in Addis, I'm sure. Women don't travel alone in this part of the world, you know."

"I'll be fine, Henri. They do know I'm coming. My godfather is the American minister in Addis and he will meet me. Thank you for all your help."

"The boxes contain your food and water," Henri said, pointing to several string tied cardboard boxes on the rack above the window. "We didn't know what you'd like so we gave you several choices. Your trunk will be on board; do not worry." He took her satchel and put it on the wooden slats that overhung the window.

"That's very kind," Ceseli said, looking at the bleakness of the compartment. "You don't have to wait. I'll be fine," she added, mustering more conviction than she felt. "Oh, Henri, I'll be coming back in a few weeks."

"Just wire the office, Mademoiselle, and I'll meet you. It shouldn't be long now. Maybe ten minutes, or fifteen at most," he said, checking his watch. "Why was the ship so late?"

"We took several hours longer than scheduled unloading in Massawa," she said, handing him a generous tip.

"The war I suppose," he said, saluting as he climbed down off the train. "Please lock the door." His warning only reinforced the trepidation she was feeling.

Ceseli looked around the small compartment of the express train that would carry her through five hundred miles of feudal, landlocked Ethiopia. The railroad, the brainchild of a Swiss engineer who worked for Emperor Menilek II at the end of the nineteenth century, had been seen as a way to connect the capital of Addis Ababa with the Djibouti port in French Somaliland. Work on the railroad began in 1897 and was finished in 1918. Because of the complexity of the undertaking that spanned a desert inhabited by warlike tribes not wanting to have their caravan trading threatened, only one track was laid, meaning that the train went only to Addis and then came back.

She noted the two worn coach chairs facing each other at the sides of the large window. They were so bleached that it was difficult to guess what the original color might have been, but now they were a sort of an ochre tinge. She remembered her father's advice: "The past is done, you can't undo it, choose the future, be creative." So Ceseli chose the seat facing forward.

She leaned out the large open window and looking along the train, noticed her trunk being loaded into the baggage car along with six of what looked like shipping crates for grand pianos.

The shrill whistle blew again and now the second and third class passengers thronged to board the train pushing and shoving to get through the narrow gate before climbing up into the cars. All of them seemed to be carrying large bundles tied with rope, some balanced precariously on their heads. Children squirmed in every direction. One withered old lady was carrying a live chicken, its legs tied to her belt, its beady eyes looking terrified in its upside down position. Armed guards climbed up onto the roof. Some seemed to be right over her head.

Abdullah pulled closed the doors to her compartment, slamming them shut with a dull thud. Ceseli turned the lock into place from the inside. The train whistle blew again. As the train started to move out of the station, she watched a gray-blue baboon grudgingly relinquish its seat on the rail.

Turning to look back toward the end of the train, she saw a man sprinting along the platform chasing after the train. He carried a small black bag in his left hand. He was catching up and instinctively she jumped back from the window as the bag came plunging through it. She watched, aghast and fascinated, as the man grabbed the handgrips on either side of the window and jumped onto the narrow step. He was hanging suspended above the tracks as the train gained speed. Slowly, he pulled himself up, steadied himself, and then climbed in through the open window.

"*Scusatemi*," he said, panting as he turned to her. "I don't usually climb in windows, but the next train is in two days and it's not an express. Is this place taken?" he asked, still out of breath.

"Maybe you should ask the porter," Ceseli answered, shocked by this new event.

"I will," he said, putting his bag on the shelf above. Then, without asking, he closed the window.

She felt extremely annoyed at this intrusion. Wasn't this her compartment? And he didn't even bother to ask her if he could close her window.

"It's hot, but the wind and dust make it worse. Trust me. It'll cool down when the sun sets. I'm Marco Antinori. I'm a doctor at the Italian hospital in Addis Ababa."

"Ceseli Larson," she replied, piqued at his arrogance.

"Glad to meet you. And thank you for your open window. If it had been closed I would have to wait another two days. That's not an ideal way to use my time."

Abdullah opened the door and looked at this young white man. He seemed unsure of what to do as Dr. Antinori fumbled in his pocket for his crumpled ticket.

"Is this seat taken?" Marco asked him.

"Mademoiselle?" Abdullah looked at her clearly apprehensive. He knew he was under Henri's orders to guard her at all costs.

"*Va bien*, Abdullah," she said, reassuring him. He took Dr. Antinori's ticket, checked it and handed it back before leaving the compartment.

Marco Antinori sat down in front of her.

Well, she thought, *if someone is going to climb in my window, it's nice that he's so handsome*. He had a warm genuine smile, she saw, and lively gray-blue eyes. He was tall, and slender unlike most of the Italians she knew in New York, who were often from the south of Italy. He was wearing a blue short sleeve shirt, khaki shorts and long khaki socks slipping out of heavy leather sandals. *He doesn't look like a doctor*, she thought, *but then what does an Italian doctor in Africa look like?* The only doctor she knew was Dr. Hunt, who had cured her childhood illnesses with chicken noodle soup, soda crackers, and daily doses of cod's liver oil.

"You're going to Addis?"

"Yes, but only on my way to Axum. I'm an archaeologist and I'm writing my dissertation on the obelisks of the ancient Kingdom of Sheba."

"Sheba?"

"As in King Solomon and the Queen of Sheba."

"Oh, that Sheba. Axum is supposed to be a very beautiful place. You're not going alone?"

"I'm not sure. My godfather is arranging it. He's the American minister to Ethiopia."

"But surely he won't send you alone. Beautiful young women don't travel alone in a country like this. Any woman for that matter. It's too dangerous. Surely, you've been told that."

"I have, yes. My father and I had planned to come together," she said, pausing. "But he died recently. I knew he would want me to come anyway."

"My condolences," Marco said, holding her gaze. "How did it happen?"

"He was giving a speech at the League of Nations in Geneva and he just fell over and died."

"A heart attack. That must have been very hard for you. It's easy on the person who goes, but very hard on the family."

"They said he didn't suffer. I was in New York at the time. That's where I live."

"He didn't suffer, I'm sure, but that doesn't make it easier to accept. You're sure he'd want you to travel around this *desolato* country alone?"

"I am sure," she said, with more conviction than she was feeling.

"That's very brave of you. I hope you know best."

Ceseli turned to look out the window, breathing deeply, trying to control her emotions. *Funny*, she thought, *there is a kindness about him, a sort of compassion and such expressive eyes. Don't be silly. There is nothing more in those eyes than in any others.* But as strange as it was, she was talking to him as if she had known him all her life. She had just told him about her father as if it were not the most painful thing she'd ever had to live with.

Now out the window, she could see a gently ascending tawny desert stretching to the horizon, broken here and there by outcroppings of huge rocks. In the distance was a red spiral joining the desert with the sky and she saw a long line of camels, tied from head to tail, patiently following each other with large packs on their humps.

"That's a sand tornado," Marco said, pointing to the cone of sand. "You see a lot of them, and that's a caravan carrying salt. The nomads take it to the highlands, where it's worth its weight in gold. The Afar people live out there. They're very tough and very jealous of their salt pans and of course their watering holes. A man would die quickly without water when the temperature reaches one hundred and thirty degrees."

"The National Geographic says it's the hottest place on earth. It's supposed to be five hundred feet below sea level," Ceseli added. "How do they live in such heat?"

"The body adapts. They raise sheep, goats, and camels. They adapt, too. You're American?" Marco asked.

"Yes, I am. And your English is very good."

"I went to a British school in Florence. That's where I live. Do you know Florence?"

"I went there with my father when I was twelve. He was attending an archaeological conference. That was one of his passions. My father told me I needed some culture so we went to all the favorite tourist places: Ponte Vecchio, the Uffizi, and the Duomo. It's a beautiful city."

"My father was probably there. He's a doctor and an expert on Renaissance gardens. We live just above the city in Fiesole. My father knows where every plant and tree comes from, and what it can be used for," he smiled. "I guess that's why I got so interested in tropical medicine. I used to curl up in his big old leather chair and read his books on Africa. I've never tired of that," he smiled. "You see, it's getting cooler."

It was getting cooler she realized as she took down her satchel and pulled out a well-worn navy sweater. As she pulled it on she thought she could feel his eyes on her. The sweater was much too large for her slender body, but it had been her father's favorite and she liked to wear it.

She settled back into the chair wondering what this handsome young man would be like. Outside, the evening light accentuated the panorama with heavy shadows. She noticed a Danakil herdsman standing with one leg crooked into the knee of the other, heron-like, and etched against the setting magenta sun. Then, in a heartbeat, it was dark.

Ceseli closed her eyes, and lulled by the rhythmic clickity-clack of metal against metal, fell into a deep sleep.

CHAPTER 2

AT DAWN, THE TRAIN entered Ethiopia and as if by magic the scenery changed dramatically to black volcanic stone and sand with an almost apocalyptic feel about it. This was the Danakil desert.

The abrupt breaking of the train woke her. Ceseli rubbed her eyes and saw that Marco was still sleeping. Looking out the window she saw a huge wooden water tank perched on the cut off stump of a very old Wansa tree. Other Wansa trees were on all sides of what she was assuming must be an oasis. She saw the men attaching a hose from the train to the water tank. She wondered if it was safe to get off the train, decided it was and climbed down closing the door quietly behind her.

Despite the early hour, native hawkers were offering bite-size pieces of raw sheep and goat meat, small eggs, scrawny chickens, and the milk from camels or goats carried in animal skin bags. Other hawkers sold cactus pears, tea, coffee, and sugar cane. There was a lot of talking and haggling going on, but she could not understand most of it.

Ceseli walked over to a short young woman selling coffee in tin cups. The woman wore a clean *shamma* and had a small baby strapped on her back. Fumbling in her pocket for change she noticed an African man smiling at her as he gave the woman some coins.

"*Endemen Adersh*, Miss Larson."

"*Awo Semeshehen Awekalehu*."

"Yes. I do know your name. Please let me."

Ceseli remembered seeing him at the train station in Djibouti in an immaculate white suit, now rumpled. He had removed the jacket and now wore a safari style blue cotton shirt that emphasized his strikingly blue eyes. He had a slender aquiline nose and a light, coffee-colored complexion. His hair was short and straight.

"Thank you, but I have money," she said, taking the hot tin cup and juggling it from hand to hand.

"My treat this time. If we walk over there we can sit down. I know you Americans are good at balancing plates and cups, but I like to sit."

"And you know I'm American?" Ceseli asked, following him to a long makeshift table made from wide rough boards with five chairs around it. There was a huge Wansa tree next to it providing shade from the burning sun even at this early hour.

"That your name is Ceseli Larson and that you've come from Naples. My name is Yifru."

"Yifru," Ceseli said, trying out the name. She knew that Ethiopians have only one name and that most of them have a meaning. "What does Yifru mean?"

"Let them be afraid of him."

"And are they?"

"Only those I want to be," he laughed easily.

"I see." She sipped the coffee. "It's strong, isn't it?"

"Coffee comes from Ethiopia. From the Kafa region. That's why it got the name."

"I didn't know."

"It's a well-kept secret," he said. "What brings you to Ethiopia? Spying for the Italians?"

"Nothing so dramatic," she laughed. "I'm an archaeologist. I'm doing my dissertation on the obelisks at Axum."

"Well, you've come to the right place, but it would make a perfect cover," he said, winking at her as he sipped the coffee.

"Yes, it would," she smiled over the rim of the cup.

"You'll need special permission from the emperor for any travel outside Addis. He won't let foreigners travel in his country without his permission."

"Oh." She frowned. "I didn't know that. I just assumed that if I could get all the way to Ethiopia, then I could get to Axum, too."

"Not anymore. Where are you from?"

"New York."

"I know New York. I studied law at Columbia for three years."

"I don't suppose there were very many other East Africans at Columbia."

"You're right. And yes, I had a difficult time fitting in, but I went there for the education and that was excellent."

"Did you like New York?"

"I was homesick. Three years is a long time to be so far from home, especially when the culture is so different. But I was lucky. One of my professors took me in. I spent a lot of time at his house. He and his family were very good to me."

"Your family must be very rich."

"Not at all. The emperor paid for it. He wants his advisers to have the best education they can get."

"You must know him well."

"I'm his personal assistant. The Keeper of the Pen."

"The Keeper of the Pen? For the emperor? For Haile Sellassie?"

"Yes, for Haile Sellassie. It means that I have to write his correspondence and keep a record of everything he signs."

"Oh," Ceseli said, at a loss for words.

"You came through Naples?" Yifru asked.

"I was only in Naples long enough to get off my ship from New York and get on the one coming to Djibouti."

"Is it true the wharf is full of troops and equipment?"

"It was very busy. It's an Italian ship and it was completely full. Most of the soldiers got off in Massawa in Eritrea."

"I know Massawa and it must have been just as busy."

"There were dozens of ships waiting to unload. That's why we were so late getting to Djibouti. The ship went on to Italian Somaliland."

"Another Italian stronghold. We're very much surrounded. The young man you're traveling with, he's Italian?"

"He's a doctor at the Italian hospital in Addis. But we're not traveling together. Just going to the same place."

"I thought I recognized his face. There aren't that many foreigners in Addis. It's a good hospital and we are grateful for it. Where are you going?"

"My godfather is the American minister in Addis. He's meeting me at the station."

"Ah, Rutherford. I know him well. You'll be in good hands."

Ceseli smelled the strong odor of goat and sweat. Turning, she saw a tall native man with a pet kid goat trailing behind him. He wore a bright red woolen toga and carried a long spear. His frizzy hair was matted and bleached to a glorious Titian red.

"It's plaster of lime," Yifru explained. "He puts it in his hair to kill the lice. He's an Afar. The Afars are nomads and salt harvesters who live between here and the Great Danakil Depression."

"I've read about them," Ceseli replied quietly as she saw a young girl perhaps eight years old peeking out behind the man.

Her eyes were almost black beneath beautifully curved eyebrows and her dark skin and delicate features attested to her Hamitic ancestry. She wore a red woolen toga and her hair was braided tightly around her head in small herringbone patterns with beads at the tips.

Ceseli's eyes met the girl's. Watching Ceseli's face from the corner of her eye, the girl approached and put a hesitant finger on her skin. Ceseli held herself very still, fearing that she might frighten her. The girl reached up to touch her blond hair.

"She's probably never seen a white woman," Yifru said, turning to the young girl.

The girl pushed the skin on Ceseli's arm, making white spots appear under her tanned skin. She pulled the light golden hair on her arm and cocked her head slightly as she gazed into Ceseli's blue eyes.

"Her hair is dressed in ghee, a clarified butter that protects her from the glaring sun. Men often tease their hair out to halo their heads."

The train whistle startled the girl. The moment was destroyed and the girl stepped back. Yifru stood up and took the two empty cups, almost tripping over a very big man intent on taking photographs.

Climbing back onto the train, Ceseli was joined by a very thin Ethiopian porter wearing Abdullah's same starched khaki uniform.

"Mademoiselle, welcome to Ethiopia", he said in French, his clipped pronunciation turning his t's into z's. "Please keep this door locked, if you need anything just ask me. My name is Tariku."

"Thank you, Tariku," she said climbing into her compartment.

She was surprised to see that Marco was still asleep. *His hair is brown and curly and soft, and he looks like a sweetly tousled Renaissance angel,* she thought. *One that Raphael or Leonardo might have painted.*

When the train actually started, she was amazed that the clanking and chugging did not waken him nor did the noise she heard herself making opening the window so she could take some photographs.

Through her camera's lens she watched as a flock of wild guinea fowl whirred up near the window of the train. She caught her first sight of the dik-dik, the tiny antelopes not much bigger than small dogs that, scared by the passing train, jumped in and out of the bush. Far out to the right she saw a herd of antelope grazing. The oncoming train set them leaping and careening away. In the distance, a herd of giraffe was running in their rocking-chair gallop, their long necks like sunflowers, waving in the wind.

Closing the window, she took a leather book out of her satchel and began to read. This was her bible, the book that contained everything she had put together about Ethiopia, King Solomon and the Queen of Sheba. It had started out as a journal, but over time all kinds of vital information had been added like the National Geographic description of the Danakil desert and even a recipe for *injera,* the pancake like bread from an Ethiopian restaurant in New York.

"What are you reading?" Marco asked, yawning as he straightened up in his chair

"The *Kebra Negast*. It's the story of King Solomon and Makeda, the Queen of Sheba. It's about how Solomon seduced Makeda and how their son, Menilek, stole the Ark of the Covenant and took it to Axum."

"You read Amharic?"

"My father thought it was a sign of respect to be able to speak to someone in his own language. I learned a little Amharic to come to Ethiopia."

"I've tried to learn it so I can speak with the patients, but I'm not so good. And the rest?"

"A little of everything. I call it my bible. If you're hungry have one of my boxes."

"Thanks. And you?"

"I'll have the water for now." She stood up to stretch and look out the window. Suddenly, she caught the sound of distant shots. She heard a screeching sound of metal grinding against metal as the train ground to a halt and the lurching motion catapulted her sharply against the window. She crashed backward to the floor hitting her head hard on the armrest of her chair. Outside there were more rifle shots.

"Are you okay?" Marco asked, kneeling down next to her. "Can you hear me?"

"Yes," she moaned, her head in her hands.

"You understand me?"

She tried to nod, but couldn't speak.

"How many fingers?"

"Three," she whispered.

"And now?"

"Still three, Doctor."

The rifle fire was intensifying and it was now on all sides of them. The pitter patters of a machine gun seemed just over her head and mixed with yells and screams of the passengers along the length of the train. The women in the closest car were crying out and wailing.

A heavy rapping on their compartment door startled them. "Miss Larson, lock this door and don't come out. And keep away from the window." Ceseli recognized the voice as Yifru's.

"What's going on?" Marco yelled.

"I don't know," Yifru yelled back, running along the corridor.

Marco rose to lock the door and window.

"What's happening?" Ceseli asked.

"I'm not sure. The people around here often derail the train. They think its great fun," he said, reassuringly. "They also take down the telegraph lines. They use the copper wire for amulets and trinkets. I think we'll be fine, if we stay put. The head still hurt?" he asked, as he got his medical bag down from the rack.

"Not as much, but I feel like I have cotton inside it. What kind of amulets?"

"The kind that magically protect you. It depends on what you believe. Rabbit's feet, the cross, St. Christopher, there are all kinds of them. You're going to get a nasty bump there. I'm sorry, but this is going to sting," he said, as he knelt and started to clean the area on the side of her head.

"Ouch. Take down the wires?" she asked, trying to mask her feeling of uneasiness at his physical closeness. "That must make communications difficult."

"Just wait till you get to Addis. The lines can be down for hours, even days," he said, trying to downplay the intensity of the gunfire outside.

"I suppose you use carrier pigeons? The way they did in World War I."

"No need. Nothing ever happens. How's the head now, Miss Larson?"

The rifle fire had become more sporadic and finally ceased altogether. Marco got up, opened the window and looked out.

"You think that's safe? He said to keep the window locked," she said, but joined him nonetheless. In the front of the train, she could see that there was an animal trussed up on the rails. Toward the end of the train they could see a truck next to the train. The heavy knocking on their compartment door interrupted them.

"It's okay now," Yifru said. "Just some local bandits. We'll be starting again shortly. Doctor, I wonder if you could help us? There are several injuries."

"Of course," Marco said, grabbing his black bag.

"Maybe I can help," Ceseli said, following him out of the compartment.

"You don't feel dizzy?" Marco asked, over his shoulder.

"I think I'm fine," she said, as the two of them followed Yifru toward the front of the train. Many of the passengers were now crowded near the first wagon anxious not to miss a show that might prove interesting. They were surrounded by a mass of inquisitive people. *I wonder if they're more interested in the wounded men or at the two of us,* she thought

Yifru pushed through to where three men were lying on the ground. Marco knelt next to one after the other, evaluating their wounds. "Do you know anything about first aid, Miss Larson?"

"Basic Red Cross."

"Then take this and put a tourniquet around his arm. We need to stop the bleeding. Then I'll remove the bullet."

Ceseli took the strip of cloth he handed her and wrapped it around the man's arm just below the shoulder and held it as the blood slowed. She squinted against the sun as Yifru stooped down next to them.

"Can I help?" he asked.

"You can keep the audience back," Marco said, as he threaded a needle.

She was not going to be sick at the sight of blood, she told herself, fighting the impulse to retch. She managed to hold the tourniquet as Marco extracted the bullet and started to suture. The man's eyes were locked on Marco's hand and he never grimaced from the pain of the stitches.

"He'll have an ugly scar, but that will probably improve his reputation." Marco smiled at his patient as he cleaned the needle and put it back into his bag. "Tell him that he should get those stitches cut out in a week. He can come to the hospital. I'd be glad to see him."

"I'll remember this," Yifru said, signaling some of the guards to help the injured man up onto the train. Three of the guards in their khaki uniforms with rifles across their backs came forward to help. The other two men had only superficial wounds, and they were taken care of quickly. Soon the train was ready to resume the trip.

CHAPTER 3

"That was very impressive," Ceseli said, after they returned to their compartment. "You've had good training."

Marco shrugged, but seemed pleased by her approval. "I don't do a lot of that, Miss Larson . . ."

"Don't call me Miss Larson, please. It's so formal and I'm not formal at all. Call me Ceseli."

"Si, Ceseli, I don't do a lot of this. I work with tropical diseases. I'm that ultra-idealist who wants to discover the vaccine against malaria. Then we can get it out of Italy."

"I didn't know there was malaria in Italy."

"South of Rome, all along the coast where the Pontine Marshes used to be. It's been a problem for thousands of years. Julius Caesar thought of reversing the Tiber River into the marshes to flush them out. Several popes had plans too, but Mussolini has done it. Several thousand families live there now."

Ceseli smiled thinking of Mussolini, known as Il Duce, who had been the Italian dictator since 1922. He was openly caricatured in the American press, credited with getting the Italian trains to run on time and for draining marshes, but not much else. *Just my luck,* Ceseli thought, *an ardent young Fascist.*

"And there's malaria even in Rome," Marco continued. "Near the Coliseum."

"Roman Fever, right? Has Mussolini been draining that area, too?"

"Trying to."

"Does that make him feel like Caesar?"

Marco looked around. "Whether one likes it or not, he is our elected leader and everyone in Italy is now a Fascist whether they want to be or not. My family is not Fascist, but that means very little."

Ceseli looked across at him and decided not to continue. She knew what her father would say: Don't argue when you're up against a wall.

Their conversation was interrupted by the heavy knocking on the compartment door. Marco went to the door, and unlocked it. Tariku, the porter, was trying to restrain a man twice his height and at least four times his weight from breaking open the door. Without waiting for an invitation, the man pushed his way inside.

"Mademoiselle Larson," the porter looked at her in exasperation. "Help me!"

Ceseli looked at Bruno Zeri realizing he was the man she had seen photographing at the watering station. "It's okay, Tariku. You can wait outside."

"Congratulations, Doctor," the intruder began." My name is Bruno Zeri. I'm a journalist with the *Corriere della Sera*. That's a Milan paper," he said, turning to include Ceseli. "I'm actually based in Rome, which is where I'm from. I apologize for my English, *signorina*."

Ceseli looked at this man carefully. Bruno she knew was the Italian word for brown and often a name. Zeri was very tall and he did look somewhat like a large, gruff brown bear. A gladiator, perhaps, or the statue of some Roman nobleman with his swarthy skin, abundant black curly hair and penetrating dark brown eyes. But the statues she was thinking of were of marble and they had nothing to do with the animation of his long slender hands as he spoke. His beard was long and in need of a trim, his clothes were rumpled and the blue cotton pants were extremely baggy, although Ceseli didn't know whether it was the style, some recent diet, or just from sleeping in them. His light blue shirt looked well-worn around the collar. The sleeves were rolled up revealing powerful arms. Around his neck were a silver chain and a Star of David. An unlit cigar hung from his lip.

"My paper has sent me here to do some background stories about Ethiopia," he said, looking at Marco.

"What kind of stories?"

"Local color. Like what you just did. 'Young Italian doctor in the wilds of Africa.' Saving that guy. That kind of story."

"I extracted a bullet. It was not life threatening. I can't see how that would be of much interest."

"Let's talk about you for a moment," Zeri smiled. "Judging from your accent, you're from Tuscany."

Marco smiled at Ceseli before answering. "Florence. I guess that gives us something in common. I see you smoke Tuscan cigars."

"*Toscani* are my favorite," Bruno smiled, chewing on the unlit cigar. "And your name?"

"Marco Antinori."

"As in the Florentine vineyards? The best Chianti wine in Italy?"

Marco shrugged in reply.

"Where did you study medicine, Antinori?" Zeri asked, writing in a small pocket-sized notebook.

"In Bologna. I graduated in 1930. I spent two years at the hospital there. Another in Florence, and I've been in Ethiopia almost two years."

"How did you get here?"

"I volunteered. I'm at the Italian hospital in Addis."

"Are there other Italian doctors?"

"Three."

"Do you treat many Ethiopians?"

"That's why the hospital was started. But most of my time is in research. Smallpox, malaria, typhus, and cholera."

"I read that Emperor Menilek had a pox-scarred face."

"Si, I think that's true."

"Do you find it difficult to treat Ethiopians when we are facing the probability of war?" Zeri asked, with his pencil poised.

"I'm a doctor. My duty is to heal. I'm not a politician and I have very little patience for politics. I'm trying to find a cure for malaria. If that happens, it will benefit both the Ethiopians and the Italians. Now if you'll excuse me, I'd like to spend these next few hours practicing English."

Zeri seemed to get the hint, snapped shut his notebook and stood. "I admire your work, doctor. And your politics. *Arrivederci,* signorina," he said as he pulled open the heavy door and then let it slam after him.

As Zeri walked back to his own compartment he couldn't help wondering what a Florentine aristocrat was doing working as a doctor in Ethiopia. It was something he was curious to explore.

Ceseli turned back to look out the window. Bruno Zeri intimidated her, she knew, but besides his physical size, she couldn't decide why that should be. He was a journalist and her father had told her that there is a very strong censor in Fascist Italy, but certainly it wasn't that. He was clearly Jewish, but she lived in New York and it couldn't be that either. That he was Italian? Marco didn't intimidate her at all. She felt at home with him. Was that because he was a doctor with what her father would refer to as a bedside manner? He was also refined, perhaps that was it. Whatever it was, she felt vulnerable in Zeri's company and she didn't in Marco's.

"Shall we eat?" Ceseli asked. "I'm starved."

"*Certamente*, let's see what we've got," he said, reaching for the cardboard boxes.

"Start with the box on the bottom, please."

"Why?"

"I think it was the travel agent's first choice."

"That's a good enough reason," Marco said as he handed the first to Ceseli.

"Wow. He said there was some choice, but look at this," she said, showing him the box. "Canned meat, hard-boiled eggs, bread, crackers, cheese, canned pate. Now I am impressed!"

"Is there a can opener?"

"Do I detect a bit of sarcasm in that question?" she asked, looking at his rueful grin. "Yes, there is a can opener and napkins and plates, forks and knives."

"Let's try this one too," Marco said, handing her the next.

"Eggs again, another canned meat, but a different kind. Let's leave one of the boxes for Tariku," Ceseli suggested.

"That's a nice gesture. What did you think of Zeri?"

"Not sure," she answered, with her mouth full of bread. "Seems a far-fetched subject for an article."

"I just hope he doesn't embellish it too much. I don't want readers back home to get the idea that I'm an ardent Fascist. Do you want to try this meat?"

"What is it?"

"I can't answer that, I'm afraid. But someone went to the trouble of canning it and your travel agent put it in your box, so it must be edible. And if you get sick, you have a doctor with you." He paused, and she felt he was about to say something about Fascism.

"Can I ask you something?" he began. "Is Ceseli a real name?"

"Probably not in the way you mean. When I was born, both of my grandmothers wanted me named for them. Daddy couldn't decide whether it should be Frances or Elizabeth. He compromised. Ceseli. Why did you choose to come to Ethiopia?" she asked as she cracked the shell of one of the eggs.

"My father always wanted to live in Africa, but my mother wouldn't leave Florence. I thought I could do some good. Ethiopia desperately needs doctors. So I volunteered. I've got another six months." He paused.

"This is actually pretty good," he said, handing to her half of the canned meat.

"Florence will be pretty tame after Ethiopia."

"I'll get used to it. I'll go home and marry my high school sweetheart. One of them that is" he said, smiling mischievously. "And have a hundred children."

"Sounds like Solomon," Ceseli laughed. "With his four hundred queens and six hundred concubines."

"Well, maybe not a hundred. Five or six."

"I'm sure you'll be a wonderful father. Five or five hundred."

Since Djibouti, the train had climbed steeply up the western rim of the Ethiopian Great Rift Valley, where the volcanic lava flow from Mt. Fautalle spread over the plain. It worked its way up the six thousand foot escarpment through hidden valleys from the Akaki River Valley past the crater lakes of the Bishoftu hills to emerge onto an eight thousand foot plateau. Soon the train picked up speed, entering a gentle plain surrounded by a lush forest of eucalyptus. In the distance, across a vast rolling, grassy plain, Ceseli could see Addis Ababa crowned by Mount Entoto.

The Ethiopian flag waved jauntily on the red tiled roof as the train pulled into the yellow stucco and brick station. *I'm here,* she thought, *I've arrived at Addis Ababa.*

CHAPTER 4

"NOT SO BAD," MARCO said, stretching and pulling the window down. "But I'm glad it was the express."

"Now you can understand why I had to catch this train. I'll pass our bags out through the window," he said, as the train lurched to a final stop.

"You seem to like windows much better than doors," Ceseli laughed and climbed down off the train. Once outside the window, she had her satchel in her arms and steadied it, but as she drew it down to her she realized it was being taken out of her hands. She turned almost tripping over a slender young man standing on the platform next to her.

"Welcome to Addis, Miss Larson. I'm Standish Forsythe. I work with Minister Rutherford. He sent me to fetch you. Is this all the luggage?"

"No. There's also a steamer trunk, I'm afraid."

In the meantime, Marco had come up beside her with his black medical bag. "This is Dr. Marco Antinori. He's a doctor at the Italian hospital. And--"

"Standish Forsythe," Standish answered. "Do you need a ride into town, Doctor?"

"No, someone from the hospital will be here. They meet every train. Ceseli, nice meeting you. Please, drop by the hospital and let me look at that head."

"I'm fine, I'm sure, and again thank you," she said, watching him turn and walk away. A feeling of loneliness came over her. He had seemed like a protector, like her father, and now he, too, was leaving.

"Thank you for your help," she said, turning back to Mr. Forsythe.

"What's this about your head?"

"We had a rendezvous with some bandits and I fell badly. Dr. Antinori thought I might have a concussion. It was extremely exciting. Bandits and trussed up animals to stop the train. Thankfully there were a lot of guards and they beat them off."

"It happens a lot. You're lucky it was the express. When I came for the emperor's coronation in 1930, the ride took three days. We didn't travel at night because of the bandits. We stayed in rather primitive hotels and ate cold Greek food, but I got here," he smiled.

"I'm glad things have improved."

He was of medium height, she saw with a shock of light brown unruly hair slicked back from his forehead. The sun was glinting so against his steel-rimmed granny glasses that she had difficulty seeing the hazel color of his eyes. He wore a light blue shirt that was peeking out from under a safari jacket.

The same first class travelers she had seen in Djibouti were now climbing down from the train and jostling each other on the narrow platform anxious to enter the small station and to exit on the other side.

As Ceseli looked into the crowd of passengers, she saw Yifru approaching and to her surprise, Standish and Yifru hugged each other, Russian style, like two upright grizzly bears.

"Welcome back. I didn't know you'd be on this train," Standish said, still holding both his hands. "We missed you."

"I got finished earlier than planned and managed to catch the express. Hello again, Miss Larson," he said, turning to her. "Standish's father was my professor at Columbia. You'll need to see the emperor about that trip to Axum. Drop by and see me when you come to the palace. By the way, how's the head?"

"Just a little sore. I'll be fine."

"Good. We can't have our archaeologist laid up before she even gets started. See you soon, Standish," he said, walking out of the station.

Standish reached for her satchel. "Thanks, but they're my cameras. I'm used to carrying them."

The smell of disinfectant was overpowering reminding her of the new smell of Africa. She followed him into the station, and as soon as her eyes adjusted to the darkness, she saw the bales of hides and skins, stacks of coffee bags, and piles of elephant tusks that were ready for the return trip to Djibouti. They would be replaced by the incoming bales of imported American bleached cotton ready to be sewn into the traditional white shamma, the toga like clothing all Ethiopians have worn since the period of the Kingdom of Axum.

Off to one side, workers were unloading the six piano crates straining with the weight, their bodies glistening with sweat as the crates were transferred up onto a heavy duty open truck ready to be pulled by a team of four oxen.

Outside, in the brilliant sunshine in front of the station she looked up at a magnificent gilded statue of a lion with its Ethiopian scepter and sword.

"What's that?"

"Beautiful, isn't it? It's the Lion of Judah. One of Haile Sellassie's many titles. The statue was a gift to the emperor from the railroad company in honor of his coronation. The scepter and sword are his heraldic signs."

A long string of brown plateau camels tied neck-to-tail were sleeping contemptuously on their flat feet to the left of the station. They seemed to pay no heed as their handlers piled cotton goods, coffee, and clanking tin ware on their pack saddles. As Ceseli slithered through to get past, one brayed and spat in protest against its handler. She brushed the swab of spit off her arm and wondered if it brought good luck like pigeon shit in Venice.

"Where are we going?" she asked, hurrying to keep up with him.

"Directly to the United States Legation where Minister Rutherford is waiting for you. An urgent telegram came in and he had to stay behind to answer it." Standish helped her into the old, but well maintained, black Ford model A. After several grunts and hissing noises, the engine finally came alive and he drove up the hill away from the station.

"This is the main street," he said, "and one of only a few tarred ones. There's another road that leads up to the palace. Next door is the police station, and that's the Hotel De France over there," pointing to indicate the hotel. "Add to that a coffee house, a butcher shop, and a bazaar and that covers the downtown. There are three hospitals, a school named for the emperor, and an Italian one run by missionaries. If you like to walk, it takes one and a half hours to walk across the city from the American mission to the British compound. If you want to get there in half the time you can ride a mule, or take our car for that matter."

As far as she could see, the city was hidden in a forest of Eucalyptus trees peeking out from every building and along the sides of every street and pathway. It was an enormous network of green through which one could see the thatched roofs of the round mud-and-manure native huts known as *tukuls.* Other than the blanket of the Eucalyptus trees were the snowflakes of the bleached white shammas togas the people wore.

The Ford was the only car on the road, but lots of people were walking or riding on donkeys and mules with their leather saddles and trimmings.

There was a heavy smell from the pack animals that jostled against the car and she felt thankful that she was looking out over the heads of the donkeys and was not right in their midst. Standish honked hard at a stray mule that had come up on the roadbed and turned sharply to miss it.

"Where will you be staying?"

"Uncle Warren said he'd take care of that."

"He'll give you a choice. Either the legation compound, or the Imperial Hotel, which is there on your right."

"The Imperial Hotel? That sounds very grand," she said as the car slowly passed the imposing Swiss chalet style dark green building, with its delicate white latticework balconies.

"Names can be deceiving!"

"What do you suggest?"

"Our little acre of the U.S. I prefer American cockroaches. At least you know what you're getting." She looked across at him, trying to judge how serious he was. "This is it," he said, turning into a driveway. "It's not as big or as old as the British, French and Italian compounds, but it's comfortable. The building belongs to a wealthy *ras.* A ras is the equivalent of a medieval warlord. The emperor urged him to rent us the villa and the emperor is rarely refused. It's handy because it's close to the palace. We even have our own hyenas."

"Hyenas?"

"They came with the villa. Now they're used to American garbage."

She got out of the car and saw the sprawling two story building with an American flag fluttering from its nearby pole. The Legation was white with brick trim and a large front door painted blue. Behind she could see well-kept gardens with a wide lawn leading out to the Eucalyptus woods. A white picket fence boxed in what looked like a vegetable and herb garden. A magnificent purple *Bougainvillea* vine crawled up one side of the building making a smashing prismatic clash with the yellow and pink roses. *Someone loves to garden,* she thought looking at a large group of avocado trees. Ceseli remembered how she had once tried to raise avocados by precariously perching the pit sustained by three toothpicks over a glass jar filled with water. It did work, she could guarantee that, but these trees were large enough to bare fruit.

"I'll lead the way," Standish said, over his shoulder, walking into the building and then striding down the hall past the faux marble columns and yellow stucco moldings of the entranceway. Lots of indoor plants were in terracotta urns. Through the long French doors she could see the clouds above Mt. Entoto.

"Here we are," Standish said, opening a door and allowing Ceseli to precede him into the room.

At the far side of the room, Warren Rutherford, the fifty-year-old United States Minister to Ethiopia, turned, smiled, and walked toward her. "Ceseli, my dear. Ceseli, it's so good to see you," he said, bear hugging her with real warmth and kissing her on the cheek. "Welcome to Addis."

"Thank you, Uncle Warren," she said, looking into his familiar eyes. They seemed darker and more tired than she remembered from his many visits with her father in their New York apartment, but his smile, as always, was engaging. He exuded friendship and authority.

"Ceseli, please accept my condolences again. Hamilton was my best friend. I can hardly believe he's gone. What a shock that was. I'm so very sorry I couldn't get back for the service," he said, beckoning her to a seat in front of his desk. He walked behind it and took a briar pipe from a rack filled with them. "When you write, please express my condolences to your grandparents. And a special word to Sotzy, of course."

"I will."

"How was your trip?" he asked, once she and Standish were seated.

"Very long. I came from New York."

"You haven't been to Geneva then?"

"I'll do that after I leave here. I've been very busy completing my studies at Penn and planning my dissertation."

"The obelisks of Axum, right?" Rutherford said, interrupting.

"Yes. It sounded really exotic. And knowing my godfather was here was reassuring. And then . . ." Ceseli paused, her voice trailing off. She looked around for a moment trying to suppress the hot tears, overwhelmed with emotion at actually sitting here in Rutherford's office in Addis, without her father.

As she looked around to gather her thoughts, she noticed that the room was light and airy, the walls painted a butter yellow with a large bow window looking out onto the garden. On either side of the window were wide bookcases full of what looked like important official publications. The wide mahogany desk was a French style partner's desk with two chairs on the side where Ceseli and Standish were sitting, and one for him on the other side. Along one wall was a comfortable chintz covered couch with two wing chairs at its sides and a mahogany coffee table.

Persian rugs with a blue and gold motif covered the hardwood floors. Along the shorter wall was a huge fireplace with imposing wrought irons with brass decoration and matching fire tools. Displayed on the wide and handsome mantelpiece were Rutherford family photographs in silver frames.

Over the years Ceseli had grown to know Warren Rutherford well. At a certain age she began to wonder how the two men had become such good friends. They were so different in every way. Hamilton had been blond. *That's where I get my hair color*, she thought, and was six feet tall and very slender. Warren was dark and solid. While Hamilton loved to play tennis, hike, swim, and ride horses, Warren preferred sitting by the pool and doing the crossword puzzle, or painting, or playing the piano. They had been roommates for seven years in New Haven, Connecticut somehow making a perfect match during their undergraduate and law school days at Yale.

Warren had married extremely well after he fell in love with Marnie Winthrop Barber, the only child of a cereal baron from Chicago. Her handsome dowry meant he could enter the diplomatic community early on. He was a full minister in Ethiopia and after reposting to Washington in a few years would surely acquire a good ambassadorship in a key European capital.

Warren Rutherford was also a good godfather, never once missing her birthday. She and her father had spent a week every summer at Warren's ancestral oceanfront family compound at Quogue on Long Island in the Hamptons.

Finally, Ceseli regained her composure and continued.

"I won a doctoral fellowship at the American Academy at Rome for next year and I've accepted. I thought a lot about whether I should change the subject of my thesis or come here as planned, and decided that would be exactly what my father would expect."

"Hamilton told me of your plans some time ago. I'm sure we can get you to Axum. You'll need permission from the emperor, of course." Rutherford turned to Standish. "I want you to arrange a meeting with Yifru."

"Actually, sir, Yifru has already met Miss Larson. They were on the same train. We'll go to see him first thing tomorrow morning."

"Excellent. Yifru can probably slip you in to see the emperor. As for accommodations, Ceseli," Rutherford said, turning to her, "most

Americans have preferred staying here in the compound. We can give you one of our tukuls."

"I'd like that very much. I shall enjoy hearing the hyenas."

"Indeed. The hyenas," Rutherford laughed. "I'm sorry my Marnie isn't here. She would love to see you, but Abigail is getting married soon and I guess young ladies like their mother's help. Unfortunately, this is no time for me to leave so Standish and I will be bacheloring it for a few months. You'll be most welcome to join us at meals and add a little luster to our existence. We can discuss everything else when you get settled in. At seven?"

"Thank you," she said.

Standish led the way walking from the main building behind which there were several of the round tukuls on a wide expanse of garden. "I'm right over there," he said, pointing to another tukul. "Holler if you need anything. The minister is very precise, as you know. I'll stop by for you a few minutes before seven."

Ceseli walked into the tukul, put her camera bag on a table and looked around. There was a large window overlooking the garden with mosquito netting neatly tacked around the edges and a double bed with a native blue and white cotton bedspread. A print of St. George and the dragon hung on the white wall. On the simple nightstand were a candleholder, matches and a good supply of candles. A book of the birds of Ethiopia was on the bureau next to a vase of freshly cut white, yellow, and cornstarch blue wild flowers. She would put the photograph of her father next to the book. She stuck her head into the bathroom to find a large zinc tub and shower that looked like something that Tarzan might have used.

Her steamer trunk, she noticed, was already waiting for her. *I guess they didn't think I'd stay at the hotel, Imperial or not,* she thought as she walked back to the verandah. There was a small table and two slat-back Adirondack style chairs, which looked locally made and rudimentary, but comfortable.

She sat down in one of them and, resting her head on the chair's hard wooden frame, thought briefly of the train ride and of Marco. She closed her eyes and remembered the trip with her father to Florence when she was twelve.

"Where are we going, Daddy?"

"We're going to climb to the top of the belfry."

The stairs were very steep, the polished marble slick under her feet.

"What do you see?" he asked.

"The whole city is red, Daddy."

Hamilton Larson hesitated for a minute then smiled.

"You're absolutely right, my dear. Those are the red tile roofs. And that is the Arno River. Florence was a trading center. They brought wool here from the Cotswolds in England and from Portugal and dyed and spun it into the most expensive fabric in the world. That's one of the ways they made this city famous. Trade brought a lot of money to Florence during a period of years known as the Renaissance."

"What's that, Daddy?"

"It means rebirth. It was a time when a wealthy banking family named the Medici paid artists to make their city the most beautiful one in the world. They lived in a palace over there across the Arno. We'll go there this afternoon." He smiled at her affectionately as they studied the city below them.

"I'd like an ice cream, Daddy."

"Ask for it in Italian, my sweet."

"Un gelato. Per favore."

"One gelato coming right up," he said as they started back down the steep stairway.

A low *wu-wu-wu-wu-wuoo* startled her. Ceseli looked out to the lawn, but she saw only a huge tortoise. It stopped in its grazing and looked at her with sorrowful almost doe-like eyes. Suddenly, she could hardly control the feeling of anxiety that crept over her. Until now, everything she had done was concentrated on getting here. The long journey from New York, the Italian ship from Naples, and then the drama of the train. Now she was in Addis Ababa. For the first time in her life, she actually felt afraid and alone in a place where she shouldn't be alone.

From a tree she heard again the *wu-wu-wu-wu-wuoo* of a mourning dove. Despite all her efforts to hold them back, her eyes filled with tears.

CHAPTER 5

"THOSE HUGE TURTLES?" CESELI asked as they sat on the verandah having a gin and tonic before dinner.

"Land tortoises. Huge, yes, but very docile. The British ambassador gave them to us when we moved in," Rutherford said, adjusting himself more comfortably in his chair. "He's got quite a few of them. We have four and they certainly do eat!"

"My father bought me two of those little green sea turtles in Chinatown. They were in a green glass bowl in my room, but somehow managed to get all the way to the kitchen and hide behind the icebox. It took us months to find them. They were hibernating. Daddy said they were on vacation."

Rutherford laughed, "Hamilton had a wonderful sense of humor. How do you like the tukul?"

"It's fine. Thank you for letting me stay here in the compound."

"I'm sorry Hamilton never got to come out here. He was quite an authority on Ethiopia," he said as he pulled a pipe from his breast pocket. "You'll like it here, Ceseli. It's considered a hardship post, but we do have some amenities. There's a decent library, and a phonograph in the sitting room. There's electricity at times. There's a curfew for his majesty's subjects. You'll hear the bugle each evening. Foreigners are exempt, but the city is blacked out. There's no place to go in any case. Right Standish? If you like to play, there's even an upright piano. The only other is at the British compound. We get together now and then to have some fun."

"There were six piano crates on the train. I saw them being unloaded at the station."

"Interesting," Rutherford paused. "Must be for the emperor, but why waste money on music? He should be buying guns."

They were interrupted by a young Ethiopian girl wearing the traditional shamma, but in a very pale blue. "Dinner is ready, sir," she said, curtsying gracefully.

"Thank you, Hilina," Rutherford said, pushing back his chair and walking into the dining room. "This is Miss Larson, Hilina. She'll be staying with us for a few weeks."

"What does Hilina mean?" Ceseli asked.

"I'm named after Saint Hilina," she replied shyly, her head bowed.

"The mother of Emperor Constantine," Ceseli said.

"Ceseli, my dear, why don't you sit here," Rutherford said, as he pulled back her chair.

Ceseli looked around her. Despite her absence, this room was very much Marnie Winthrop Barber Rutherford. It did not look somber despite the eggplant purple walls. The four large windows were outlined by grey and white stripped silk drapes. Over the sideboard was a huge mirror inside a mahogany frame. On each side of the mirror was a Tiffany glass sconce with stained glass shades. On the sideboard sat an elaborate Gorham silver tea and coffee set on a twenty-four inch tray. *I wonder how long that takes to polish,* she thought, *and who does it? Hilina?*

Two large oil landscape paintings were on the short wall. She wondered if they were painted by Rutherford, who she remembered as a very good painter. She remembered that on one trip to a dude ranch in Wyoming that her father had taken her, Marnie, and Abigail riding through the mountains while Warren painted them. Warren Rutherford's paintings, like the crossword puzzles he not only solved, but constructed, all had a theme. This painting had a cerulean sky with wisps of yellow, a string of purple mountains, and wheat fields. She wondered what it meant.

When they were all seated, Rutherford turned to Ceseli, opening a small brown leather diary on the table next to him.

"Axum. Let's presume the emperor approves. I don't think he'd refuse us anything right now. I know he thinks that President Roosevelt will come to his rescue and I know he will be disappointed. How many days do you think you will need up there?"

"I think I could finish in five, or at most, six days."

"A week. That shouldn't be hard to arrange. By the way, you mentioned going to Rome next year. You came through Naples, so you saw the number of Italian soldiers coming to Eritrea?"

Ceseli nodded.

"Ethiopia is in grave danger right now," Rutherford said. "Mussolini has big dreams. He's using a border clash at WalWal as an excuse to invade Ethiopia. The emperor, unfortunately, is in no position to fight the Italians."

"WalWal?"

"WalWal is an oasis of several watering holes in the south of Ethiopia in an area that borders Italian Somaliland. There was a stupid border clash there last November. Mussolini is saying the Ethiopians were responsible because they provoked the Italians at the wells, but the emperor quite rightly maintains that the Italians had no right to be on Ethiopian soil in the first place."

"Were they?"

"We believe that WalWal is about sixty miles inside the border of Ethiopia, even on the Italian maps," Standish said.

"The League of Nations is trying to arbitrate a settlement," Rutherford continued. "Since this is his only excuse for invasion, Mussolini won't give in easily. The emperor wants the League to stand up to Mussolini, but that's not going to happen. Even though, in theory, each member of the League has a vote, the League is dominated by its two strongest members, England and France, and they are too busy courting Mussolini and hoping to entice him into an alliance to protect them from Germany."

"But why would Italy want Ethiopia?" Ceseli asked.

"Having Ethiopia would link together Italy's two colonies, Eritrea and Italian Somaliland, and that would be good. But what Mussolini really needs is good farmland. He has forty-two million people in a country one-eighth the size of Ethiopia and the highlands here are very fertile. And Ethiopia has less than eight million people so it wouldn't be hard to govern."

"So you believe that war is coming?" Ceseli asked.

"I'm afraid so," Rutherford said. "Roosevelt does not want to get involved. But how can he avoid it? Most discussions we've had are on how to stay neutral in the face of a European war. We seem to forget about the rights and wrongs of the crises that threaten war. But since we are sitting here in the middle of one of these crisis, my opinion may be somewhat biased. This isn't meant to be a first year college history course," he continued. "In my next reincarnation, I'll be a college professor. Then I can give vent to my pedantic talents."

Ceseli smiled. "I'm here to learn everything I can."

"You don't have to flatter me, my dear. Standish, I never asked you. You were stationed in Geneva. Did you know Ceseli's father?"

"I never worked with him directly, but I studied his paper on WalWal. It was a very sound analysis," Standish replied, looking at Ceseli.

Ceseli stifled a yawn. "Uncle Warren, I think I'm more tired than I thought. It's a lot to digest all at once. I'll retire, if you don't mind."

"Sweet dreams. Oh, Ceseli, one thing. Let's do away with this Uncle Warren thing. It makes me feel like a relic. Why don't you and I have breakfast tomorrow morning? We'll let Standish sleep an extra hour. That's okay with you isn't it, my boy? 7:30?"

Standish walked with her to her tukul. "If you need anything, just call."

"Thank you," she said wondering, in practice, how she could do that.

"Don't mention it."

Inside she fumbled for the candles and lit one. She undressed and climbed into bed. For a moment she wondered if she could leave the candle burning. She decided against that, and gathering as much courage as she could muster, blew out the candle, turned over and slept immediately.

A short time later, Rutherford knocked on the door of Standish's tukul. "We need to talk, Forsythe. You do know that I'm not going to let Ceseli go to Axum alone. It would be possible if Hamilton were with her, of course." Rutherford stepped inside and paused to look around for a second as Standish pulled a foot-high stack of books off the only other chair in the room. The diplomat sat down while Standish stacked the books along the wall. The minister's eyes travelled to the garden as he thought about what he was going to say. "You know, I've known Ceseli from the day she was born. Hamilton and I lived relatively close to each other in New York and we spent a good deal of time together with our families.

"The minute she was born he called me and I went to the hospital. By then things were starting to go bad. He handed me a cigar, but then told me that they didn't expect Alex to live. Frances, Alex's mother, who everyone calls Sotzy, was already there. Neither Sotzy nor Hamilton were ones to show much emotion, but it was a dreadful moment. Then you know what Sotzy did? She took Ceseli from the nurse. She was in a pink cotton blanket and carried her over to Hamilton and said 'Look at this absolutely beautiful creature Alex has given us. We will have to be worthy of her, won't we' and with that, she put Ceseli in Hamilton's arms and gave him a big hug. Alex died less than an hour later. Hamilton never remarried. The most tragic part of it all was that Alex was a doctor and had chosen a young woman protégé to deliver her. Hamilton never blamed the doctor, for that would have meant questioning Alex's judgment. He would never have done that."

When Warren Rutherford stood up, his eyes were moist. "And now we are going to have to be worthy of Ceseli. Which is to say, you're leaving for Axum with her. I'd go, but honestly you know I just can't," he said. His eyes were focused tightly on Standish as he moved toward the door. "Make the arrangement with Yifru. And watch out for her."

CHAPTER 6

"How WOULD YOU LIKE your eggs, Ceseli? Sunnyside up, like your father?"

"That would be perfect, thank you."

"Hilina, you've heard that?"

"Yes, sir. It'll be a minute."

"So, my dear, tell me how you're managing since Hamilton's passing?"

"Some days are okay. It's been four months. Sometimes I feel like sobbing. There are moments when I feel deserted. It was so sudden. There are so many things I'd like to have asked him and now I never can."

"What were the questions, Ceseli? Maybe I can help you find the answers."

"Well, I was wondering how my parents met. He told me a bit of that a long, long time ago, but I've forgotten most of it."

"Oh I remember that very well. He and I met Alex at the same time. We were juniors at Yale and had been invited to a debutante ball in New York City. The dance was given by the New York Junior League. There were twenty-three lovely young eighteen year olds walking to the center stage and curtseying before they walked down the stairs to the dance floor. They all wore floor-length white satin gowns, white kid gloves to the elbow and held a long ostrich plume dyed green. We had a long wait before we met Alex because the presentations were alphabetical. Alex was very pretty of course, but there was something in her smile that was captivating. I remember that Hamilton was smitten from the moment he laid his eyes on her. He cut in during a waltz and introduced himself."

Warren Rutherford paused as Hilina put the eggs and toast in front of Ceseli. "Afterwards, I asked him what he'd said and he smiled and repeated to me what he had said to her. 'Miss Alex, my name is Hamilton Larson. Please remember that name, Miss Alex Sheraton, because I hope it is going to be yours.'"

Ceseli listened as she used a spoon to open the yolk of her eggs.

"She told him he was going to have a long wait because she planned to be a doctor. He told her he thought it would be worth the wait. After he finished the dance, Hamilton came back to me. 'Warren, I'm going to woo that young lady,' he said, never taking his eyes from her. And I told him "Hamilton, it looks like she has already wooed you.' Oh, did he laugh when I said that. 'Yes, she has,' he told me. And then he said that while I could dance with her, she was absolutely off limits. He made me promise that." Warren chuckled. "Over the next seven years, we all spent time together, especially after she introduced me to Marnie, who was one of her best friends. So that's how they met. More questions?"

"And they got married right after she graduated from medical school?"

"The first Saturday, actually. There was a big party at the Metropolitan Club in New York with dancing, champagne, and the whole thing. Marnie and I had already been married for several years. Four I think, and my Abigail was the perfect flower girl. I've never seen two people so much in love, Ceseli; they were devoted to each other. That's why he never remarried. No one could live up to her. Except maybe you, my dear. Do you remember coming out to our house on Long Island?"

"Oh, yes." For a minute, Ceseli was back there on the beach building sand castles on the dunes of Long Island Sound.

"What is that, Daddy?"

"It's where the king and queen live." Hamilton said as he built a castle almost as tall as his five year old daughter. "And this is a moat," he said as he dug out a trench so the ocean water could rush into the moat.

"What is a moat?"

"Castles have a moat to protect them from people who might want to hurt them."

"Why would they want to hurt them, Daddy?"

"Maybe because they want something the other person has. Like a doll."

"But if someone wanted my doll, I'd give it to them."

"What if they wanted your heart, sugar?"

"They can't have that, Daddy. You already have it."

"Remember what I'm saying, dear. Don't build a moat around your heart."

I wonder if that's exactly what I have done, she thought, and why her father's death had left her feeling so empty.

"I was just remembering the sand castles."

"And when you were older, the tennis games. You were quite the little champion."

Ceseli took the napkin and dabbed at her eyes. "Thanks, Uncle Warren. Excuse me, Warren. This makes me feel a lot better."

Warren Rutherford looked at her affectionately before continuing. "You will see a great deal of poverty in the next couple of weeks, Ceseli, but that shouldn't be anything new to you. Hamilton wrote that his mother had been organizing a soup kitchen for those living in the Hooverville in Central Park."

"She's been wonderful. I learned to ride my bike on the Great Lawn. Now it's a shantytown. I help Nana when I'm in the city, but for the past three years I've been in Philly. Not to say that life there is any better these days."

"No, I'm sure it's not. Just smaller. Enough of this. Now we're going to move you along. You're going to meet the emperor," Warren smiled. "I hope you like him."

CHAPTER 7

"THESE ARE MEN OF the Imperial Guard," Standish explained as she saw that they were dressed in well-tailored European style khaki uniforms. They saluted smartly, presenting arms with their various guns, some of which looked very old indeed.

"They're barefoot," Ceseli noted. It was the next morning and Daniele, the driver for the United States mission, stopped the Ford at the gate of the new, but unfinished, Ghibbi Palace. Ceseli and Standish were going to meet the emperor. She was dressed in a blue linen skirt with a white cotton short-sleeved blouse. She had her wide-brimmed straw hat with her, but she had removed it at the gate.

She looked to the right and left at the painted sentry boxes, striped diagonally in the Ethiopian green, yellow, and red colors. The car drove up the long elliptical driveway passing a circular marble fountain with its sea nymphs and rearing horses that was beautiful even without water.

At the door of the palace, an aide met them and escorted them up the steep set of stairs into the palace and along the yellow hallways decorated with large gilded mirrors. Deep rich red Persian carpets were soft under her feet. On the landings of the gray marble staircase were other smartly uniformed guards, also barefoot.

The Little Ghibbi, the emperor's new palace, to be distinguished from Menelik II sumptuous palace, was unpretentious. On the ground floor was a square dining room and two large salons for dancing and receptions. On the second floor to which they were led, was the emperor's study, his bedroom, his library, and his documents room.

All of these rooms were connected more by heavily curtained doorways, but without real doors. In cold weather, fires were lit in braziers in each of the rooms.

On the walls of the study, where they were taken to await the emperor, she noticed autographed sepia photographs of several European monarchs including Italy's King Victor Emmanuel III. Ceseli studied the leather-bound books lining the walls. Most of them were in French, but several were in English or Latin. They gave the impression of being well read.

She joined Standish looking out the window to the European style gardens where rows of English roses stood somewhat out of place in these surroundings. Some were abundantly flowering and trained over iron trellises. They were a prism of whites, yellows, pinks, and reds melding together like a spring bouquet.

She didn't count them, but she saw that a long chain of men were passing buckets of water to the flowerbeds. Up until now, the only Ethiopians she had seen were, well, scrawny, but these men looked very fit; their muscles taut and their bodies strong with the white toga-like shammas hooked up to the waist. She thought of the roses at her grandmother's house in Connecticut and of the gardener, Roger, who watered the huge garden himself with a hose.

Standish tapped her arm and pointed to the diminutive man walking alone, lost in thought. He was wearing a black flowing cape over white Jodhpur pants. At his heels, two lion cubs played like kittens.

"The emperor keeps several lions as symbols of the Lion of Judah," Standish explained. "At times, he had full-grown lions sprawling on the carpet at the door of his study so that visitors had to climb over them as they came in. Yifru told me that one of the British consuls was so unnerved that he shot one of them."

They turned as Yifru came up behind them. He had exchanged his white linen suit for a khaki safari jacket and slacks. *How blue his eyes are,* she thought, *and his smile is so open and friendly.*

"The emperor will be here shortly," he said. "About Axum," he said, turning to Ceseli, "How did you plan on getting there?"

"Minister Rutherford has asked me to accompany Miss Larson to Axum," Standish answered. "I hope we can drive the truck at least as far as Dessie."

"The minister called me this morning. He wanted to know how far the road actually goes. I told him I'd find that out," Yifru said, tapping a silver pen with his index finger. "Eventually it will link up with the Italian road from Eritrea. As you can imagine, it's not one of the emperor's fondest projects just at the moment." Yifru winked at her as he led them into the emperor's study.

Directly facing the door and with his back to the window, the Emperor of Emperors of Ethiopia, the Negus Negusti, the Conquering Lion of

Judah sat behind his large antique French desk. Hanging from a standing gilded base was a large cage with a blue and yellow parrot watching them.

"The emperor! Long live Haile Sellassie!" The parrot's raucous cry was so unexpected and startling that Ceseli had to pinch herself to keep from laughing. She felt thankful that he had exchanged the two lion cubs for cocker spaniels. One of them walked over to her and wagged its tail as she patted it.

"The Duke of Abruzzi gave them to us. He is a cousin of the king of Italy. We are very fond of them," the emperor said, calling the dog, which took its place obediently under his feet.

Ceseli had seen photographs of the emperor and knew what to expect. *He's even shorter and slighter,* she thought, *and looks much younger than his forty-four years. He had a high brow and the full mass of hair above the quick eyes and slender, handsome features of his face. Though his skin was dark, the fine high-boned features were Caucasian.* As she studied him, Ceseli saw his movements were quick, and when he spoke, he gesticulated with his hands. She smiled to herself wondering where he had picked up this very Italian habit.

"Minister Rutherford says that you wish to visit Axum. May we know for what reason?" the emperor asked as he took the parrot from its cage.

"I'm doing my graduate work in archaeology, on the obelisks of Axum. Whether or not there is one for the Queen of Sheba. I have studied them through the many archaeological explorations to Axum."

"The Germans and the English?" the Negus asked.

"And even further back. James Bruce, the Scot, who traveled there in 1769."

"We know of James Bruce," the emperor smiled, going to a shelf and taking down a leather-bound book. "Bruce lived at the Ethiopian Royal Court of Gondar."

"I've read his travel log about finding the source of the Blue Nile at Lake Tana. He thought the Blue Nile was more powerful than the White Nile," Ceseli said.

"Alas, history has proved him wrong," said the emperor, sitting down again. "Please go on."

"I have been awarded a graduate fellowship at the American Academy at Rome next fall. That's where I will complete my dissertation."

"We visited Rome in 1924," the emperor interrupted. "Our trip was in the capacity of regent for the Empress Zauditu, not as emperor. We gave the king a lion and a zebra. He was starting a zoo. Our relationship was very different then. You have heard of Monsieur Mussolini?"

Both Rutherford and Standish had warned Ceseli not to get caught up in political discussions and so she sidestepped the question. "I am an archaeologist, your majesty, not a militarist. I know only that there is talk of potential war. You have become a very sympathetic person in the American press."

"We have gotten many letters from people in America giving us advice on how to proceed. We wish that there had been more official communications," he said. "We will allow you to go to Axum," the emperor said, returning to the subject at hand. "Perhaps when you return you will come and tell us what you have found. We intend to set up a university center to study the history of our country. What ideas you might contribute would be important for us to hear. Is there anything else we can assist you with?"

Ceseli looked at the emperor, her eyes moistened by emotion. "I'm so thankful to you for letting me go. I've come such a long way. I never thought if we, I, got all the way here, I couldn't go to Axum. It just never entered my mind. Yes, I know you're the emperor. And it's your country and your decision."

"We are letting you go to Axum," the emperor repeated as he tried to interrupt.

"Yes. Thank you. I understand, it's just I was so afraid you might say no."

He smiled warmly. "Is there something else we can help you with?"

"There is one thing," she said. "I was wondering whether there is a place where there is information on Axum and the Queen of Sheba that might not be easily available outside of Ethiopia."

"We ourselves have a very extensive library. When you return from Axum, let us talk. Perhaps there is information we could exchange."

"I would be very happy to do so," Ceseli said.

Yifru stood and Ceseli and Standish followed suit. "I urge you to go at once before the rains come." He turned to Yifru. "You can arrange this to their satisfaction."

Ceseli and Standish walked backward out of the emperor's office careful not to bump into the wall.

CHAPTER 8

"So you met the emperor?" Rutherford asked at dinner that night.

"He was very impressive," Ceseli answered.

"I agree," Rutherford said, puffing on his pipe. "He is an absolute monarch like those in Siam and Afghanistan. He is not vastly rich. He lives within his means like a gentleman and spends the state's money on the state. He's a good father and loves his children. He likes good wines, books, music, his private cinema, horses, and his dogs. Before all this WalWal business, he had thought of importing sailboats to use on Lake Zwai. That is the limit of his extravagance."

Rutherford paused, intent on his reflections. "Right after his coronation he set up a constitution and a parliament so leaders would gain experience in running the country. He has been trying to centralize the government, but it's a slow process because tribes like the Azebu Gallas resist his rules. But he is moving forward. And don't underestimate for a minute the Empress Menen. She is not only the mother of his six children, she is his closest confidant and advisor. She's also an extremely astute business woman, right Standish?"

"The emperor, Princes Menen and others took a huge track of two thousand acres near the railroad to Djibouti and irrigated it to grow coffee, citrus, grapes, nuts, sugar cane, and kapok. They earned huge profits. Menen governed a vast area down there. They also let farmers of the Oromos tribe become sharecroppers and join in some of the well-being."

"Decidedly a very shrewd woman." Rutherford added. "And a good match for Tafari. But everything about this man is extraordinary, including how he became the emperor."

"How do you mean?" Ceseli asked.

"Succession in Ethiopia is not like it is in Europe. The eldest child does not automatically inherit the crown. You do have to be a direct descendent of Solomon and of the Amharic people, but it is the most powerful person in the family who becomes the king of kings. Menilek had no sons so he designated his grandson, Iyasu, as his successor and that proved to be a real disaster."

"What happened to Iyasu?" Ceseli asked.

"He decided to convert to Islam, wanted to deny the Amharic people their traditional power and make Islam equal to the Coptic Church. Everyone opposed him, particularly the Church. There was almost a civil war. The solution was to depose Iyasu and make Menelik's daughter, Zauditu, the empress. Installing Tafari, that's his baptismal name, Haile Sellassie is his throne name, as her regent was also a very popular and politically astute move," Rutherford said. "Let's sit outside. It's such a beautiful night and I could use a brandy," he said as he walked out to the verandah. "Tafari became emperor only five years ago, you realize. By the way, get Standish to tell you about the coronation. It's a wonderful story."

"The emperor told us that he took a lion to the king of Italy."

"I wish a lion would satisfy them now," Rutherford looked up at the sky and sipped his brandy.

"But why WalWal?" she asked.

"Water," Rutherford answered. "Controlling the southeastern Ogaden desert can only be done by controlling the water supply at WalWal. The emperor has his own reasons for wanting the League to find in his favor. If WalWal belongs to him, he can trade it to the British in exchange for a port on the Red Sea. He has tried several times to acquire a port, but for one reason or another, France, England, and Italy have all turned him down. They own all the land along the Horn of Africa. This is his last chance."

"And that's why Italy doesn't want him to get it."

Standish and Rutherford nodded together.

"Do you have a copy of my father's paper on WalWal?" Ceseli asked Standish.

"Yes. Come to my office tomorrow morning."

The next morning, Ceseli opened the door to Standish's office, surprising him sitting with his feet up on the desk and his chair tilted backward. It was the first time she'd been to his office. She sat down on the only wooden chair not covered by books, as he went to a shelf and began rummaging through papers. Next to the wall map of Africa was a photo of President Roosevelt. The floor-to-ceiling bookcases were all jammed. More books were piled on the floor. Outside the French doors she could see that the tortoises were sunning themselves.

"Here it is, a little worse for wear. If you want you can read it here."

"I understand what he's saying about WalWal, but I don't understand why the United States didn't join the League of Nations?" Ceseli asked after she had finished reading.

"We were afraid of getting involved in other wars. Then President Wilson had a stroke. He was the real inspiration for the League."

"But we fought in World War I."

"Only at the end. There was no alternative. But the Republicans hid behind the isolation issue. You know what that means?"

"That a nation should not get involved in the troubles of other countries," Ceseli answered as she studied Standish.

"The founding fathers believed that the oceans would protect us, and our ideals of freedom and equality. We didn't want other countries to dominate us, particularly, Great Britain." Standish added. "Let's not forget the Boston Tea Party."

"That was a long, long time ago."

"But the principle is the same. We like to get involved only when it comes to expanding our markets. I'm here to work on Ethiopia's economic development, stimulate the trade in coffee, and develop the project for the dam across the Blue Nile. That would earn the U.S. a great deal of money."

"But getting back to the League. Daddy argues that the basis of the functioning of the League is that each country, big or small, has only one vote."

"That's part of the Covenant of the League of Nations. But in reality, the League is dominated by its two strongest members, Great Britain and France."

"Standish, what made you come to Ethiopia?"

"Yifru used to come to our house every Sunday for dinner. My father and he would discuss ways to improve life here. Then when I finished graduate school at Princeton, Yifru invited me to come for three months and help him in the preparations for the coronation. That was in 1930. It was an amazing experience. Afterwards, I joined the State Department and was posted to the League in Geneva. While I was in Geneva, the League was still involved in some important issues as a result of the World War I. Fifteen, even twenty years though it may seem a lot, is not much time to settle all the problems that started because of that war. There were problems with new borders and new frontiers. We needed to find a place for refugees and decide how to limit the trade in narcotics."

"You were involved in that?"

"So was your father. We were observers. The only real difference between being an observer and being a member was that the U.S. didn't have a vote. But your father was a very influential person and he was consulted on several important issues. He believed in collective security, that by joining the League, each country would be protected. That's also what the emperor believes and why he joined the League. After WalWal, I actually advised the emperor to send a telegram to the League denouncing the Italian action at WalWal."

"Standing up to Mussolini?"

"Your father was against Mussolini. He thought he was a bully and you had to stand up to him. And Hitler as well."

"You think that the British and the French will stand up to Mussolini?"

"I certainly hope they will."

After Ceseli left, Standish put his feet back onto the desk and stared at the map of Africa. On his desk was his most treasured possession: a hardball of the New York Yankees, signed by Babe Ruth, the Sultan of Swat, and next to it a signed photo of the Babe. Standish picked up the hardball and clenched it in his hand, remembering.

It had been a beautiful warm day. He sat in the bleachers at Yankee Stadium between his father and Yifru. It was his birthday. He offered the popcorn to Yifru who was dressed in a long blue *kaftan*. It was his native costume, he told Standish, and showed him that there were pants underneath. *It looks more like something my mother would wear around the house,* Standish thought.

Standish had carefully explained to Yifru all the rules of baseball. You hit the ball and run to first. Then the next batter tries to hit the ball. If you're really lucky someone will hit a homerun and that meant at least another point. The very best that could happen would be a homerun with someone on each base. But the Yankees weren't doing so well this afternoon.

"What do you think, Standish?" Yifru asked him, taking a handful of popcorn.

Standish's father winked at Yifru over his head. "It's okay."

Suddenly the ball was flying out over center field. Lots of people were on their feet. You could hardly see. "Wow!" Yifru yelled, jumping to his feet and clapping enthusiastically. "Look at that. Did you see that, Standish? That was some homerun."

Standish looked up at him. Tears were prickling his eyes.

"Well! You said you wanted a homerun," Yifru shouted, above the din and looking at the young boy. "What did you think?"

Standish's father caught Yifru's eye. Standish looked up at Yifru. "It's the White Socks." Standish looked at him miserably. "Not the Yankees."

"Oh."

Standish pitched the ball into his left hand. He had forgiven Yifru after a while. You can't know everything about baseball the first time. Yifru had redeemed himself in Standish's eyes by buying him the photograph of Babe Ruth. The ball he had caught himself at another game. There was certainly going to be a game of hardball in the near future. He wondered who would win.

CHAPTER 9

HUGE TORCHES SET OUT all along the drive flamed heavenward as the black Ford stopped at the front entrance of the Ghibbi Palace. Ceseli felt like a glorified Cinderella. She was thrilled when Rutherford asked if she would like to join them, particularly because state dinners were not common. Ceseli had been to many receptions and dinner parties with her father, but not in Africa. She was curious to know what this one would be like.

As she waited to be presented at the receiving line, she looked at the wide yellow room with its white stucco columns, gold-highlighted ceilings, mirrors, blue patterned Persian rugs, and crystal chandeliers. The room contained elaborate Louis XV style chairs with embroidered cushions. An ornate vermeil clock with a lapis lazuli face was on the mantelpiece, with gold, wide-branch candelabra as sentinels on each side.

Her Majesty Menen, the Empress of Ethiopia, wearing an embroidered blue silk dress and a tiara stood next to Haile Sellassie in the receiving line. Empress Menen Asfaw was now forty-four years old and had borne the emperor six children: three princes and three princesses. Whereas he was angular with high cheekbones, she was plump. They were about the same height and shared the same background as both were descendants of the House of Solomon. She had married Ras Tafari at the age of twenty.

As soon as they had passed through the receiving line, Ceseli was happy to see Marco across the room. *He looks so handsome in a black tuxedo with a floral cummerbund,* she thought. *He has shaved.*

"I was hoping you'd be here," he said, kissing her hand.

"I thought you were going to call me. To see your hospital."

"I thought it was the other way around. You'd come and show me your head," Marco smiled. "Can I get you something to drink? There's everything except Italian wines. The emperor is not interested in helping the Italian economy," Marco said taking her elbow and steering her to a long table set up overlooking the garden illuminated by more torches.

Bats flickered and soared in the semi-darkness almost in unison with the bows of the string quartette playing on a platform in the rear. Here instead of violins, cellos, and violas, the chordophones or stringed instruments were the *masengo*, a one-stringed lute, a *begena,* a large ten-string lyre and a five-string lyre. Ceseli stopped to listen to the music she had never heard before.

"Try this," Marco said, handing her a gold goblet of champagne. "The French are still in good favor."

Ceseli took it and followed him to a quieter area of the terrace.

"How do you like Addis?"

"I can see what you mean about the pace of life."

"You'll get used to it."

"I'm not going to be here long enough to get used to it."

"How about your trip? Is that working out?"

"I was really afraid that the emperor would find some reason to prevent me from going, but he was very helpful. I like him."

"By the way, you look ravishing. Is that the right word?"

"Thank you, it's certainly one that's nice to hear," she said, remembering what a long time it had taken her to get herself ready. Hoping that Marco might be there, she had indulged herself in a luxuriously long hot bath. She had plaited her hair into a French braid and chosen a tortoise shell clip to hold it together. The uplifted braid accentuated her long neck and small ears. It wasn't that she had a great deal of choice for her formal dress, but the clean, long line of a white cotton one would compliment the black morning coats the gentlemen would be wearing. She put two gold bangles on her wrist, and replaced her father's beloved World War I dog tag with a thin gold chain. *I'm ready to go to the emperor's party,* she thought.

Ceseli and Marco were abruptly interrupted by the man she remembered as the journalist on the train ride from Djibouti. He had exchanged his worn blue shirt for an elegant black silk tuxedo. She still felt unnerved by his physical size.

"Ah Antinori! And our American signorina. Not much Italian wine, I see, even if Antinori. Oh, Signorina Larson, I was hoping to find you here," Bruno Zeri said, handing her an envelope. "I took a photograph of you and the Afar girl. I hope you like it."

"It's for me?" Ceseli asked, looking more carefully at Zeri as she took the photograph out of its envelope.

"Look at the girl's eyes," he said softly.

"Where did you take it?" Marco asked, looking at it over Ceseli's shoulder.

"At the first watering station."

"I must have been sleeping."

"Soundly, like an angel," Ceseli smiled at him.

Marco looked at the photo and then at Ceseli. "The way she looks at you," he said, studying the photo more carefully. "It's almost as if she were looking at something from another world."

"The girl had quite obviously never seen a white woman before," Zeri said.

"I think it's beautiful," Ceseli said. "Thank you."

"What kind of stories are you writing?" Marco asked.

"Local color. What an Italian doctor is doing in Addis. Trust me, I'm not saying he's an Antinori. That might create undo problems for you," he said patting Marco on the shoulder. "I've heard the people here eat raw meat."

"It's considered a delicacy when it comes from a freshly killed animal," Marco said, sipping his champagne. "There are many accounts of the Empress Zauditu serving raw meat at her banquets."

"She was Menelik's daughter, right?"

"Yes, and the empress before Haile Sellassie," Marco clarified.

"Well, my assignment is to do some stories about local customs. I guess that eating raw meat might be one of them," Zeri smiled.

"But the French eat raw meat too, as I'm sure you know," Marco commented. "Steak tartare and Florentine steaks are pretty raw too, for that matter."

"I wasn't meaning to start a gastronomic war," Zeri laughed as he lit his cigar.

Ceseli studied the two men. Even though Marco was tall, Zeri towered over him. His sheer size was threatening. She felt his intense and mocking eyes, his disciplined expressions, and his unreadable countenance. She felt uneasy in his presence.

"I'm wondering what you'll do if there is a war. Will the hospital continue here?" Zeri asked.

"I guess that depends on our leader," Marco replied.

"I've just spent four months in Geneva covering the League of Nations. I'm sure that there'll be war."

"You think so?" Ceseli asked.

"Everything points in that direction, Miss Larson. I can't believe that Mussolini would be spending so much money on what he claims is a purely defensive action. He is spending that money so he can defeat Ethiopia. He's taking no chances on another defeat like the one at Adowa. The only question is when."

Ceseli was thankful when their conversation was interrupted by the commotion from the next room where they could see that the emperor was leading the empress into dinner. Ceseli took Marco's arm and followed him toward the dining room where an elaborately laid U-shaped table awaited them. Most of the guests were European and she calculated that of the almost fifty guests, men outnumbered women by three or four to one. She was pleased to find herself seated between Standish and Marco.

"Be careful of the wine. It packs a punch," Marco said, holding her chair.

"And no raw meat?" Ceseli smiled.

When it was served, the six-course dinner was in the French style of well-chosen dishes, prepared by an accomplished chef and served faultlessly by waiters in elaborate burgundy velvet jackets. The beef bourguignon was superb, as was the lentil and *teff* soufflé and the fruit tart. The French wine came from the emperor's extensive cellar. No detail was missing, and if there were anything about it that might be deemed barbaric, it was only the display of golden tableware that was dazzling. Plates, serving dishes, flatware, and high double-decked fruit dishes all were solid gold. The gold was of Ethiopian origin, but the elaborate design was that of fine European craftsmanship.

"Look at the goldfish" Marco said, indicating the large golden fishbowl on the table in front of them.

"I'm pretty sure we're not meant to eat them," she smiled. "I think I'll remember this for a long time."

"So finish the story about Axum. How are you getting there?"

"The road is supposed to be finished as far as Dessie, but after that it may be by mule. I wouldn't mind that. I'll do just about anything to get to Axum."

"Surely the Americans have one of these big overland trucks? Or you could fly."

Standish had turned to listen to their conversation. "I doubt the emperor will agree to that. Gasoline is very costly right now."

"I don't know," Marco said, weighing the alternatives. "The press has reported that the emperor wants to get his university started so there'll be a higher level of trained Ethiopians. If the Negus wants a university and you're willing to help him, a very good case could be built for getting you there. Besides, the United States minister is probably not willing to have his chief assistant gone for long, at a time like this," Marco added.

"His only assistant," Standish corrected, smiling.

"His only assistant. Agree to give him copies of your photographs and write a report. That should do it."

Standish hesitated, looking again at Ceseli. Clearly this idea was inviting. Their discussion was cut short by Yifru who was standing to propose a Champagne toast. *He looks so stately*, Ceseli thought, in a white dinner jacket with an aquamarine tie that set off his vibrantly blue eyes.

"To the oldest Christian nation in Africa," Yifru said, raising his glass and nodding in her direction. "And to Joe Louis, and the mighty punch that felled Primo Carnera."

Ceseli looked at Marco. Marco whispered that Joe Louis was the American Negro boxer who had just defeated the Italian heavyweight champion, Primo Carnera.

"I wish it were that simple," Standish said.

Ceseli looked down the table at Bruno Zeri. Although his hand was raised, he wasn't drinking. She felt again that he was studying her and it increased her sense of insecurity. Worst of all, she didn't know why this should be.

Ceseli turned back to Marco. "That's a very good idea. I'll ask Yifru what he thinks. He seems to be not only the Keeper of the Pen, but the Keeper of the Purse."

"He knows how far the emperor will go, I'm sure."

Their conversation was interrupted by the sounds of distant thunder. BOOM . . . BOOM . . . BOOM. . . .

The satiated guests walked out to the terrace as the dark sky lit up. The offshoots hung like great open flowers in the night sky. Noiselessly as a morning glory opening with the light, a rocket burst above the garden. Then BOOM, the night air resonated with the delayed report.

A second rocket soared up into the black sky, and showers of red, yellow, blue, and emerald bloomed with tendrils. As soon as the dropout was falling, another flash fired up between the hangings and burst into a magenta-red parasol. Then three altogether, each one of a different color. BOOM went the nurturing air. BOOM. BOOM. BOOM. The air smelled like firecrackers and aerial fountains of light.

She half turned to Marco among the showers of the prism. "How do they make the colors?" she asked as the fountains of light continued their booming sermons from the sky.

"Magnesium salts, I think. The yellow is from sodium, the white from magnesium, and the red from calcium. The green may be copper."

"They're lovely," she said, leaning back against him.

"They are," he whispered.

As the grand finale ended, she looked at him over her shoulder. "Thank you for your good advice. I'll go to speak with Yifru."

"Let Forsythe do it. This is very much a man's country."

"I accept that. Thank you."

"When are you coming to see how the Italians live?"

"When you invite me."

"Consider yourself invited. How about Saturday? At one."

CHAPTER 10

"How do you find anything, Danielle? The streets have no names and the building no street numbers," Ceseli asked, bewildered.

"Areas are given names for the church they are near and then you just have to know. I was born and raised here in Addis, Miss Ceseli, and I've watched each new street be built."

"I can see how you are worth your weight in gold, Daniele," she smiled.

"Thank you, Miss Ceseli, but soon you will see there are differences."

"I hope so," she answered with little conviction.

Nothing could have prepared Ceseli for the reality of Addis Ababa. Warren Rutherford said there were some decided assets: the climate, at eight thousand feet, was exhilarating and the setting was beautiful, with green hillsides stretching up to mountains on one side and down to a great valley on the other. Distant ranges and peaks in the background added majesty and variety. It was lavishly verdant, blanketed with Eucalyptus and bright with flowers.

But as Daniele drove Ceseli around the city those first days, she was quick to notice that the city was smelly and dirty, had clouds of insects, herds of goats along the streets and that beggars and lepers were everywhere. The shadows of carrion birds darkened the sky as they floated on the wind and at night hyenas howled in the streets.

The imperial capital of Addis Ababa was unassuming, unpretentious, and unfinished. While the emperor lived in his palace, the common people lived in the mud and wattle tukuls that sprawled up and down the steep ravines. These were small, round one room dwellings with thatched roofs. Cooking was done inside which made the air very smoky and bad for the eyes. There was no plumbing. Garbage and feces ran through troughs up and down the ravines and people bathed in the rivers.

But despite the poverty and all the other contradictions, the strongest plus for the Ethiopians was that they governed themselves and were not governed by the Italians, English, French, or other foreigners like other African countries.

The city had become the first fixed capital in 1886 at the request of Menelik's wife, Queen Tatou, who chose the site because of the Entoto Mountain and the rich hot mineral springs at Filwoha where she and ladies of the Shoan Royal Court liked to bathe. She named it Addis Ababa, or "new flower."

Before Addis, the capitals had been at Axum and later at Gondar and these places were abandoned when the fuel supplies were exhausted. Everyone assumed that the capital would soon move like other Shoan capitals had such as Ankober, Angolala, and Entoto. In those times, an emperor's capital was a grouping of elaborate tents, both round and rectangular, made from red, white, or black material, or from multi-colored ornamental brocades. The monarch would have several tents to serve as his residence, his court, his administrative offices, and even smaller ones for his servants. These tents were usually pitched on the highest ground with smaller tents belonging to his rases lower down the hill.

This all changed when Menilek was able to fulfill his fuel needs by planting the hillsides with the fast growing Eucalyptus trees imported from Australia. The Eucalyptus when cut down quickly pushes up new stems as strong and virile as the original. The decision to stay at Addis Ababa marked a turning point in Ethiopian history. To develop a modern state as Menelik intended, he needed a fixed capital.

The center of town was the great octagonal Cathedral of St. George. It was the handsomest of the European style buildings built by Menilek using the Italian prisoners of war captured after the defeat of the Italians at Adowa in 1896. Walking through the garden of Eucalyptus trees surrounding the cathedral, there were flocks of mourning doves scavenging on the ground for food. Women and children sat on the stairs on all sides of the church.

Removing their shoes, Daniele and Ceseli walked into the interior on the soft carpets. It was light and airy and he led her to the altar where a painting of St. George hung. The saint was on his rearing horse and had just finished slaying the dragon.

"The Emperor took this *tabot* into battle against the Italians," Daniele explained, pointing to the picture. "When he won the battle and defeated the Italians, he promised to build a church for St. George. And he always kept his promises."

Walking out the front door of the church, Ceseli saw the magnificent bronze equestrian statue of Menilek II that dominated the view out over the city. It had been commissioned by Haile Sellassie and unveiled at his coronation in 1930. Behind the church, a young lady was selling long amber colored tapers. They were several feet long and looked very rudimentary with bunches of wicks rather than one. *They look too thin to hold a flame without melting down the wax completely and causing a fire*, she thought.

"And your English, Daniele?"

"A missionary school and lots of practice," he smiled. "And Mr. Standish lends me his books."

"I didn't bring many, but you are welcome to them."

"Thank you, Miss Ceseli."

On the Saturday morning after the Emperor's reception, Daniele drove Ceseli to meet Marco at the Italian compound, a large shady enclave where Italians lived and spent their time when they were not working. It was much larger than the American one, straddling the hill leading up to Mount Entoto. The Eucalyptus were huge and brooding, with a sharp pungent odor. The small residential building was made of large blocks of tuft volcanic stone covered with plaster and painted Pompeii red. The green, white, and red Italian flag hung from a brass pole.

Marco was waiting for her at the door and took her hand to help her out of the car.

"Shall I come to pick you up, Miss Ceseli?" Daniele asked.

"No, I'll take her home, but thank you," Marco answered as he lead her inside the small villa.

"This is one of the original land grants Menilek gave to the Europeans," he said, leading the way through the living room to the terrace where there were chairs and tables. "I hope you're hungry."

"I'm always hungry."

"Yes. I remember that from the train," he said, holding her chair. "The pasta is made in Eritrea, but to our specifications. It's funny what you need to have in a colony for it to be considered Italian. Pasta is our first, but what would the British Empire do without its teatime?

"I don't know," Ceseli said, looking at the spaghetti on her plate and starting to eat.

"I'm a pretty good cook, don't you think?"

"Excellent," she said with her mouth full.

"My mother is the good cook. She says the best food only comes from the best ingredients. She puts a lot of love into everything she makes."

"Well, she was a very good teacher. My father was a surprisingly good cook, too. He liked to wear one of those white chef's hat. You know the ones with the balloon on top. He said people respect hats. Give someone the right hat and they feel important. Like policemen or mailmen," she paused. "I don't think I've had food this good in a long time."

"You're just hungry."

She looked at him while he ate. The spaghetti was neatly coiled around his fork, like hay in round bales. *Why can't I do that*, she thought noting the long strands of spaghetti drooping from her own fork.

"Just take a few at a time and twirl."

Ceseli tried, but still ended up with an unruly looking mouthful. "In Italian restaurants in New York they give you a spoon to help you."

"I can get you a spoon if you want one."

"No. I'll do it your way. I hope it just needs practice, like eating with chopsticks."

"I don't think I could manage that," he smiled. "But it's not crucial. There aren't any Chinese restaurants in Addis, or in Florence."

"There are certainly a lot in New York. Kung Hei Fat Choy!"

"What's that?"

"Happy New Year's in Chinese, I think. Daddy and I, and my grandparents, never missed Chinese New Year's celebrations in New York. There's a large Chinese population in China Town. It was a lot of fun and great food."

"Then when I come to New York you'll have to teach me."

"That's a deal."

They ate for a few minutes in silence, but it wasn't a heavy one. "On the train you said your family wasn't Fascist."

"That's why they sent me to a British school, so that I wouldn't be brainwashed by the Fascist propaganda. My father told me I'd thank him for it one day. I remember being with him in his office in Florence one summer day when there was a rally outside in the square in front of the railroad station. It was jammed with waving black banners and blaring music. The Fascist boy scouts were in their starched black shirts and perfectly pressed pants. They were going to a youth camp. It was exciting, but it was scary, too. Lots of my friends were going and I wanted to go. They kept telling me how much fun we would have." Marco paused, remembering. "My father would not allow it. I argued with him at dinner every night for a week. There was a sad expression in his eyes that day. He told me that he and my mother had decided to send me to the British school. I was very upset. All my closest friends were going to the Fascist school, but he wouldn't budge." Marco paused again. "He was right, of course. But I only wanted to do what other boys my age were doing. I didn't want to be different. Can I ask you something?"

"Sure," Ceseli said, wondering what had interrupted his thoughts.

"You speak often of your father. But you've never mentioned your mother."

Ceseli put her fork down. "I never knew her. She died right after I was born. I'm sure she was a wonderful person because my father loved her so much. The only thing Daddy regretted was that he never got to say goodbye." She looked up at the sloughing trees. "He never made me feel guilty. But there were times that I did blame myself. I didn't want to be different either. But children do a lot of things with their mothers that I couldn't do. I lived with Daddy and his parents, Nanna and Poppy. They were wonderful to me. And I was lucky because my mother's mother spent a lot of time with me. She was the Frances of the grandmothers. Every Saturday morning, she took me to the Museum of Natural History. And we'd do a lot of other things too, like pull taffy or go to the Washington market; that was the biggest food market in New York. You could buy anything there, buffalo meat or even ostrich eggs. She loved to bet, so we'd bet on who could find the most French cheeses or the smelliest ones."

"She sounds like fun."

"She is. The moment she weaned me from Santa Claus she got me looking for dressed fleas. Mexican dressed fleas. Only Mexican fleas were big enough to dress."

"There are such things?"

"There are Mexican fleas, that's for sure, but I'm just not sure if what I was seeing were actually fleas. I could never see the fleas, but she could, of course. She'd bet me she could train them to jump. Sotzy likes to bet, but she doesn't like to lose."

"Sotzy?"

"Something her younger sister started calling her. I don't know how you get Sotzy from Frances, but it was her nickname. She is remarkable. In Connecticut, we'd get little green tree toads and she'd make a big chalk circle and put them in the middle, then see which one jumped out of the circle fastest. Do you have tree toads in Florence?"

"I don't know."

"Sotzy could always find something to bet on. She lived in Florence for a while when her mother was there being treated by a doctor."

"Did she like it?"

"I think she did. I saw one of her sketchbooks of the bridges on the Arno River. She has a lot of talent. She has tried to teach me, but I'm not anywhere near as good."

"Your grandmother sounds like a special kind of person. She's still alive?"

"Yes, and if it weren't for Sotzy I wouldn't be here. She didn't think I should cancel the trip. She encouraged me to come. My father would expect me to get on with my life and Axum is part of my plans."

"Did she like your father?"

"Oh yes. In the summer she took me with her to her farm in Connecticut. Daddy would come up to the farm on weekends and we'd go sailing or fishing. He was very serious when he was fishing. I didn't like putting the worms on the hook or taking the fish off. I hated catfish. They always stung me. But I liked being with him. So did Sotzy." Ceseli tried to fight back the tears that felt hot behind her eyes.

"It's okay," Marco said, smiling with that same sense of compassion she had felt on the train. "Grief is a very normal emotion. You don't have to hold it back. Mourning is just as much work as being a painter or a writer. You have to leave enough time. Eventually it will get better."

Ceseli smiled at him, wiping away the tears. "Sotzy took me to the ship and saw me off," she continued. "I asked her if she wanted to come. She said she'd slow me down. As always, she was probably right." Ceseli waited a moment before asking, "How is your work going?"

"Pretty well. I've been gathering herbs for my medicines. Hey, that's a fine idea, even if I do say so myself. When you get back from Axum, come and gather flowers with me. There's a hot thermal spring just out of town. At Filwoha. It's where Queen Tatou went to bathe. When the water comes to the surface it's boiling."

"That sounds like fun. I'll count on it."

The afternoon was fading as Marco drove her back to the American compound. "I'm looking forward to hearing about your trip. Good luck," he said, holding her hand and kissing it.

"That's something I'm always long on. Sotzy taught me that."

As she walked toward her tukul, she couldn't help wondering what she was feeling. Marco was so easy to talk to, not like so many men she knew who were so caught up in their own lives that they weren't interested in hers.

She realized that she didn't find it easy to be with men. She had been so protected by her father and his parents that she didn't feel easy with strangers, but somehow it was hard to think of Marco as a stranger. She felt like she'd known him forever and she knew that she was looking forward to seeing him again.

CHAPTER 11

"Can you smell that?" Ceseli asked.

"What?"

"You can almost smell it. The cradle of Christendom."

"I thought you meant the mules," Standish said, looking at her and kicking his mule to keep up.

Ceseli and Standish looked out over the spectacular Valley of Axum. The huge valley was lush, watered by the wide Mai Chan River. It was an astoundingly lovely day, with clear aquamarine skies and the few clouds overhead were thick, like giant sea turtles floating upside down.

Ceseli thought back on the previous days. The embassy's truck had behaved admirably on the long drive from Addis up to Dessie. They drove through great forests of weeping Cedars, Podocarpus gracing the lower slopes along with Hagenia, St. John's Wort, giant heath, and everlastings. The trip was alive with the flights of guinea fowl, herds of graceful gazelle, antelope, and eland. She had seen a buzzard almost as big as an ostrich. She could still smell the intense fragrance of the flowers and hear the songs of the small, brightly colored birds.

The emperor's sky blue Puss Moth had met them in Dessie. It was a high-winged monoplane capable of flying at one hundred sixty miles per hour and carried a pilot and two passengers in a tricycle arrangement, with the pilot up front in a cabin under the broad sweep of the wings.

The handsome pilot was Yifru's nephew, Yohannes. His handshake was firm and decisive. He was a bit taller than his uncle, slender, well built, with an open friendly smile and the same startlingly blue eyes. His hair was combed out into a huge halo setting off his high cheekbones and fine features. A white silk scarf and a mauve shirt under his smart khaki uniform accentuated the café latte color of his skin. On anyone else the color mauve would seem effeminate, but there was nothing effeminate about Yohannes. Both his English and French were excellent. Ceseli liked him immediately.

"Have you ever flown in a small plane, Miss Larson?" Yohannes asked.

"I've never flown at all."

"I'll take it very easy, no acrobatics. You'll be fine."

"Thank you for the reassurance," she smiled.

Once they were airborne, Ceseli and Standish could see that the land was as unique as any in the world. A relief map could not do it justice. Sometimes it was lunar and sometimes infernal, but never merely earthly. In the north, the Ethiopian plateau rose sharply within a few miles from sea level to eight thousand feet. Representing the most gigantic swath of erosion in the world, this highland was cut through by innumerable gorges and valleys, many of them on the scale of the Grand Canyon. Extraordinary rock formations bore witness to the volcanic activity that had shaped the skeleton of this incredible landscape, its topography imposing isolation and with it timelessness.

Below, they could see that on the spurs and mesas that rose from the canyons, even when their sides were vertical and their surfaces just a few acres, there were fields and sometimes villages and round Coptic churches. On each plateau there were squat, toad-like tukuls made of piled fieldstone, all kraaled with a thorn fence and speckled around with grazing sheep and cattle. Each flat mountaintop was ringed with cactus euphorbia or wild lemon to prevent the cattle from falling over the edge of the plateau as sacrifices to the Gods of the Cliff.

"Look at that," she yelled above the roar of the engine. "The highland protected them for thousands of years."

"Who?" Standish shouted back.

"The Axumite people. The Axumite state covered this whole area from the Sudan to Somalia and all along the Red Sea coast and as far as the Nile. Their only rival was Rome."

"How do you know that?"

"A sixth century Christian monk came here and wrote about it. He claimed that the Axumite merchant navies sailed as far as India, China, and even Gaul. They carried gold, ivory, rhinoceros horn, frankincense and myrrh, and in return imported cloth, glass, iron, olive oil, and wine."

"Why did it end?"

She shrugged. "That's what we're trying to find out. Problem is that with one exception, there is no documentation. The only things we know are from a brief account written by a Greek traveler named Cosmas Indicopleustes, who after his trip to Axum reported that the King of Ethiopia's four towered palace was adorned with four brass figures of a unicorn, as well as the skin of a rhinoceros stuffed with chaff. He wrote that the king dressed in a short toga with gold necklaces and armbands, rode about in a golden chariot pulled by elephants, and kept several giraffes as his pets. That was in the fifth century. I'm not sure one could call that barbaric splendor befitting a capital of what had by that time become the most important power between the Roman Empire and Persia."

Today, as Ceseli and Standish rode their mules toward the center of the valley she could see the obelisks in front of her. Then in a large nearby field they finally found all the others, lying on the ground like a complicated maze of giant matchsticks. It was a horizontal forest of huge monolithic pieces of dark granite. Some of them were rudimentary, but others were elaborately carved.

"Each of the obelisks is a single block of granite. This could weigh three or four hundred tons," she said, drawing her hand over the rough-hewn surface. "How do you think they carved them, brought them here, and erected them?"

Standish was walking around the side of an obelisk. "Like the pyramids, I guess. Elephants, or maybe slaves. What did they do with them?"

"They're grave markers and they honor a celestial god," Ceseli answered, feeling awed by these surroundings. "Sun worship was very popular in the towns of Yemen in Arabia. Queen Makeda ruled a part of southern Arabia in Sabea that is known as Sheba. That's how she got the title of Queen of Axum and Sheba. People forget the Axum part and she is usually referred to as the Queen of Sheba. Do you believe that the Queen of Sheba was Ethiopian?" Ceseli asked, turning back to the present.

"I'm not very good at believing."

"No problem. Do you know anything about obelisks?" Ceseli asked as she circled one of the standing obelisks.

"Only that there are lots of them in Rome, and one in New York."

"In Central Park. I used to play near there."

"That's where I learned to ride my bike."

"Do you remember all the impromptu baseball games in the park?"

"I was an avid baseball fan. I wanted to be a professional pitcher," Standish smiled.

"Yankees or Dodgers?"

"Yankees, of course."

"Me too. I didn't want to be a pitcher, but I loved playing softball with Daddy during the summer. Hey, look at this one," she said, pausing to look more closely at a huge obelisk broken into four pieces. "It's carved as if it were a tower. This is meant to be the door," she said, pointing to the carved sham door which had a stone lock carved into it. "Count them. It's thirteen stories tall."

"They weren't superstitious."

"I guess not. The Sun God lives up there in the firmament at the top. These flat basins collected the blood from the offerings."

"What kind of offering?" Standish asked.

"I'm sure they weren't human," Ceseli said as she took out her sketchpad and began drawing one of the standing obelisks. She looked up to the height of the obelisk. "Maybe sixty or seventy feet? What do you think?"

"You want to measure it?" he asked, shading his eyes from the sun.

"I was thinking of a small boy and a coconut tree."

"And that I'd like, a coconut right about now."

"I'm very serious," she smiled.

"So am I! Must have been very impressive when they were all standing," Standish said as he ventured looking out over the valley. "That's very good," he said, walking behind her to look at the sketch.

"Thank you. Drawing is one of the first things you learn as an archaeologist." She turned to a new page and walked to a huge altar stone.

Standish stooped to look more closely at the carvings on the stone. "It's like a house of cards. Any idea why the obelisks fell?"

"A group of German archaeologists who came here in 1906 thought it could have been the silting up of the Mai Chan River. That one," she said, pointing in the direction of the river. "They lost their balance and toppled over. Or, razed to the ground by some Muslim army."

"Or an earthquake?"

"That might explain why they go in every direction. Razing them would probably mean deciding in what direction."

Ceseli had returned to the fallen obelisk and was stooping over one of the pieces. "This is carved on three of the surfaces. Do you know how rare that makes it? Think there's any chance to look at the fourth side?"

"What were you thinking of?"

"Tunneling under just enough to see if the carving continues? Or lifting it."

"I don't know how many elephants or slaves we can count on."

"What about oxen?"

Standish stooped to look at the thorns and grass matted around the edges. He walked around the obelisk and looked at the other broken pieces. "Perhaps down from this edge. We can try that tomorrow."

Remounting, they galloped the mules over the meadow with its sky high grass. It could have been a sea with two ships, their sails trimmed neatly. The gait of the mule and the wooden western style saddle were different from those she had ridden before, but wasn't uncomfortable. She looked across at Standish who was holding his own.

She felt exuberant, free, wild, transported. It was not yet hot and she had been right to wear her blue jeans rather than a pair of jodhpurs. Her hair was lightened by the sun, and braided in two thick tresses that barely contained its volume. As they rode, the wind blew her straw hat, held in place by a cord knotted under her chin onto her shoulders and she felt the wind warm against her face.

As they rode, they passed two young boys whipping an ox as it tilled the field with an archaic wooden plow pulled behind it. The ox was small by American standards, but so were the children, who looked to be seven or eight, but were probably several years older.

Finally they reached a magnificent tank, or reservoir, where the waters of a stream were artificially confined and from where the town got its water. It was an open deep water reservoir dug down into the red granite of the hillside and approached by means of a rough-hewn stairway.

"It's known as the Queen of Sheba's pleasure bath. Since the beginning of Christian times it was used for baptismal ceremonies to celebrate the Holy Epiphany, or Timkat."

"Some bath! This must be one hundred fifty square feet," Standish said. "Half of the ladies of Axum could have bathed in here with ease."

As they watched, three women descended the rock-hewn steps carrying gourds balanced on their heads to collect water. Their stature was so regal, their balance so perfect that they could easily have been royal women in waiting rather than modest peasant women.

Ceseli looked at him before removing her boots, tucking her legs over the edge, and dangling them in the cold water.

"Can you hand me my bag?" she asked while making herself comfortable. Standish handed her the bag and was not surprised when she pulled out her bible. She opened it and began flipping through the pages. "You know why this place is so important?"

"It's the place where the Ark of the Covenant is supposed to be."

"That too. But because of its holiness, it has the status of a sacred city. Axum is the only place in Ethiopia where a man or woman can take refuge and be safe from justice. He only has to go to the porch of the sacred enclosure, ring the bell and declare three times in a loud voice his intention of taking refuge. And all Christian kings were crowned here up until the 1870s."

"I wonder how many people actually take advantage of that," Standish mused.

"I don't know. Let's go see St. Mary of Zion."

CHAPTER 12

THE LIGHT WAS DIMMING as they dismounted in front of the holiest church in Ethiopia. Ceseli had already read that the "new" St. Mary of Zion was a Portuguese style structure, with some fragments of the earlier Byzantine church set into the walls. It had a flat top and battlements on a little bell tower. The church had been built on a raised platform above the ancient temple that existed in the days of sun worship.

The few stones still in place were drafted stones with chiseled edges put together without mortar. Inside, the church had one large vestibule and a sanctuary known as the Holy of Holies. It was this sacred chapel that contained the Ark of the Covenant.

"What does your bible say about this?" Standish asked as they studied the ruins.

"A Portuguese chaplain, Francisco Alvarez, was here in 1520. He was the first European to come to Ethiopia and he left very detailed accounts. He said that King Ezana built the church when the Axumite kingdom converted to Christianity in the fourth century AD. Parts of it have been destroyed and rebuilt several times. The first time was by order of Queen Gudit in the tenth century. Then again in the sixteenth century by Muslims who were trying to conquer the whole area from the coast up. The most powerful of them was Ahmad ibn Ibrihim al-Ghazi. He was a warlord and his battle name, Gragn, meant left-handed."

"But he didn't succeed."

"No. But they did drive the Portuguese out, and with them all their efforts to convert the Ethiopians to the Roman Catholic Church."

"Do you get the idea that history is about to repeat itself?" Standish asked.

"How do you mean?"

"Don't you think Mussolini has the Pope's blessing? It would give him a holy mission. Bringing the Catholic Church to Ethiopia."

"You think that's his plan?"

"It would be mine," Standish said as he looked at the church. "It's where the Ark of the Covenant is supposed to be." Standish rubbed his forehead, trying to reconcile his thoughts. "But if your story of the Queen of Sheba is correct, and if Solomon sired a son, and this son you call Menilek did steal the Ark of the Covenant and brought it to Ethiopia, then it must have been here well before the time of Christ."

"Legend says it was kept protected in a monastery on an island on the east coast of Lake Tana. Then when King Ezana converted to Christianity, he sent for it. Now that we're here, let's go see where the Ark is supposed to be. Women aren't allowed in the Holy of Holies so you need to take wonderful visual notes."

On the doorstep of St. Mary of Zion was an ancient deacon, leaning on a prayer stick, his back almost parallel with the ground. He wore a black robe and had a long, straggling patriarchal beard. As they walked toward him, Ceseli was sure that the cloudy cataracts completely dimmed his sight. He turned hearing, but not seeing them approach. He held out his right hand and she noticed it was like a dried prune, and his grip was delicate as if he were offering a tiny bird.

The smile she gave him was in her voice and he reciprocated, his face creasing like precious papyrus. "Good day, Father, may peace be with you."

"And with you, my daughter." The eyes followed her words. "You have come to see the tabot? The Ark?"

"Father, I know I cannot enter this holy place," Ceseli answered, "but my friend will go if he can. He has come from across the ocean to see the tabot."

"He cannot see the tabot. No man can look at it. Only at the holy of the holies, where it resides."

"Yes, father, we know. You alone among men can look upon it."

"I am the Keeper of the Ark, but even I cannot look at the face of god, only at the container of his laws."

Standish followed the priest who, although disfigured to such an extent, did not lose his noble bearing. While he was gone, Ceseli walked in the vestibule noting a huge collection of varied drums, banners, and crutches all given by the faithful worshippers who had been cured. She took several photos of the inscriptions carved into the stone.

Looking around, she found a comfortable spot on the wall of the enclosure and reread the entry she had made in her bible.

'God himself inscribed the ten words of the law upon two tablets of stone. These were the Ten Commandments. Moses put the stone tablets into the Ark of the Covenant, that was a chest made of wood and gold.

The Ark accompanied the Israelites during their wanderings in the wilderness and their conquest of the Promised Land. It brought them victories. King Solomon placed the Ark in the holy of holies of the temple he built in Jerusalem. The Ethiopians called the Ark a tabot. Really, it is an altar slab. In an Ethiopian church it is the *tabota Zion*, not the building itself, that is consecrated.'

Ceseli opened her bible and began to read the *Kebra Nagast* from where she had left off on the train. According to the story, Queen Makeda, also known as the Queen of Axum and of Sheba, had little experience in government when she became queen in the tenth century BC. One of her closest advisors suggested that she should travel to Jerusalem, where a famous King Solomon was known for his wisdom. Solomon was also a healer and Makeda had a clubfoot. So Makeda set out with seven hundred ninety-seven camels, mules, and donkeys laden with precious gifts. When she arrived, Solomon received her with great pomp for she was a beautiful queen. He agreed to let her learn as long as she paid her own way and took nothing without permission.

As it is said in the Book of Kings, Solomon was a lover of women and he married wives of' the Hebrews and the Egyptians, and women who were reported to be beautiful. He had four hundred wives and six hundred concubines. This he did not for the sake of fornication, but with the thought that perhaps God would give him male children from each one of these women and his sons would inherit the cities of the enemy and would destroy those who worshiped idols.

The queen stayed in Jerusalem and studied Solomon's religion and his rule. When she was ready to leave, she sent a message to Solomon. Solomon answered inviting her to a banquet. When she accepted, Solomon rejoiced and ordered the royal table set according to the law of the kingdom. He spread near his place purple hangings and laid down carpets, he burned aromatic powders, sprinkled oil of myrrh, and scattered frankincense and other costly incense in all directions.

The queen came and passed into a hidden place set apart just behind the king where she could see everything, but not be seen. And with intent, Solomon sent to her meats that would make her thirsty, drinks that were mingled with vinegar and fish and dishes made with pepper. *He's a dirty old man*, Ceseli thought.

And after the meal ended, the king went to the queen, and he said, "Take thine ease here until daybreak."

And she said unto him, "Swear unto me by thy God, the God of Israel, that thou wilt not take me by force. For if I, who according to the law of men am a maiden, be seduced, I should travel on my journey home in sorrow, affliction, and tribulation."

Solomon answered, "I swear that I shall not take thee by force, but thou must swear unto me that thou wilt not take by force anything that is in my house."

The queen laughed and said unto him, "Being a wise man, do not speak as a fool. Do you imagine that I have come hither through love of riches? My own kingdom is as wealthy as yours, and there is nothing that I wish for that I lack. I have only come in quest of thine wisdom." And she said unto him, "Swear to *me* that thou wilt not take me by force, and I on my part will swear not to take by force thy possessions."

And he swore to her and made her swear. And the king went up on his bed on the one side of the chamber and the servants made ready for her a bed on the other side. Solomon instructed a manservant to wash out a cup and set it in a vessel of water while the queen is looking on and then to shut the door and go to sleep. The servant did as the king commanded. Solomon pretended to be asleep and watched the queen intently.

The queen slept a little, but when she woke her mouth was dry and she was thirsty. She moved her lips and sucked with her mouth. She wanted to drink the water. She looked at King Solomon thinking that he was sleeping soundly. She rose and making no sound, went to the water bowl and lifted the cup to drink the water.

Solomon, of course, was not asleep. He was waiting for her to take the water.

He seized her wrist before she could drink the water, and said, "Why hast thou broken the oath?"

She answered, "Is the oath broken by my drinking water?"

"Is there anything under the heavens that is more valuable than water?"

"I have sinned against myself and thou art free from thy oath. But let me drink some water."

And he permitted her to drink the water and after he worked his will with her and they slept together.

The day of her departure, Solomon took her aside so that they might be alone and he took off his signet ring and gave it to her as a remembrance. If she should bear a son, then this ring will be a sign of recognition.

The queen did bear a son, whom she named Menilek I. When he became a man, he traveled to Jerusalem to meet his father. Solomon was pleased with him and offered to make him crown prince. Menilek, however, was determined to return home and Solomon graciously anointed his son King of Ethiopia. He chose from the oldest sons of his highest noble families to go with his son to Ethiopia and to establish there a kingdom. Among these young courtiers was Azarayas, the first born of the High Priest, Zadok. Yet these young men, who had grown up in Jerusalem, could not think of living without their god and the Ark of the Covenant. So Azarayas stole the Ark and hid it in the caravan destined for Axum.

Ceseli put down the book. Did Menelik revenge his mother and steal the Ark? "So that's who did it," she said aloud, understanding what had happened.

"Who did what?" Standish asked, startling her with his presence.

"Azarayas, the son of Zadok. He would have had access to the keys of the temple."

"You mean to steal the Ark?"

"Yes. To steal the Ark. How was it?"

"It's really run down, and it's very dark. Even with candles you can't see much. There are some paintings on the walls. But almost nothing else."

"And the Ark?"

"Ceseli, there's a big box. The priest seems very concerned about its safety. It looks like it's made of wood. How do I know whether that's what you call the Ark? It's a big moldy box, but I can't tell you anything much about it."

"Bezaleel made the Ark of Acacia wood and plated it inside and out with pure gold. It was two and a half cubits long and one and a half cubits high and wide. A cubit is the length of a forearm from elbow to the tip of the second finger. Approximately eighteen inches, I guess. Like this," she said, indicating with her hands.

"So it would be almost four feet long and more than two wide and high. Well, the moldy, old box was about that size. If they were so proud of being converted to Christianity, why would the Ethiopians build a church to protect a pre-Christian relic?"

"It contains the Ten Commandments. Christians believe in them as well."

"And you really believe it's here."

"That's what I'm trying to find out. Daddy believed I was right. The box must contain something, otherwise why not throw it out?"

"I don't know what to say. I know you must be very disappointed. I'm sorry women aren't allowed inside."

"There is only one day I could see it, that's when it is brought outside and paraded around. But that's not going to work because it's on the Epiphany in January. I'll be in Rome long before that."

CHAPTER 13

"LET'S TRY TO FIGURE out just how big Axum really was," Ceseli said early the next morning. As they rode north of the obelisks, everywhere they looked there were traces of buildings with large stone foundations, structures of considerable size that must have been temples or palaces or other public buildings. They found another field of monoliths, rough-hewn like the menhirs of Brittany in France and Stonehenge in England. Ceseli photographed them carefully, marking down in a ledger a description of each photo so that she would not forget.

Later, southwest of the town. they found the Mount Gobederah granite quarry. It was a huge semi-circular quarry, almost like an amphitheater or football stadium, and it seemed to be the source of all the obelisks. On one side, there was an obelisk that had not been freed from its excavation site. It hung with five sides cut free like a sculpture waiting to be released.

On the granite boulder, Ceseli found the carved frieze of a leaping lioness. She had read of it in a book by a British traveler and amateur archaeologist, J. Theodore Bent, who had visited Axum in the 1890s and had discovered the frieze. She had copied the account into her bible.

"*It is halfway up the steep hill at the foot of a massive granite projection,*" *he had written,* "*from which I imagine the ancients obtained their large blocks of granite for their monoliths. It is a very spirited work of art, measuring ten feet eight inches, from the nose to the tail. The running attitude is admirable and given the sweep of the hind legs show that the artist had thorough command of his subject.*"

"I need to photograph this. Do you have any matches in that saddlebag?"

"What are you going to do?"

"Just what Mr. Bent did!"

Despite the fact that Standish claimed to have been an eagle scout, it took some time to get the fire started. When the twigs had become charcoal she rubbed them along the carving so that the lines were visible to her camera.

"What's this?" Standish asked, pointing to a small circle near the nose. "Shall I rub this as well?"

"Let me see," Ceseli said, kneeling to study what appeared to be two rays of sun. "Yes, let's get this too."

While Standish rubbed in the charcoal, Ceseli opened her book to Bent's description. "*A few inches from the nose of the lioness is a circular disc with rays, probably intended to represent the sun, and the whole thing impresses one strongly with the knowledge and skill possessed by the artist in depicting animal life.*"

As she looked more closely at the gray stone the small circular sun now looked very different. She kept tracing her finger over the points and the carving.

"Not the rays from the sun, although that's an honest mistake considering the people here were sun worshippers. It's a cross. A very stylized cross. A Christian cross on an obviously pagan subject."

"Why do you say pagan? It could just mean that there were lions in the area."

"The question is why the cross, not why the lioness. Why a cross? I don't know. But I'm willing to bet that I'm right. Can you see it?"

"Yes," Standish said, looking more closely where she was tracing the carving.

Later in the afternoon, they rode back to a promontory about a mile and a half up the valley to a hilltop fortress with deep dungeons and underground chambers.

These were ancient tombs, called by the local people the Tombs of Kaleb, the king who according to Abyssinian story, led his victorious army into Yemen in the sixth century.

As they talked, Standish lit a candle and they descended into the dungeon where the blocks of stone were very large and seemed to be much older than the sixth century. The stones were wet and slippery underfoot and smelled of dank. The underground chamber was full of large stone coffers. Standish passed the light across the end of one of the coffers and then stopped. Carved into the stone was another cross.

Ceseli stooped to see it better. *It's much too dark for a photograph, but not for a rubbing*, she thought. She took a page from her sketchpad and started rubbing the pencil along the cross so that the image was clearly visible. In the next large rectangular chamber, they found two more crosses. One quite crude, but the second high up on the ceiling was beautifully rendered.

That evening, Ceseli leaned back from the fire in the small room they were sharing. Here, they could cook over a fire pit. They each had a bedroom with a shuttered window. The beds were made by stretching a dried camel's hide across a wooden frame. It was like sleeping on an army cot, but surprisingly comfortable. They also shared a bathroom, if you could call it that, with a pitcher of water and a large earthenware bowl. The toilet was of the Turkish style, really a squat hole.

The days have been rewarding, she thought. Following Standish's suggestion, they found an agile young boy who climbed the standing obelisk to measure it with a cord held to the helmet at the top. With equal ingenuity, they found a pair of oxen and successfully lifted the side of the smallest of the pieces of the broken obelisk. By digging under the slightly elevated edge, she was able to make a rubbing and confirm that the carving continued on the fourth side. It was the only obelisk she had found carved on all four sides, and from an archaeologist's point of view, unique.

But the most important part of the trip had happened quite unexpectedly. When they were about to lower the piece of obelisk, Ceseli saw several pieces of what she thought were metal disks. "Don't lower it yet," she shouted, as she started to scrape the disks out from under the obelisk. "They're coins."

Standish bent down and looked where she was pointing. "Coins? Get your hands out of there before something happens."

"This is the last," she said, scrubbing her hand over the hard earth.

That night, Ceseli sat with the coins and a small bowl of water. The mud and debris of centuries washed away to show beautifully worked gold coins.

"What are you going to do with them?" Standish asked.

"Give them to the emperor."

"What are you thinking?" Standish asked, somewhat later as he fed some small pieces of wood into the holes left by the fire between the other logs.

"About how time does heal," she answered. "I wouldn't have believed it a few months ago."

"Doing something completely different can help too. Come on," Standish said, handing her a plate of injera, the crepe-like bread made from teff with the hot, spicy wot sauce.

"This is hot," she said, her eyes beginning to tear as she scooped up the spicy hot tomatoes and chili sauce. "Daddy would have loved to be here," she said a few minutes later. "Hey, as long as I have you as a captive audience, tell me about the coronation. You said you would, and Warren says it's a wonderful story."

"I'm going to bore you. I'm not much good at storytelling."

"Fishing for compliments?"

Standish sat down and was silent for a moment. "It was any typically sharp blue Ethiopian morning. You could already smell the pungent odor of the breakfast fires. On the Ethiopian calendar, it was Tekemt 23, 1923. On our calendar, it was Sunday, November 2, 1930. Either way, it was Coronation Day.

"Addis had been lavishly prepared for the Coronation. Ras Tafari Makonnen was already the Prince Regent and had been since 1912. He had decided to use his baptismal name, Haile Sellassie, as his throne name. So he would be known as Haile Sellassie I, King of Kings of Ethiopia, the Conquering Lion of the Tribe of Judah, Negus Negusti, the 334th of all the kings of Ethiopia and 134th of the Christian Kings of the Empire.

"Workmen were still busy on the final completion of the coronation monument which was being erected on a newly built triangle in the center of the city. The three pronged propeller blades suggesting the title of the emperor: Power of the Trinity."

"What about Menelik's statue? The one in front of St. George's Cathedral?"

"That one was already finished. It just needed to be unveiled. Yifru had taken the time to explain to me what to expect during the coronation ceremony. Our delegation had received a detailed schedule so that we could follow it in English. I knew that the emperor and empress had already spent the night in prayer and meditation with the priests in the Cathedral of St. George.

"The Coptic Church was revered and all-powerful in Ethiopia I had been told, but that day it showed its impressive might and splendor. Our legation is only a five minute drive from St. George's, but we had to be ready and in our places before 7 a.m. that morning. All of us were wearing a morning coat with a flower in the lapel. We looked pretty shabby next to the brilliant military uniforms of the English, French, Germans, and Italians.

"Through the early morning, the prayers continued in Ge'ez. The chanting was accompanied by the dancing of the priests with their great pulsating drums, cadence of cymbals, and brass *sistra*. One of the men in our delegation said they were like the ancient Jewish rites that were in use at the time when King David danced before the Ark of the Covenant.

"All the important European powers were represented. So was the Ethiopian nobility. I knew that Tafari didn't want to offend any of the major European powers, so he bought six matching bay horses from Austria to pull a ceremonial coach previously used at the coronation of Kaiser Wilhelm of Germany. A British naval band played music. The city police were outfitted in khaki uniforms from Belgium. Some of the things were quite comical."

"Such as?"

"Well the police and bodyguards wore beautiful new khaki uniforms, but no shoes. They stood at attention ready to direct traffic. But there wasn't any. There were several great triumphal arches, like the imperial arches of Rome, except they were of papé maché, not marble. Oceans of green, yellow and red bunting lined the streets trying to hide the tukuls.

"Yifru said that there would be forty-nine bishops and priests in groups of seven, who had held place for seven days and nights in the seven corners of St. George's Cathedral. That morning it seemed that they were joined by hundreds of others chanting continuously the Psalms of David.

"We couldn't all fit into St. George's Cathedral so a large temporary pavilion had been built on the west side of the cathedral and that's where the ceremony took place. There was seating for seven hundred officials and guests. The sidewalls of the building had been draped with white cloth, decorated only at the pillars with clusters of small flags. The lofty ceiling was made of orange and yellow cloth in several drapes and across the entire front were rich gold-shot red curtains falling in loose folds to divide the inner sanctuary from the main portion of the hall.

"Facing me across the space in front of the throne chairs was a row of imposing large gilded chairs. The Prince of Savoy, Italy's official representative sat on one. I wondered what he felt like sitting in a church built by Italian prisoners of war. Next to him sat the Duke of Gloucester, representing the king of England, splendid in his guardsman uniform. The representative of France was Marshal Franchet d'Espérey, who was balancing a gold baton on his knees. Next to me on each side were two gaunt and venerable feudal chieftains who had lion mane headdresses that continued to scratch and tickle me."

Ceseli smiled listening to his tale.

"I remember the rich colors of the hangings, the thick floor rugs, and the costumes. It was the most awesome thing I'd ever seen. In front of the sanctuary were the large thrones of the emperor and the empress. The throne at the left, for the emperor, was decorated in scarlet and gold and the throne for Her Majesty Menen, in blue and gold.

"Shortly after 7:30, and just as it had been planned, the studded doors to the Holy of Holies opened and through them came the muffled distant chant of hundreds of priests. Dressed in white silk communion robes, his imperial majesty entered the ceremonial hall. In front of him came the clergy waiving incense burners. As he took his place on the throne, the ceremony began. There were a few minutes of silence, then it was broken by his holiness the Abuna Kyrillos, the Archbishop speaking in Arabic. As a result, I didn't understand a lot of it."

"Arabic?"

"The Ethiopian Coptic Church depends on the Coptic Church in Alexandria, Egypt."

"Sorry. I'd forgotten."

Standish raised his voice as he continued in the lilting words of the Archbishop. "Ye princes and ministers, Ye nobles and chiefs of the army, Ye soldiers and people of Ethiopia, and ye doctors and chiefs of the clergy, ye professors and priests look Ye upon our Emperor Haile Sellassie the First, descended from the dynasty of Menilek I who was born of Solomon and the Queen of Sheba, a dynasty perpetuated without interruption from that time to ours.

"Before the questioning of the Abuna, the emperor had made his sacred pledge to uphold the orthodox religion of the Alexandrian Church, to support and administer the laws of the country for the betterment of his people, to maintain the integrity of Ethiopia and to found schools for developing the spiritual and material welfare of his subjects. After that he was presented with the royal insignia.

"Then the Abuna anointed His Majesty's head with seven different ancient scented ointments, one for each of the seven ornaments of the coronation."

"Again sevens," Ceseli observed.

"One by one, in token of his position and responsibility, the emperor received the gold embroidered scarlet coronation robes, the jeweled sword, a gold and ivory imperial scepter, the orb, the diamond encrusted ring, and two gold filigree lances. Seventh, and last, came his magnificent crown made from pure native gold, encrusted with diamonds and emeralds.

"Then the Abuna finished, 'That God may make this crown of sanctity and glory. That, by the grace and blessings that we have given, you may have an unshaken faith and a pure heart, in order that you may inherit the crown eternal. So be it. Blessed Be the King of Israel.'

"Then for the first time in Ethiopian history, the crown prince was installed, followed by the empress and other members of the royal family, signifying that the emperor was intent on creating a dynasty. He was the 134th of the Christian Kings of the Empire. He intended for his son to be the 135th."

"It's a wonderful story. And it's all based on a myth, isn't it?" Ceseli asked. "That the emperor is the descendant of Solomon and Sheba?"

"Some people feel very passionately about it."

"I know. Thanks."

"Don't mention it."

CHAPTER 14

"Hurry up, Ceseli, we'll be late and Rutherford doesn't like that."

"Just a minute. Let me at least wash my face and change out of these jeans. I've been wearing them for a week. I'll meet you on the verandah."

Ceseli looked around the tukul. It seemed like ages since she left for Axum and yet it was only eight days. She pulled off her jeans and put on her linen skirt and a clean blouse and exchanged her boots for red leather sandals. As she walked up to the terrace ten minutes later, the two men were busy talking.

"What is the purpose of the obelisks?" Rutherford asked as she joined them and they walked into the dining room.

"I can answer that," Standish said as they sat down at the table. "They're grave markers."

"I always thought they were giant phalluses. And you found the one for the Queen of Sheba?"

"She shouldn't have had one, at least if what she told Solomon was true. She told him she was a sun worshipper, but that she meant to convert to his religion and intended to set up a Jewish state. So, if she kept her word, she must have worshipped Yahweh, not the sun."

"What century are we talking about?"

"Solomon ruled from 970 BC for about forty years."

"And he built a temple and had a lot of gold mines."

"Um."

Ceseli looked down the long polished mahogany table to where Hilina was taking the teff from a matching sideboard. "Can I have some more, please, Hilina?" The girl smiled and came back.

"When did Ethiopia become Christian?" Rutherford asked.

"In the fourth century AD," Ceseli answered as she brought her attention back to the subject of Christianity.

"Ethiopia accepted Christianity before Rome did?"

"Quite a bit before."

"What about the story of Constantine? The vision in the sky."

"Constantine didn't convert until he was on his deathbed in 337 AD. But the story that he converted the Roman Empire to Christianity is just untrue. He did no such thing. Did Standish tell you about the coins we found?"

"No, we were talking about the news of Mussolini."

"What news is that?" she asked. "If you can tell me, that is."

"Well, the Germans and the British have signed a naval treaty by which the German navy can build up to thirty-five percent of the British navy."

"What's news?"

"It allows Germany out of the arms restrictions imposed by the Treaty of Versailles at the end of World War I, and it was signed without consulting either Italy or France."

"So Mussolini is angry, is that it?"

"That, my dear, is the understatement of the day," Rutherford said, chuckling. "So why are these coins important?"

"Axum was the only state in Africa to mint its own coins over a three hundred year period. Those coins give us a complete chronology of the Axum rulers. Through the coins from the rein of Ezana, we can pinpoint the exact date of his conversion as 331 AD. Before that date, all his coins bore an image of the full moon. After 331 AD, they are stamped with a cross. These were the earliest coins to bare the Christian symbol. The ones we found . . ."

"*You* found, Ceseli!"

"Okay, the ones I found are all stamped with a cross."

"Why did Ezana decide to become a Christian?" Rutherford asked.

"There were two Christian brothers at his father's court. They were Phoenicians from Tyre in Palestine. They were shipwrecked off the coast of Ethiopia and brought to the court as slaves. The oldest was Frumentius and the king appointed him as his treasurer and secretary. He held him in very high regard. Then the king died abruptly leaving his son, Ezana, as an infant. The queen asked Frumentius to stay on and to become Ezana's tutor. So of course he had a great deal of influence over the boy while he was growing up. During this time, Frumentius invited Christians to settle in Ethiopia to build their own churches and to worship in them, not in catacombs as they did in Rome. Somewhere along the line, Frumentius was appointed a bishop of the church in Alexandria and he succeeded in converting Ezana."

"What are you going to do with the coins?"

"Standish asked me the same thing. I'm giving them to the emperor."

"I'm sure he'll like that," both men said at the same time.

Three days later, Ceseli was asked to go to the palace and meet again with the emperor. Yifru told her that the emperor had already read her report and that he had expressed interest in having her do some work for him.

The following day, after speaking at some length with the emperor and giving him the coins she had found, Ceseli took possession of a small office near the library. Working for the emperor would give her the opportunity to look at historical papers and letters, many of which had not been catalogued.

"Can I stay on here with you?" she asked Rutherford.

"Of course you can. Your father would be very proud of you. But what about Geneva?"

"Geneva can wait. It's not far from Rome. I'll go over the Christmas break."

"Just one thing. Please don't let anything you hear here be repeated at the palace. We must follow very clean lines in our relationship with the emperor, and with Yifru."

"I'll be very careful."

Ceseli was very pleased. The archives were meticulously arranged chronologically and a wonderful source of information. She had access to the library, to all the bound letters and correspondence of the former emperors, and to the books in the emperor's extensive collection. Her task was to gather all the obelisk references together and while doing so she was free to use any of the content as she saw fit for her dissertation.

Down the hall in his own office, Yifru took Ceseli's report and reread it. She reminded him of another young American girl he had known many years before in New York. Her name was Debra. It was the only time he had thought of defying his emperor.

It was the spring of 1917. Yifru was graduating from Columbia that June, and he would be returning to live and work in Ethiopia. That was the repayment for studying abroad.

Then he met Debra, and all his ideas of young American ladies changed. Standing in line outside the college on Broadway and 116 Street, Debra was picketing for a woman's right to vote. She had masses of dark curly hair under a jaunty sailor's hat and was waving an American flag. He stopped to look at the flag. It was cut diagonally from the top left tip of the stars to the bottom right of the stripes. Half of it was missing.

"Half of our people have no vote," she shouted, waving it energetically in his face. "Women!"

She was a student at Barnard College, he learned, and wanted to be a doctor like her father, and her grandfather.

"You don't like it here?"

"Yes, I do."

"Then why are you going back to black Africa?" she asked some days later while they shared a hot chocolate in one of the small coffee shops on Broadway.

"Because I made a promise to help my country."

"Ask them to let you stay another bit."

"I have no right to ask. I made a promise."

She looked at him over the whipped cream. "Well that's noble. When I'm a famous doctor, maybe I'll start a hospital there like Dr. Schweitzer."

"Dr. Schweitzer didn't work in Ethiopia. It was in . . ."

"Yifru. The trouble with you is that you take everything so seriously," she laughed, mischievously sticking out her tongue at him.

"I'm a serious person."

"Oh I know. I know."

It was the only time, ever, he had questioned Tafari. That one time he wanted to refuse his order and to remain with Debra. And he had for a month. He had fallen in love and it was excruciatingly painful for him. After he had been in Addis for several months, he was able to offer to pay for her ticket if she came to marry him. She declined.

CHAPTER 15

"Be careful. The water is boiling," Marco said, offering his hand so she could walk across the slippery stepping stones.

"So I see, Doctor," she said, watching where she was going. "I'm watching very carefully."

"You have to, or you'll end up like cooked spaghetti," he grinned. "Let me carry the saddlebags."

"Thanks. I get the point. So this is why Queen Tatou decided to settle in for the stay?"

"What do you mean?"

"I read that she asked Menelik to build a capital here because she loved to bathe in these springs with the ladies in waiting." Ceseli looked around her noting that mountains now forested in Eucalyptus surrounded the plain. "It is a beautiful place."

"Look around when we get to the other side, please," Marco shouted, above the whishing of the bubbling water. "Otherwise you might become the Queen of the Boiling Spaghetti!"

"Okay, okay," Ceseli laughed to herself. "I think I might not like that title." She followed him to a small grove of Eucalyptus on the far side of the spring where they put down the saddlebags and sat down. They had already gathered the flowers he wanted.

"How was your trip?" Marco asked.

"Really, really wonderful," Ceseli answered.

"That sounds optimistic."

"I'm an optimistic person."

"That's what I like about you," he grinned.

"I'm glad there's something you like about me!"

"I haven't got time to make a list. Just let's content ourselves with that. The obelisks are all lying on the ground?"

"There are about fifty standing, and many more on the ground."

"Why do you think?"

"I don't know. The silting up of the river, or an earthquake maybe. Some say a Muslim army."

"Like the leaning tower of Pisa? That's what they say is happening. The ground is settling differently than one would have expected. Did they all come down at the same time?"

"I have no idea. But they're sort of like a house of cards. Not in any one direction, just any which way."

"I'll bet on the earthquake. Armies follow orders. Nature doesn't."

"Well, there's a chance we'll find out. I'm going to work with the emperor."

"What? Tell me more!"

"I'll be trying to catalogue everything there is to know about the obelisks."

"So you're not going home?"

"Not right away."

"Working for the emperor? That sounds impressive. Does he pay well?"

"Does he pay at all? I forgot to ask, but money isn't the issue. My father left me quite well off."

"So, tell me about Axum."

"You know Axum is to Ethiopians what Rome is for the Roman Empire. It even has a lot of hills. I wonder how much of all this is true? Sociologists believe that behind every legend there's some part that is true. Unless it's Jack and the Beanstalk, or Johnny Appleseed."

"Who was he?"

"A man who wandered around Massachusetts planting apple trees."

"I thought horses do that?"

"They do. That's the scientific part. Sure the Bible says Solomon had four hundred wives and six hundred concubines. We don't have to take that literally. Everything he touched didn't turn to gold. It meant he was a wealthy king. And he was a wise man. Remember the story of the two women who were claiming they were the mothers of the same child? He ordered the child cut in two so each one of them could get her half. The real mother gave up the child rather than have it cut in two."

Marco laughed. "I guess I don't know much about Solomon, or Sheba. But Solomon sounds pretty smart to be able to keep four hundred wives. Do you believe that there ever was a Queen of Sheba?"

"I doubt that we will ever be able to prove that the Queen of Sheba who visited Solomon was a pure blood Abyssinian, or an Arab queen from Yemen or Sheba, or any other part of the Arabian Peninsula. But the folk tales that some queen did visit Solomon are so old and so widespread that there must be some kernel of historical fact."

"Why do you say that?"

"Because the caravan men and the scribes would certainly have told the tale around their fires. The way they did for Homer."

"Are you hungry?"

"I'm always hungry. I've told you that. Daddy said it was not very ladylike."

Marco took a bottle of white wine, and some cups and napkins from his saddlebag. Ceseli took from hers some chicken, bread, and a piece of cheese. They settled down and ate for a while in silence.

"What was it like going to a British school?" Ceseli asked, breaking the comfortable silence.

"Well, they don't cane you, if that's the question. It was near my home in Fiesole. There's a large British colony living in Florence. The school was small. My brother and sister go there now."

"You haven't mentioned them before."

"They're much younger. My brother, Paolo, is fifteen and Chiara, my little sister, is thirteen."

"I would love to have a sister and a brother."

"Where did you go to school?"

"I grew up in New York. I went to a school for girls."

"That doesn't sound like much fun. Why didn't you say no?"

"You don't say no at six. It was what Daddy wanted. My mother went there. And it was a lot of fun. Boys didn't exist of course. I also went to a women's college. It was also where my mother went."

"So you had no serious loves?"

"Oh I did. Peter Jennings. He lived near Sotzy's house in Connecticut. We'd play together every day."

"Doctor and nurse?" Marco asked.

"You probably did that."

"I certainly did. I always wanted to be a doctor."

"And marry your high school sweetheart?"

"There were quite a few of them."

"I believe you," she said, laughing as she struggled with a chicken leg.

"Well, not as many as Solomon," Marco laughed. "Tell me about Peter."

"He had red hair and lots of freckles. We played with other farm kids in the area. We played baseball almost every evening. When my father came he'd be the pitcher. I was quite a tomboy. I loved to climb trees and watch birds. In college I had a few boys that I liked, and a few liked me. They just weren't the same ones."

Ceseli leaned back on the grass and looked up to the sky where huge thunderheads were massing. "You know the first time I knew that clouds moved, I was leaning back on a swing in Central Park and I thought I was being chased by the clouds." She lifted her finger tracing the path of the clouds. "Giant thunderheads like these moving very fast. As I was swinging, they were moving." She smiled across at him. "Have you ever thought about miracles?" she asked.

"How do you mean?"

"Like the birds flying away in the fall. One day they're there, and the next they're gone. Or butterflies. The next year they're back again."

"We have swallows in Florence that come out in the late afternoon and fly all over trying to find food. They fly very low over the squares and even along the bridge at Ponte Vecchio. Then one day, they're all gone."

"Swallows are so graceful, but I've often wondered how they get any food. You know, flying around blindly with their beaks open. It must be pure luck."

"One summer I found a baby swallow that had fallen out of its nest. I took it home and I fed it freshly ground flies. It grew tremendously big and I tried to launch it so it could be with its friends. But I think it was too heavy. Or it didn't have enough strength in its wings. It kept falling and I'd have to find it again before some cat did."

Ceseli smiled at him as she turned back to the clouds. "There's a marsh along the shore in Connecticut. One minute the marsh was full of water and the next it was empty. The water rose and fell every six hours. If you tied up a rowboat it would either float or lie on the bottom. Over and over again. Do you have a tide in Italy?"

"It's not like the ocean. The Mediterranean is calmer."

"Where did you spend vacations?"

"In Viareggio. It's on the coast west of Florence. Lots of people from Florence go there. When I was small we'd make sand castles. Swim of course. Go riding in the pine forest that is all along that coast and very deep. It's easy to get lost."

"I had a dappled grey Shetland pony in Connecticut named Rosie. Sotzy gave her to me for my fourth birthday. There was a man who worked on Sotzy's farm and took care of her. His name was Jimmy. He was Irish.

He taught me to ride bareback like an Indian princess. As I grew older, he taught me about the land and how to track deer and woodchucks. How to get the beavers to build a dam where you wanted it, and not where they wanted. Recognize poisonous berries. Know north from south. I followed him around all day long and I loved him very much. He went fishing one day in the winter and his boat capsized. He caught pneumonia and died. That was when I was seven. I didn't know what 'died' meant. I was taken to his wake. His sister wanted me to kiss him goodbye. I still remember how his lips were so cold and smelled of flowers. He was the first dead person I'd ever seen. After that, I was terrified of death."

"You should never have been taken there." Marco looked at her. He lifted her face to him and kissed her gently on the mouth.

"Now you're sounding like a doctor," she said, drawing back. "Or rather, a psychologist. It wasn't done on purpose. But it did scare me."

"Death is scary. Even to me, and I'm trained to deal with it."

"Are you really trained to deal with it?"

"Not really. But it gets easier and it's easier when you don't know the person. That's why doctors try to stay removed."

"But can you do that?"

"I can't yet. But I think it does get easier."

"I'm not so sure."

"This conversation has taken a morbid twist," he said, looking at her and using his finger to trace the line of her eyes down to her lips.

Ceseli looked up into his eyes. He kissed her again and she felt his weight on her as she kissed him back. The moment was broken as Marco turned and looked over his shoulder at the sky that by now was very threatening. "We're in for a hell of a storm."

"I don't mind, but maybe the horses will."

"I don't know whether they'll be afraid of the lightning, but we're about to find out."

They hurried back to the horses and galloped back toward Addis. The cold rain started pelting down as it does in the tropics. The sky above them was almost black, the wind screaming. The peaceful clouds had turned into the churning of gray waters. Right in front of them lightning struck, joining earth and sky. Ceseli felt her horse balking, rearing, and whinnying in terror. She was just able to keep her seat on the wet slippery saddle.

"Are you all right?" Marco yelled into the wind.

"Yes."

"Let's head over there," he said, slowing to a trot and pointing toward a grove of trees.

Jimmy wouldn't like this at all, she thought. *Never take cover under trees. Trees are the natural anchor for lightning.* She followed him anyhow. They dismounted and held the horses tightly. The eye of the storm seemed directly above them. Lightning tore open the sky. You could see for miles despite the blackness of the storm. Ceseli counted the seconds between the flash of lightning and the crack of thunder.

"It's almost over," Marco grinned. "Have faith. Are you wet?"

"Oh no," she grinned, knowing that her thick hair was hanging, as if they had become rivers of live water running down over her shoulders. And then the eye of the storm passed. The clouds raced on. The darkness ceased.

"Well, that was interesting," Marco said, remounting his horse. "Everything okay?"

"Everything's fine," Ceseli answered as she got on her horse and followed him back to Addis.

CHAPTER 16

In the summer of 1935, there were six thousand foreigners in Addis Ababa, including some rather unsavory mercenaries and adventurers. Among them were one hundred thirty men claiming to be journalists. The *Times of London* was represented, as was the *New York Times*, *Associated Press, Reuters,* and *Paris Soire*. Some of them were anti-Fascist, some anti-Ethiopian, some both. These journalists had their own war: who got the best story, and who got it first.

The Greek owned, two floor, barracks-like Imperial Hotel, where Ceseli had not stayed, was their haven. The building had ornate lacy balconies outside almost every room, but only one bathroom in the entire hotel and no maid service. When the journalists were not running down important leads, they played chess or billiards in the lobby, or dined on greasy artichokes, sweetmeats, kebabs and copious amounts of beer, wine, and schnapps.

At thirty-six, Bruno Zeri was proud of his job as chief war reporter for Corriere

Della Sera, the prestigious Milan daily newspaper. It was the newspaper of the northern Italian industrialists, and of the monarchy. Before the total Fascist censorship came into effect, it was dedicated to excellence. Zeri liked to think it still was.

His life with the paper had been interesting, and at times exciting. It did not lend itself to a family, although he had had several tortuous love affairs. He often thought that he should have been a lawyer like his father, or a doctor like his uncle. He had thought of teaching, which his mother loved, as had his grandmother. Religion had never played an important part in his life. If he had to think about it, he was probably more like his Jewish mother than his agnostic father. When he thought sarcastically about it, his greatest loyalty was to the Rome soccer team, *Roma*.

Over the summer, the number of journalists was increasing, and now arrangements for interviews with the emperor devolved to Yifru. *The war is coming soon,* Zeri thought as he made mental notes of the interview he would conduct with the emperor. He wrote down the questions and submitted them. A few days later he received word that the emperor would see him for a few minutes on the following Thursday. Zeri realized that he was intensely interested in meeting him.

As he walked to the Ghibbi Palace, he was thinking about the two leaders. The King of Italy, Victor Emmanuel III, was only a figurehead. Benito Mussolini was now the elected leader with absolute power. Haile Sellassie was an emperor. Was there any real difference between an absolute dictator and an absolute emperor?

Zeri knew that if Benito Mussolini were compared to Caesar, he would be an armchair Caesar. With total dictatorial power, Il Duce was more and more isolated. He spent most of his time alone in his offices in Palazzo Venezia, especially the *Sala di Mappamondo,* with its world maps on which Mussolini pinned little red and blue colored flags showing whether a country was friendly to him or not.

Mussolini had already made his plans. He would need one hundred thousand Italian soldiers to conquer Ethiopia, and probably just as many natives. However, Ethiopia was not the main threat; Great Britain and France were. He ardently believed that the League alone could not, or would not, stop him. His main worry was how he could supply Eritrea and Italian Somaliland with the needed men and equipment if Great Britain and France intervened. Great Britain single handedly could stop him by slamming shut the Suez Canal.

He also knew that the quicker the invasion could be completed, the less likely the danger of diplomatic complications. It would be enough to safeguard the interests of England and France. Mussolini understood this to mean, annex Ethiopia, but safeguard the French railroad in Djibouti and the British interests near Lake Tana and the Blue Nile. Furthermore, all this must be completed before Hitler was strong enough to start his own imperialistic warfare in Europe.

While Mussolini sat and dreamed, Zeri grudgingly had to concede that the Italian people revered him. In official proclamations, Mussolini's name was above that of the king. No laws passed the senate or the chamber of deputies except his. Nobody contradicted him, even in his outlandish whims. When he complained that he couldn't see the Coliseum from his office window, the Via dei Fori Imperiale was built by leveling all the buildings around the Coliseum.

And nobody would contradict him now. It was far too late.

Yifru was waiting for Signor Bruno Zeri as he walked up to the palace and accompanied him to the emperor's study. "Welcome, Signor Zeri," he said, pleasantly shaking his hand.

"*Grazie.*" Zeri answered, surprised at the warm welcome. "Thank you for letting me interview the Negus."

"It was his majesty's decision, I assure you."

Yifru guided him up to the second floor and indicated the seat in front of the emperor's desk. He walked behind the desk taking a well-worn leather seat behind the emperor, and to his left. The dogs lay obediently at the emperor's feet.

Haile Sellassie studied Zeri for a moment before beginning. "You represent an important newspaper. That is why we have granted this interview. We hope you will record it faithfully."

Zeri nodded in acceptance as he studied the small man seated in front of him. He knew he was facing a man of authority and intelligence. He saw that he economized gesture and sat perfectly straight. Only the jeweled hand moved a little under his black cloak. Zeri sensed the great dignity of his bearing. *How different from the ranting and posturing of Mussolini,* he thought.

"On methods of negotiation," the emperor began, taking the single sheet of questions. "Great Britain has not made proposals to Ethiopia, but we are delighted with the attitude of Sir Samuel Hoare and Mr. Anthony Eden."

Zeri already knew that the British had sent Sir Anthony Eden to Rome to negotiate the trade of the Ethiopian Ogaden desert area near WalWal to Italy in exchange for the port of Zeila on the Red Sea in British Somaliland. It was a last ditch effort to avoid hostilities. He also knew that Eden had failed. It was common knowledge that Mussolini detested the British diplomat and that he already possessed one hundred thousand square miles of desert. He didn't need any more.

Yifru, sitting behind the Emperor, remembered the number of times the two of them had discussed the frontiers that had been set up by Menilek through negotiations with the predatory European governments. Frontiers had become an urgent necessity. The idea of an encircling border, a kind of watertight state, which could be shown on a map in a separate color was new even in Europe. Innumerable frontier problems were an inheritance of the recent past, and were moving and shifting because of war. Political borders were even vaguer and sometimes meaningless in Africa where huge areas, empty and unmapped, separated nomads and tribal villages. But now well demarcated frontiers had become essential in Europe, and if Ethiopia was to survive as a modern state, it too must have them.

The frontier lines had already been drawn, but many of them had never been surveyed or demarcated, and the territories they ran through were often unexplored. This was the case for the much disputed frontier between Ethiopia's Ogaden and the Italian colony of Somaliland. Where exactly were the wells of WalWal? In Ethiopia, as the Ethiopians claimed, or in Somaliland as the Italians asserted.

"We have in mind only an exchange of territory," the emperor said. "If the Zeila offer is accepted, we are willing to surrender to Italy an equivalent amount of land. But the Zeila offer must stand. We still regard a seaport as much more important than loans or other financial assistance. But," he added, "we have received no proposals of a territorial nature from any source."

The emperor paused as he read the next question. "We learn from press accounts in some parts of the world that Mussolini told Sir Anthony Eden, the British Secretary for League of Nations Affairs, that Italy's minimum demand were the expulsion of Ethiopia from the League and an armed Italian protectorate over Ethiopia. You ask will Ethiopia accept an Italian protectorate?"

The emperor paused looking at Zeri. "Monsieur Zeri, only a country which fails to accomplish its duty may be expelled from the League. Ethiopia has always respected all its international obligations. Only the League, not Italy, can decide as to the exclusion of Ethiopia. Concerning an armed Italian protectorate, an old proverb says '*one shouldn't sell the lion's skin before killing the lion.*'

"In reply to your question concerning the Italian threat to raise the question of slavery at the League of Nations in Geneva, we are gratified that Italy would use Geneva for any question whatsoever. You are well aware that slavery is not confined to Ethiopia, since it flourishes too in Italian Eritrea and in Libya. Have you been to Eritrea or Libya?"

"I have been to both, your majesty."

"Then I do not need to tell you that the fact of slavery is not denied by the Italians themselves, and a fact the League is well aware of. We believe it is an insufficient argument for the annexation of the so-called colonial provinces that have been member states of Ethiopia by treaty and in historical fact."

The emperor paused looking Zeri straight in the eye. "The Italian threat to peace appears to me to be flagrant. If Italy declares war, or her troops dare to cross the borders, Ethiopia will fight immediately and simultaneously appeal to the League."

The emperor paused letting the impact of his words speak for itself. "We believe these are our answers to the questions you put forth. Is there anything else?"

Zeri hesitated. He wanted to ask about the rumor that Hitler was supplying arms. He thought better of it. He knew that even if it were true, the emperor would have to deny it.

"We hope your article will be faithful to the spirit in which we have answered your questions," the emperor said, still holding Bruno's eyes with the magnetism of his own.

Zeri, as he put down his notebook, studied the leader he could not help, but respect. "Your majesty, I will write this interview faithful to the way you have explained to me your views. I need to warn you though that there is a powerful censor in Italy. My paper is not as free as I, or your majesty, would like it to be."

"We ask only that you do your best."

"I promise you that I will." Zeri said, nodding as he stood up. "Thank you again for seeing me."

"We deemed it necessary."

Zeri bowed and walked backward from the emperor's presence, following a red carpet that had been placed to guide him.

Outside the office, he turned to shake hands with Yifru. "Thank you for arranging this," Zeri said as he put his notebook into his breast pocket.

"It was entirely the emperor's decision."

"Thank you anyhow." Zeri started down the corridor to the stairs. *Did the emperor grant this interview to issue a veiled threat,* he thought. *Yes, no doubt of it.* He was still mulling over this when he almost bumped into Ceseli Larson coming out of one of the rooms. "Miss Larson. How are you?"

"I'm fine, and you look well yourself."

"I've just been interviewing the emperor."

"That must have been interesting."

"I was very impressed. I didn't think he'd see me. Just curiosity, but what are you doing here?"

"I'm cataloguing the emperor's papers on Axum that mention the obelisks."

"You mean you're working for the emperor! Does that give you access to him?"

"Through Yifru. Yes."

"His faithful amanuensis."

"That doesn't do him justice," Ceseli answered, a little piqued. "He handles everything the emperor does."

"The Keeper of the Pen. Rather Ethiopian, isn't it?"

"Any different from the British Lord Keeper of the Seal? Except that that man usually has a title and a seat in the House of Lords."

"Maybe you're right," Zeri said. "Can I ask you something? Do you mind if we go somewhere where we can talk?"

"You can come to my office," Ceseli said, preceding him down the hall.

Zeri followed her into the small office and as he walked over to the open window, Ceseli could not help again thinking how tall he was. She was five foot seven inches and he made her feel like a midget, but despite his size he was very lithe, almost like a panther might be. His eyes were alert and somehow troubling.

Outside he could see the gardeners weeding the yellow and red roses. Farther on, the home guard was drilling. *Gra-Gra-Gra-Ken-Gra! Gra-Gra-Gra-Ken-Gra*!

"What's that?" he asked.

"That's their drilling cadence. *Gra* means left, *Ken* means right."

"Some look like they're children," Zeri said as he watched them march back and forth with their smart uniforms and no shoes. He looked back into the room, and walked over to study the photos on the wall. The office was small, but adequate. The walls were white and she had covered one wall with her own photographs. Outside the window was the circular fountain, still without water. Besides her photographs, the unique part of her office was the Swiss made cuckoo clock that cuckooed ten minutes after the hour, not on it. Ceseli, and half the guards at the palace, had all tried to adjust it so that it ran on time. It wouldn't. The amusing thing was that when the cuckoo finally burst out of its little peaked roof house, the parrot in the emperor's office started calling to it as if the birds, one wooden, the other live, could have some meaningful communication. It was, Ceseli conceded, certainly not emblematic of Swiss efficiency.

"It's in Axum," she said, answering the unasked question and noting his attention as he looked at the photos of the fallen obelisk. "It's the only one carved on all four sides."

"Was that, what we say, a coup?"

"Yes," she smiled despite herself.

"The picture is very good, you know. You use a Leica don't you? And you're good at it."

"You wanted to ask me something?" she asked, not wanting to be rude, but wanting to shorten the meeting.

"I was curious about what you feel working here. I mean is the emperor upset? Testy? Worried?"

"If he is, he keeps it well hidden. He's always very gracious and polite."

"So you get to interact with him?"

"He has stopped by a couple of times to make sure I don't need something I'm not finding. Yifru on the other hand comes by at least once a day."

"What's he like?"

"He's totally loyal to the emperor. He's the only one who knows him as a man, as well as a figurehead. Except his wife, I guess."

"You've met with the empress?"

"I don't see her at all. She and the princesses live in a separate pavilion."

"There's something else I was interested in. I heard about the *Falasha*, the Jews of Ethiopia. Have you come up with anything in your research?"

"Why are you interested in the Falasha?"

Zeri shrugged as he took out his notebook.

"I do know that they're a native Jewish sect," Ceseli began. "The name is Amharic for exiles, or landless ones. The Falashas refer to themselves as Beta Esrael, which means House of Israel. One Falasha tradition traces their ancestry to Menilek I, the son of King Solomon and the Queen of Sheba."

"As does everyone else it seems," Zeri smiled, taking notes.

"The bible of the Falashas is written in an archaic Semitic dialect known as Ge'ez. It's ancient Ethiopic. Ge'ez is to the Amharic language what Latin is to Italian."

"That I didn't know," Bruno said, writing it down.

"It is also the liturgical language of the Coptic Church. Most of the old manuscripts were written in Ge'ez, and services are still in Ge'ez. The Falashas live in the area above Lake Tana, but we ran into a community near Axum. They're farmers. Until the seventeenth century, they had their own independent province at Semien in the north. But Emperor Susenyos expelled them from there. Sorry I don't know more. But you should ask Yifru. I'm sure he'll know."

"I was curious about what I heard about the animal sacrifice. My mother is Jewish, but I know that animal sacrifice hasn't been used in Europe for thousands of years. That is why one thinks of this sect as being segregated for centuries. How many Falasha do you think there are?"

"I read a book by a Reverend Henry Stern who was sent to convert the Falashas living in the Gondar area in the early 1890s. He thought there were about two hundred fifty thousand then. But there have been several famines since and many were forced to convert to Christianity. I'm afraid I don't know how to calculate the numbers."

"That's a good beginning," he replied. "And keep up the good work with your camera."

After he left, Ceseli went to her desk, and started to read a letter she had taken from the archives. She paused thinking about Bruno Zeri. *There is something about him that I don't trust,* she thought. It troubled her that she couldn't understand her own feelings and it wasn't the only time she had had these misgivings. Was it because he was a Fascist, or a journalist? An Italian? She felt that there was something missing. What was it?

CHAPTER 17

"IT'S THE LIONESS ISN'T it? The one you mention in your report," Yifru asked, studying the photograph. It was the day after her talk with Bruno Zeri and she was working on some reports of the German expedition to Axum at the beginning of the century.

"This is what looks so interesting," she said, showing him the tiny cross above the lioness's nose. "There was a British traveler who said it was the rays of the sun, but I think he's wrong. I think it's a cross. And these," she said, bringing his attention over to the rubbings she had done in Kaleb's tomb. "See what I mean? But why a Christian symbol, such as the cross, on a pre-Christian tomb?"

"If I'm not mistaken, these are the *croce patté* of the Knights Templar."

"The Knights Templar?"

"I'm almost positive. But we can check. I have a book of Christian crosses. Don't move," Yifru said, going out the door.

Ceseli did move over to her desk. She was sorting out some papers when he got back. Yifru took the seat in front of her and started to thumb through a small book. "Who were the Knights Templars?" she asked.

Yifru hesitated for a minute, but when he answered it was clear he knew the subject well. "They started out as a pious group of French nobility who went to Jerusalem after the First Crusade in 1099. There were nine of them, I think. They all came from the same area of Champagne in France and they became known as the Order of Poor Knights of the Temple of Solomon. Their job was to protect pilgrims on the road between Jaffa, the Mediterranean port where the ships landed, and Jerusalem. They were warrior monks. For their services in protecting pilgrims, Pope Innocent II granted them forgiveness of their sins."

"How could nine monks protect all the pilgrims?"

Yifru stopped and looked at her. "That, Miss Larson, was my first question, too."

"You need to call me Ceseli," she smiled. "Are these the ones who grew so rich?"

"Young men flocked to the order, but to join they had to give all their wealth and belongings to the order."

"That's how they became wealthy?" Ceseli interrupted.

"There were other ways. They owned their own ports and hospitals. As you know, the church, or maybe I should say the pope, forbade money lending with interest. That was called usury. But the Templars got around that because they became very powerful and very rich. They ended up being the bankers to the popes and to kings. That caused their downfall."

"What do you mean?"

"Here it is. In 1127, the Templars were recognized as a religious military order at Troyes by the court of the Count of Champagne. It was said to be founded in 1118, by Hugues de Payen, a nobleman of Champagne and a vassal of the count of Champagne. According to what we know Hugues and eight comrades, all noblemen from the same Champagne area presented themselves to King Baldwin I. Baldwin was the King of Jerusalem, whose brother, Godfroi de Bouillon, had captured the Holy City nineteen years earlier. They offered their services in the protection of pilgrims. The king was so thankful for their offer of help that he vacated a wing of the palace and gave it to their use."

Yifru smiled. "Notwithstanding their oath of poverty, the knights moved into this lavish headquarters that was built on top of the temple that Solomon had built. Hence the name. Am I going too fast?"

"No."

"They wore distinctive white robes with a large red cross on it. Only the Templars could wear it. Moreover, they were ordered to fight to the death, they could not be ransomed, and they could not surrender unless the odds exceeded three to one." Yifru paused. "Those are pretty stiff orders."

"This story is better than King Arthur."

Yifru chuckled as he ran his finger down the page.

Ceseli looked at Yifru. "Why your interest in the Templars?"

"When I was at Columbia I took a course in medieval history. What interested me was that one of our Ethiopian emperors had been in exile in Jerusalem from around 1160 AD when he would have been twenty years old, until 1185. He is best known for his given name, Lalibela, but his throne name was Gebre Meskal. He is famous for the eleven rock-hewn churches he had built in twenty-three years."

"Why was he in exile?"

"To protect him." Yifru said, drawing in his breath. "He was the son of the Emperor Jen Seyoum. When Lalibela was born, there was a swarm of bees on him in his cradle so his mother named him Lalibela. That means 'the bees recognize his sovereignty.' And bees are considered a royal sign so that people began talking about his future as an emperor."

Ceseli thought of other kings who used bees in their heraldic signs and came up with the Italian Barberini family that had sired two popes. Napoleon too had golden bees appliquéd on his purple robes. She refocused on Yifru.

"Lalibela had an older, half-brother, named Harbay. He was the oldest son and thought he should be heir to the throne. Harbay felt threatened by these prophesies. So he tried to have the baby killed. That didn't work. So later he tried to have him poisoned."

"And I take it that didn't work either."

"No, but it is said that he was in a coma for three days and during that time, God told him not to be afraid of dying for he had foretold great things for him during his lifetime. Including that he would build magnificent churches. Anyhow, his mother thought he might be killed in some other way so she sent him to Jerusalem for protection. In 1185, he returned to Roha, which was then the capital of Ethiopia, and persuaded his half-brother, Harbay, to renounce the throne."

"Why would Harbay do that?"

"Because it was foretold. You see, succession in Ethiopia is not directly to the eldest son."

"I know that," Ceseli interrupted. "Rutherford explained. It is the most powerful who becomes emperor. Perhaps he knew that Lalibela had a bigger army."

"That's possible too. And if he had employed the Knights Templar to return with him then your supposition would make good sense."

"Then what's the connection with the crosses?" Ceseli asked, confused.

"These are the same crosses. Those," he said, pointing toward the rubbings, "carved into one of Lalibela's churches."

"Are they signatures?"

"I can't answer that. Nobody has been able to explain how the crosses got there. The churches are excavated down out of the volcanic tuff rather than built above the ground."

"Like a cave?"

"If each cave were vertical. He built, and I put that "built" in quotes, them in twenty-three years. Legend says with the help of angels. He needed a lot of help, that's for sure. And the Templers were known as master builders and architects and they were living door-to-door for twenty years. Some friendship must have developed."

"So putting one and one together, you believe the Templers helped Lalibela?"

"Their help as warriors is not to be scoffed at either. Getting his brother, Harbay to step down was not easy. Ethiopians are not ones to shrink from battle."

"How do you know so much about this?"

"Why should an Ethiopian know so much about his own history?"

"Did it sound like that? I'm sorry." Ceseli felt mortified. The last person in the world she wanted to offend was Yifru.

"My father is the foremost authority on Ethiopian history."

"Is he still alive?"

"Still kicking, if that is the American euphemism."

"It gets the point across," she smiled. "And you of course grew up with his knowledge."

"My father was the emperor's tutor."

"Why did Lalibela build the churches?"

"The Turks had reconquered Jerusalem. He built them here at his birthplace so that Ethiopian pilgrims would not need to travel to Jerusalem. He had lived in Jerusalem for twenty years and he recreated it in Roha. Even the River Jordan. Later the name was changed to Lalibela."

"But eleven churches in twenty-three years is a master undertaking. How did he get that done?"

"The simple answer is, I don't know." Yifru smiled. "The local people will tell you that while he had crews working during the day, angels were working at night."

"He'd still need an army of angels, I think."

Yifru looked up as the cuckoo clock sprang into action. "I need to finish these papers. Let's continue this when I catch up with the angels."

Ceseli smiled as he left. That seemed just as daunting a task as building eleven churches in twenty-three years.

CHAPTER 18

At the end of June, the rains began, but nothing had prepared Ceseli for their intensity. In the early morning, when she arrived at the palace, the sky was penetratingly clear and blue. Looking out the window, she could see the Entoto hills above, the gorges below.

Around midday, the clouds would start forming into gigantic thunderheads, followed two hours later by lightning, thunderbolts and torrential rain in such force that Ceseli could barely see the huge circular fountain just below her window. There was no reason now to water the roses and the fountain actually worked. Each day when the rain stopped, there was often a splendid sunset, with a rainbow its colors so strong that one might think of a huge prism used by a favoring god.

Marco is certainly right about the pace of life in Addis, she thought. After work, there was almost nothing to do except use one's initiative. Reading, of course, was number one and thankfully there were lots of books in the library. She played the piano, despite its imperfect tuning and also spent some evenings cataloguing her photos and making notes in her bible. Jigsaw puzzles were started, but rarely finished because Hilina often moved the pieces around so that she could dust.

On the Fourth of July, Rutherford gave a barbeque inviting all the Americans in Addis as well as the members of the British Embassy, two Canadians and Marco, who telephoned from the hospital to ask if he could bring Zeri.

They dug an open pit in the garden near the Eucalyptus trees where they could roast a whole steer. There were several long tables set up with blue, red, and white bunting draped from them. They were laden with homegrown watermelons, pickles, chocolate cake, and potato salad. The smell of the roasting flesh and the smoke as the fat dripped into the pit was almost nauseous, but the meat was very good indeed. They also served corn on the cob grown from seeds imported from the U.S.

"Guess who?"

Ceseli was helping to serve potato salad, when someone covered her eyes from behind.

"You're not supposed to speak, or you give yourself away," she admonished.

"Just wanted to tell you I'm here," Marco smiled, taking some of the potato salad. "Um, this is delicious. You made this; confess!"

"I gave our chef the recipe. It's about the only thing I can cook. Except French toast. That's a warning."

"Warning received. What's French toast?"

"Bread soaked in beaten eggs and sautéed in a skillet. It was my father's favorite breakfast. Oh, I forgot you smear on jam or maple syrup."

"Maple syrup?"

"The sap from Maple trees. It's very sweet. I don't know if Maples grow in Italy, but in late winter the sap is collected. Maybe we should ask Zeri to do an article on the sap from Eucalyptus trees," she joked. "I mean, if there is sap."

"You don't seem to like him, but he's a very decent chap."

"I'm glad."

Ceseli saw Warren Rutherford not far away and waved for him to come to her. "Warren, I want to introduce you to Marco Antinori. He's a doctor at the Italian hospital."

"Very glad to meet you Doctor Antinori. I'm happy you could join us," the minister said shaking hands. "The Fourth of July is the day we celebrate our independence, but Ceseli has probably told you that."

"No, actually she hasn't, but she has said that you are her godfather."

"And her Uncle Warren, although we have dropped the uncle part of that," he smiled hugging Ceseli warmly. "Now let me greet the other guests," he said, walking off to join the British ambassador.

The harmonica music from Ol' Man River interrupted them. His harmonica playing made him an instant success. His name was Bill and he was a Negro from Kansas. "If one name is good enough for the Ethiopians, it's plenty good enough for me," he joked.

Ceseli had met him at the palace to which he delivered six chocolate brown Kansas mules and one pure white one. They were the gifts of the Negro community in Harlem and meant to show solidarity with the emperor. Bill's knowledge of mule breeding could make him a wealthy man, he explained. He liked the place and was determined to stay on.

She liked Bill immediately. He was a very big man, with a jovial smile and a kindly way with his mules, but she couldn't help wondering, if something more modern would not be more efficient on a battlefield.

Marco and Zeri were captivated by the way he played his harmonica. "You're amazingly good. Where'd you learn?" Zeri asked him.

"Doin' is all. Just listnin' and tryin' to imitate. You play?"

"Not very well. But mine is quite different. It has ten holes above and ten below."

"I've seen a lot of those. Mine is not so elaborate."

"But you're a genius playing it."

"Just passion," Bill laughed as he put the harmonica back in his mouth.

"I didn't know you could play," Marco asked of Zeri.

"Experimenting. Something to keep me busy. Trying to write a little music. My mother plays the piano and she gave me lessons. I liked the guitar better, but it's too big to carry around. The harmonica can be a lot of fun. And our friend here sure knows how to play. I'm still at the very beginning."

"Well, keep up the practice. You can't get any worse."

"No. You're right. I can't get worse." Zeri smiled.

CHAPTER 19

Marco stood on the steps of the *ospedale Italiano* waiting for Ceseli. It wasn't a beautiful building, but it was functional and because of its proximity to the center of town, it was handy. The Emperor Menelik II had built his own hospital in Addis in 1906 and that was where the Ethiopians went. Marco had been to it often never failing to wonder at the number of the family members of patients who were camping out in the hospital grounds.

Marco thought about his father's letter of two days before and took it from his pocket to reread. "*Keep a low profile, Marco, and be careful of what you say and to whom you say it. War is coming and you don't want to get accused of not being an ardent Fascist. You know,*" he had continued, "*every time I look out the window I see new trains coming from the north bringing the young conscripts. They're so eager and happy to be going to Naples and then Eritrea. They want this war. They're willing to die for Il Duce, and many will. If they only knew.*"

From an early age, Marco had known the importance of the Antinori name, of the land that went with that name and that he would inherit someday. Instead of being just landed gentry, his father had chosen to hire a manager for the vineyards while he studied and then practiced medicine. Marco couldn't pinpoint the moment he decided he wanted to be a doctor or why his special interest in malaria. Perhaps it was because his father believed that clearing malaria from the Pontine Marshes was the only thing Mussolini could be credited with.

He had kidded Ceseli about the number of girlfriends. Really he was a very shy teenager with his nose stuck in his schoolbooks. He wanted to be the best in his class and being the only Italian, that meant first learning English and then studying very hard. He had done so willingly. Recently, Marco had written his father asking him what he thought about using chloroquine as a substitute for quinine. "*It's like the search for the Holy Grail,*" his father had written and that made Marco smile. *It really is,* he thought.

While he waited, he thought of Ceseli and wondered how he could convince her to leave while it was still safe to do so. "So you've finally made it here," he joked, helping her out of the mission's car and leading her to his laboratory.

"I would have come earlier if you'd invited me," she said as she followed him up the stairs. She took off her sunhat letting loose her hair and smoothed her blue cotton skirt. She had seriously considered wearing something more flirtatious, but the reality of it was, she really didn't have anything appropriate. That realization forced her to find a seamstress at the market and she had ordered several other skirts and some blouses.

"It's nice here," she said. "I can see where you get your inspiration."

"Not much inspiration, I'm afraid. Mostly just drudgery, but that's sort of what research is. Long hours of trying to track down matches and answers. Do you know anything about malaria?" he asked.

"Only that Daisy Miller caught it wandering around Rome's coliseum."

"That's because mosquitos come out at night," Marco said. "The name comes from the medieval Italian word for *mal* and *aria* literally meaning bad air. It's also been called ague or marsh fever because it was commonly found near swamps or marshland. Unlike most African countries, Ethiopia has a long written history and it is full of documented famines and epidemics. And there have been many, many Italians who have travelled here. So there's no shortage of information."

Marco walked over to a shelf and while he was searching for a book, Ceseli looked around. The laboratory was small, but it had a large window looking out toward Mt. Entoto that provided a lot of light and a feeling of spaciousness. On the wall next to the window was a floor-to-ceiling bookcase. Facing the bookcase were several steel glass fronted cabinets all of which looked to be heavily stocked with scientific equipment. Next to it was Marco's desk with a few file covers on it and a calendar. On the wall over his desk was a map of Ethiopia with little red, green and blue dots on it and a series of circles.

"What are the colored dots?" Ceseli asked, studying the map.

"The blues are typhus, the reds are smallpox, green are cholera. The circles are famine."

"Gosh, there's so many of them!"

"So many it's hard to tell when one stops and the next begins. That big one was the Great Famine of 1888 to 1892."

"That was the worst?"

"Yes. I'm pretty sure it was triggered by an outbreak of rinderpest, also known as cattle plague. It is an infectious viral disease that affects cattle, water buffaloes, antelopes, giraffes, wildebeest, and warthogs. It was probably introduced to Ethiopia by sick Indian cattle imported by the Italians who were busy colonizing Eritrea. It spread very quickly and destroyed eighty percent, maybe even ninety percent of the cattle. In 1889, and again in 1890, the rains failed and nothing grew. There was nothing to eat. People died in the hundreds of thousands. Menelik showed himself to be a very astute leader. He went to his fields and showed by example that there was nothing demeaning in tilling one's fields with a hoe rather than oxen."

"I read that he was an exceptionally farsighted ruler. The schools, hospital, railroad all to bring his country out of the middle ages. And defeating the Italians. The Italian defeat at Adowa. Wasn't that the first time since Hannibal that an African army defeated a European one?"

"I remember Hannibal from grade school, but our books dwelt on the fact that he was a barbarian who came across the Alps on elephants."

"Well, so did the British when they came through Eritrea to free the British prisoners."

"I know little about that except that they came through Eritrea. But, it's all in here," he said, opening the navy blue leather book. "We can come back to this. Let me show you our hospital," he said, holding the door for her.

"Despite the name, it's more like a clinic. We have these two examining rooms," he said, letting her peak her head in one of them. "We have a dispensary over here, and because Mussolini has abolished patents, it is remarkably well stocked. Of course, nothing, but quinine for malaria."

Ceseli looked at the wall-to-wall shelves of boxes and bottles. "Why did he do that?"

"Rescind patents? So Italy could produce its own medicine and sell it. Money, my friend, and here we have the ward. Very few Ethiopians come here now. I'm sure that's because of the threat of war. Other foreigners still come. That man over there has yellow fever that is also spread by mosquitos. The Greeks had a name for mosquitos that translates into useless. They certainly are that. The food for our patients comes from the Italian nuns who run the school over near the compound. And it gets here by donkey."

"Like everything else," she said, following him back to the laboratory.

Marco reached for the blue book and flipped through the pages. "Malaria was once common in most of Europe, not only Italy. It has infected humans for over fifty thousand years. The reason some believe that the disease came from central Africa was that it was also common among chimpanzees and some evidence seems to suggest that the most virulent strain of human malaria might have originated in gorillas."

"Gorillas, as in Apes? Tarzan?"

"Some diseases jump from monkeys to humans quite easily. I think that's what happened in this case." Marco paused. "The most serious type of malaria, known as *plasmodium falciparum,* reached Rome at about the time of Christ. I think it travelled by Roman cargo ships from Africa. The water barrels on board could have contained mosquito larvae."

"Are you writing a book, Marco?"

"Maybe," he smiled. "Is that what it sounds like?"

"Yes."

"Would that be so bad?" he asked, pausing.

"No. Not at all."

"What we do know is that an Italian archaeologist and historian recently completed his studies that show that malaria was partly responsible for the fall of the Roman Empire. If you can believe that! He says that several regions in the ancient Roman Empire were considered at-risk and then names areas in southern Italy, the island of Sardinia, the Pontine Marshes, of course, and Rome along the Tiber River. The stagnant water in those places was the preferred breeding grounds of mosquitos," he said as he flicked back his hair and straightened the collar of the white laboratory coat he wore.

"Caesar wanted to drain the Pontine Marches, but couldn't, or didn't get the time to do it. The epidemic of malaria during the decline of the Roman Empire might have had the same negative impact as did the lead in the drinking water. It also explained the numerous pagan temples dedicated to "fever" that later would become Christian chapels dedicated to Our Lady of the Fever."

"Did people already treat malaria then?"

"Well, from what I've learned, the Chinese used a mixture of *Qinghao* to control the fever and that the slaves building the Egyptian pyramids were given large amounts of garlic and that Cleopatra slept under a mosquito net. Did you know that four members of the Medici family supposedly died of malaria? Maybe that's why Italians have always been interested in malariology." Marco stopped, looking at Ceseli and not wanting what he said to be a scientific lecture. "I'm boring you!"

"No, you aren't."

"The first effective treatment for malaria came from the Amerindians of Peru who made a tincture from the bark of the Cinchona tree that grew on the slopes of the Andes Mountains. There's no mention of it in the Mayan and Aztec histories, but it seemed to control the shivering that comes with the Malaria fever. Anyhow, the Jesuit missionaries were quick to note that it did control the fever and introduced the treatment to Europe during the 1640s. It was called Jesuit bark. Of course, everyone then wanted the cinchona bark and an English trader named Charles Ledger was able to smuggle the seeds out of the Bolivian side of the Andes. Some went to the island of Java in Indonesia from which the Dutch built up a world monopoly in quinine."

"That's what my father would have called good business," Ceseli said. "But not unlike bringing pineapples to Hawaii."

"They never made it to Italy. Either of them. But it wasn't until 1880, that a French army doctor, Charles Louis Alphonse Laveran, working in Algeria observed parasites for the first time inside the red blood cells of those people suffering from malaria. He was awarded the 1907 Nobel Prize for Medicine."

"Am I understanding that you'd be interested in a Nobel Prize?" Ceseli teased.

"I'm not anywhere near there. Yet. But I wouldn't shun it," Marco smiled ruefully. "I am boring you."

"No, you aren't. Really."

"Well, then I'll tell you that an earlier Nobel, in 1902, was given to a Scottish doctor working in Calcutta, who proved that the mosquito was the vector for malaria in humans. A Scot and a Frenchman have won the Nobel, but it's the Italians who have been pioneers in the field for centuries. But there has to be a way to find a vaccine to prevent the disease, not just to cure it."

"And that's your Nobel?"

"I hope so. By the way, can I convince you to leave?"

"Probably not," she smiled, "but do try. By the way, what about all those flowers we gathered?"

"No matches," he said, walking to his microscope. "I'll take you home. I need to be back at the hospital on duty."

"I can go by myself."

"No, you absolutely can't. I've told you that before. Women don't travel by themselves. Besides, I can show off my driving skills."

After he dropped her off at the ministry, he drove back through the darkening streets. "*Ti voglio bene*" he had said on leaving her and now he was wondering if this was true. It meant I'm fond of you, even as far as to say I love you, but without bringing into play the stronger sexuality of the *ti amo.*

CHAPTER 20

Li-li-li-li, li-li-li-li, li-li-li-li. It was the Ethiopian welcome erupting from the hordes of well-wishers waiting for the arrival of the emperor. The *li-li-li-li, li-li-li-li, li-li-li-li* grew louder as the emperor's Rolls Royce entered the square in front of the parliament building.

On July 18, news began circulating that the emperor was convening a special session of parliament. The area near the parliament building swelled with people who were waiting ankle deep in mud for the emperor to arrive. Joining them were the quickly summoned greater and lesser chiefs, who were arriving on beautifully caparisoned mules and donkeys.

Using willow wands and swords, the court officers opened a path for the emperor to move through the crowd. Proudly wearing the field uniform of the Imperial Guard, he walked into the building where members of parliament, national dignitaries, and representatives of the foreign press were already waiting. Standish and Rutherford waited in the small area reserved for the diplomatic corps.

Haile Sellassie had created a parliament soon after becoming emperor and built a large hall to house it with its own clock tower inspired by London's Big Ben. It was not modeled after the deliberative and legislative parliament in England, but similar to *Il Duce*'s Italian one, an assembly where elected members were privileged to hear, but not contest, the decisions taken by the man in power.

The emperor's box was on an enclosed balcony about fifteen feet above the assembly chamber. In the box on his left, seventy year old Ras Mulugeta, the Minister of War, took his place alongside Abuna Kyrillos, the Chief Bishop of the Ethiopian Orthodox Coptic Church. The Cabinet ministers sat in another box dressed in somber mantles of gray, blue, brown, and black.

At precisely 11:55, the Court Chamberlain wearing a chartreuse silk cape and carrying a silver-topped staff took his place in the center of the chamber. He waited while a pink silk veil dropped from the front of the emperor's box. The veil was meant to protect the emperor from the eyes of his people, who must never see him in any movement unbecoming to his stature as might be sitting or standing. When the veil was lowered, the audience saw him standing with his speech in his hand.

Speaking in Amharic, he began by outlining at length the dispute with Italy: "Ethiopia has no intention of establishing her authority over other countries. When the Italian people arrive with their weapons of aggression, claiming that it is to teach us civilization, the Ethiopian people, who are prepared to die for their emperor and their country, will await the invader mustered in unity."

Standish and Rutherford listened as he then launched a vigorous exhortation to personal courage.

"Soldiers! When it is announced that a respected and beloved leader has died for our freedom in the course of the battle, do not grieve, do not lose hope. It is better to die with freedom than without it. Our fathers who have maintained our country in freedom have offered us their life in sacrifice. So let them be an example to you!

"Soldier, trader, peasant, young and old, man and woman, be united! Defend your country by helping each other! According to ancient custom, the women will stand in defense of their country by giving encouragement to the soldier and by caring for the wounded. Although Italy is doing everything possible to divide us, whether Christian or Muslim, we will, united, resist.

"Your king, who speaks to you today, will be in your midst, prepared to shed his blood for the liberty of Ethiopia. Before we conclude, there is one thing we wish to say to you once again. And this is our earnest striving for peace. By diplomatic means, Ethiopia has continuously sought a way of reaching accord that is peaceful and in which, there is honor for both of us. It has twice asked the League of Nations to get the Italian Government to honor the treaty of friendship and of arbitration that Italy voluntarily signed in 1906.

"We shall strive for peace till the end. But even if our exertions and our goodwill have not achieved results, our conscience will not reproach us. The Ethiopian people, united in faith, stretch out their hand to God that he may strengthen the power of our valiant men, truly to defend our country's independence."

A deep murmur arose in the crowded room as Haile Sellassie put away his papers. Again, the pink silk veil now rose to cover him as Standish and Rutherford made their way to the door.

"He looks upset, doesn't he?" Standish paused.

"He has every reason to be. Eden's failure in Rome is only one of the immediate problems. The way Mussolini has been acting, it wasn't the best idea to send Eden in the first place, but I doubt if anyone else could have succeeded."

"Yifru told me that Belgium cancelled its order to sell Ethiopia ten million cartridges. They've delivered only a fifth of that. Czechoslovakia and Denmark have done the same."

"How will the emperor make up for that ammunition?"

"Maybe he's hoping we will."

"He must not count on Roosevelt!"

"Yifru says that the emperor is in an impossible position. His chiefs won't tolerate surrender without a full fight. If their fathers could defeat the Italians, so will they."

"Yifru knows what he's up against, doesn't he?"

"The emperor's adamant that he won't make any concession that would damage the integrity and sovereignty of his country."

"But he must know what it means to lead his soldiers into the range of modern weapons. We're not talking about popguns."

"Yifru says he still believes that England might yet take some action, either unilaterally or in conjunction with the League."

"But judging from what we have been hearing and reading, if any help were to be forthcoming from England, it would have to come through the pressure generated by the English people. Not from their leaders."

A few minutes later they watched as Haile Sellassie left the building. When he descended the steps to his car, the crowd broke out into the vibrant ululating *Li-li-ii-li.* The sound spread to the thousands standing in the mud, and along the roadside, as the emperor drove back to the Little Ghibbi. His officers of the Guard, with their lion's hair insignia, dog-trotted, barefoot, beside the car.

CHAPTER 21

"Busy?"

"Trying to keep up with the angels," Ceseli said, putting down the paper she was reading. "But I did find out how Emperor Lalibela got so much help."

"Really?" Yifru smiled, sitting down. Ceseli waved a book at him. "James Bruce of Kinnaird. *Travels to Discover the Source of the Nile 1768-1773.*"

"I've read it."

"I found what I was looking for," she said, opening the book. "In the reign of Lalibela, after the Saracen conquest of Egypt, there was a persecution against the Egyptian Christian masons, builders, and hewers of stone. Emperor Lalibela invited these workers to seek refuge in Ethiopia and four to five thousand came."

"That's a lot of skilled labor."

"Bruce mentions that Lalibela had seen examples of the ancient works of troglodytes, and he used those examples for his own churches to be hewn out of the solid rock in his native area of Lasta. According to Bruce, Lalibela also wanted to divert the Nile from flowing down to Egypt because Egypt was now in the hands of his religious enemy. He thought that this could be achieved by making sure that the tributary rivers did not flow into Lake Tana. Egyptian agriculture flourishes only because of the silt carried with the Nile."

"I'm not sure how reliable Bruce is," Yifru said. "I don't mean about this. But there are other things that are puzzling."

"Such as?"

"Did he come to Ethiopia to find the source of the Nile?"

"What other motive would he have?"

"Some thought he came to find the Ark of the Covenant."

"Why do you say that?" Ceseli froze. *That's exactly what I was thinking*, she thought, *but with no logical explanation*.

"Bruce was a moderately wealthy Scottish nobleman with a passion for travel. He is credited with speaking several languages including Arabic and local dialects. He claimed to have discovered the source of the Nile. That is completely false. The Jesuits were there a one hundred fifty years before he came. Not to mention that the local people have lived along the shores of Lake Tana for centuries."

"So let's take everything with a handful of salt. Is there anything he did do?"

"Visited the Ethiopian royal court at Gondar and put it on the world map."

"Significant."

"I'm not saying he didn't come to Ethiopia, or that he didn't put it on the map of European travelers, just that all he said does not seem to be factually correct."

"You mean he was a braggart or a liar? Yifru, you are a diplomat at heart. Why do you think he was looking for the Ark?"

"Because of the relationship between Scotland and the Masons. The Masons of Scotland grew out of the Knights Templar, and I believe that Bruce was a Mason."

"That's where we stopped the other day. The Templars. What happened to them?" Ceseli asked.

"They excavated Solomon's Temple in Jerusalem and took the treasure. When the Templars got their hands on that hoard, they became the richest Christian order and started lending money to European monarchies and governments. Their base remained in France. By 1295, the French King, Philippe IV, owed them so much money that he decided to confiscate all their property. But he couldn't do that because they were beholden only to the pope."

"I get this," Ceseli jumped in. "He got rid of the pope."

"Two popes, one right after the other. Philippe then put one of his own henchmen, the archbishop of Bordeaux, into the papal seat. He became Clement V. With Clement under his complete control, Philippe put his plan into effect. On Friday October 13, 1307, he had every one of the Templars in France arrested. After interrogation and torture, the Templars were tried by the Inquisition as heretics and then burned at the stake."

"Ah, Christian mercy!" Ceseli smiled.

"But some Templars were able to escape to England and Scotland, where they met with happier circumstances."

"Did the king ever find the treasure?"

"Not to my knowledge. But it's not in Ethiopia."

"You say that with conviction. You think Bruce came here to find the Ark?"

"Bruce went to Axum on Timkat 18-19. It's the Epiphany, and it's the only time that the Ark is ever taken out of the Holy of Holies. It's carried in procession down to the reservoir so that people can see it. It's part of a baptism ceremony."

"I know about Timkat. I would love to see the Ark, but I don't expect to be here as late as that."

"Well Bruce went there so that he could try to find out if it was the real Ark. I'm not sure he could do that though."

Ceseli was skeptical.

"If he had, I think he would have tried to steal it."

"How feasible was that? I know he was a very big and powerful man, but the monks would have protested. How could he get it out of the country?"

"He stole several important books and manuscripts from the imperial library and he succeeded in getting them back to England. One was the *Kebra Nagast.* And he took a priceless Book of Enoch. It was composed before the birth of Christ and considered to be one of the most important pieces of Jewish mystical literature. Scholars thought the book was lost. It was only known from fragments and from references to it found in other texts. Bruce changed that by procuring several copies of it. They were the first complete editions of the Book of Enoch ever to be seen in Europe."

"What do you mean by procured? Buying or stealing?"

"I don't know how he did it. Only that they were written in Ge'ez, and were the only surviving copies, and he smuggled them out of Ethiopia and took them back to England."

"Why would the Book of Enoch be so important to Bruce?"

"Because I think he was a Freemason, and the masons thought Enoch was the Egyptian God of Wisdom. The God's name was Thoth. And of course because no one in Europe had ever seen the Book of Enoch."

"How could the Book of Enoch be written in Ge'ez and be in the Imperial library?"

"I don't know for sure, but it is an impressive collection. Many of the scrolls and early papyri were identical to those in the library in Alexandria.

But ours did not get burned as did the library at Alexandria. That I do know."

"Are there other such unique texts still in the library?"

"You, Miss Larson, are the archaeologist. Why don't you find out?"

Ceseli paused looking at him. "Thank you, Yifru. I'll try."

CHAPTER 22

Boom. Boom. Boom.

The deafening noise of gunfire woke her. *It couldn't be the war*, Ceseli thought. Then she remembered that the twenty-one shot cannon salvo announced the emperor's forty-fifth birthday. It was July 23, 1935.

Just before 9 a.m., accompanied by his priests and counselors, the emperor, wearing a black cape embroidered in scarlet and gold and wearing the Golden Collar of Solomon, walked into Menilek's immense throne room at the old Ghibbi palace. In the center of the huge room, the *Alga*, the oriental bed throne with its four posts and a canopy, was newly trimmed in crimson velvet. In the penumbra of the chamber, as he sat motionless on the *Alga*, Haile Sellassie's face was one of enigmatic mystery.

One by one, the great leaders and *shums* walked into the emperor's presence. They laid their swords and shields by their sides, prostrating themselves before him.

The press had been invited and came. Next to each of the lions' manes and spears, the gold encrusted rhino skin shields and every elaborately attired shum there was a photographer with his magnesium flashgun. Although European statesmen might try to conceal it, through these journalists the world now knew that a cultural and picturesque Ethiopia did exist.

Rutherford and Standish were among the diplomatic corps that kissed the emperor's hand while the young officers of the Imperial Guard stood at attention.

"That's Gugsa," Standish said under his breath, indicating the arrival of the emperor's son-in-law, Haile Sellassie Gugsa, hereditary prince of the Tigre Province.

"Quite boorish, isn't he?"

"He claims to be the descendent of the Emperor Yohannes."

"I'm willing to bet he's a descendent of Solomon, but is he a traitor?"

"I find no proof of it."

"The Italian Ambassador hasn't come," Rutherford whispered.

"No. I don't see him," Standish said, looking around.

"He was offended at the emperor's speech to Parliament. He insists that saying that Italy was preparing an act of aggression was incorrect. Italy was coming to civilize the country. The emperor is very sensitive when the word "civilize" is used," Rutherford added.

"Yifru said he's holding a raw meat gebir tonight for five thousand men."

Rutherford watched as the French Ambassador approached the *Alga*.

"The Empress Zaudita loved to do that. These gebirs were her favorite kind of banquet. Raw meat, mead, you know the whole Homeric scene. Or King Arthur, for that matter."

"The press would eat that up, excusing the pun," Standish said under his breath.

"Won't be there. The emperor has forbidden any foreigners. Particularly, the press. It falls in the same category as civilization," Rutherford added.

"Tough on Zeri and his lot."

"Very much so."

The room is getting very crowded, Ceseli thought, standing off to the side.

"I was pretty sure you'd be here," Marco said a few minutes later as Yifru found room for them with the distinguished local foreigners, the hotel keepers, shop owners, bank managers, and school teachers who lined up to wish the monarch well.

"Who's the guy standing behind the Emperor?" Marco asked.

"The imperial impersonator."

"Impersonator?"

"His *Likamaquas*. I've seen him often at the palace. According to the imperial tradition, he has to dress up as the emperor as if he were in battle and wave the red parasol to deceive the enemy."

"The red parasol?" Marco winked.

"Only the emperor carries the red parasol. It's his sign of power."

"That's one of the traditions Zeri would love," he said, holding her hand.

"He's still here?"

"Oh yes. He comes over to the compound a lot. He's doing some kind of a story on the Falasha Jews. In the area north of Lake Tana."

Ceseli shrugged. "I'm surprised that the emperor let him go. Yifru says the emperor likes him. He believes that, above all, he's an honorable man and I'm not going to second guess the emperor."

Marco noticed the coldness in her voice.

"Look," she said, as forty Muslim envoys prostrated themselves before the throne. Next, it was the children of the imperial schools presenting nosegays.

"I ran into him one day at the market," Ceseli continued. "He must go there often. But I do, too. He was very nice. Showed me a couple of tricks with his camera. Very polite."

"I sense you don't like him, but he's not a bad person."

"You know him better," she said, a little piqued that they should disagree on human nature.

"Yes and no. In some ways he's everything you'd expect a reporter to be. Censorship and all. But in others, I don't know. We've done a lot of late night talking. He's very open and humorous, but it's like I do all the talking. I don't know exactly how to describe it. I have almost no idea what he really thinks. Maybe he doesn't trust me."

"Do you trust him?"

"Would I trust him? Yes, I think so."

"Maybe you should trust your own judgment."

That evening, the emperor sat at his high table poised above the feast. The huge hall was transformed with rows of tables and benches. The gebir was a way to keep in touch with his fighting men. The five thousand men had their rifles and spears by their sides. They ate a huge amount of meat and drank copious draughts of *tej*, which at the emperor's table was served in silver pitchers, to his soldiers in huge earthenware jugs.

The Homeric atmosphere increased when the raw oxen and sheep were carried from table to table on long poles. The soldiers chose the choicest pieces hacking them from the carcasses with an upward thrust of a knife.

The boasting was curtailed that night. Haile Sellassie had already recognized that the Ethiopians' superiority complex, their invincibility and lack of fear in front of an enemy, particularly the Italians, was the most serious military problem that he had to face.

CHAPTER 23

"WHAT ARE YOU UP to?" Marco asked on the phone. It was Sunday afternoon and Ceseli felt creative.

"I've been painting. I thought you were working?" she said, looking down at her pants decorated with various dribbles of color. Her hair was pulled back so it wouldn't get into the paint.

"Can I come over?"

"You'll be bored."

"I'll bring a book."

"Sure, then come. Warren and Standish have gone hunting with the British Ambassador."

"I didn't know you had such talent," Marco said, looking over her shoulder.

"What's this?" he asked, pointing to a drawing in her notebook.

"It's the drawing of a tendril motif I saw at Axum. There's another just like it in the British museum. I saw it with my father. He dragged me through every museum in Europe, especially the British Museum which has a large collection of plundered art. Most of them are archaeological pieces, like the Rosetta Stone from Egypt and the Elgin marbles from the Parthenon in Athens. You know the British Museum?"

"I've been there several times. I spent the summer in London after graduation from *liceo* and before going to medical school. It was a graduation present from my parents."

"Well every time Daddy saw the Elgin marbles he was outraged. Recovering stolen art was his hobby," she said, pausing. "He was interested in the legal issues, what countries could do to get back their own national treasures. He wrote several articles on the marbles and gave lectures all over Europe. When I was old enough, I helped him on the research. I guess I feel that I'm keeping him here with me by pursuing his interests."

"There's nothing wrong with that, Ceseli. Don't be so hard on yourself. Grieving takes time."

"I know." She paused. "I guess I'll get used to it. And I shouldn't pick on the British. They were by no means the first of the great plunderers. I'm sure they won't be the last. Roman emperors started the plundering. They captured art as booty. Sulla looted Athens, Verres plundered Sicily, and Titus brought back the Jewish treasures of the Second Temple. And later, they brought back from Egypt some of their most important obelisks. There are eight standing in Rome. I think that's where Napoleon got the idea."

"Got what idea?"

"Napoleon was building his empire. He captured treasures wherever he went. He closed the Italian monasteries and stole their art. The popes had an amazing collection of Greek and Roman marble statues. In 1797, Napoleon forced Pope Pius VI to give him some of his statues and paintings. Some of them were huge marble statues like the *Laocoön* or *Apollo Belvedere*. They were shipped to Marseille and then floated in barges up the Rhone River to Paris. I can't forget the story because Daddy was trying to teach me the laws of physics. You know the one where you put an elephant on a barge and calculate how much water is displaced. The weight of the displaced water is the weight of the elephant. We calculated the weight of every marble piece in the pope's collection."

"If Mussolini conquers Ethiopia, what booty would he take?" Marco asked.

Ceseli paused. "To begin with, he'd take the things that represent Ethiopia's heritage, her history. The Ark of the Covenant. My obelisk. The equestrian statue of Menilek II in front of St. George's Cathedral. That golden lion from the railroad station. Then someone will have to find a way to get them back."

"I'm beginning to understand your father's passion for stolen art," Marco said. "Do any of them get returned?"

"Some, I guess, but it takes a very long time." Ceseli finished the painting, got up and took the notebook into her tukul.

"Is this yours?" Marco asked, looking around the tukul.

"Yes."

Marco walked to her dresser and took the picture of the Afar girl. "It's beautiful, isn't it?" he asked, turning to hold it up to her. "You're beautiful too," he said, taking her hand and drawing her gently to him. She moved willingly to him and felt his lips on her forehead, tiny kisses down her cheek and finally her lips.

After Marco finally left, Ceseli took some notepaper and went back onto the verandah. She had a letter to write that was long overdue.

Dear Sotzy,

I want to tell you about a young Italian doctor I met on the train coming to Ethiopia. I've been seeing quite a lot of him. Well, maybe not a lot, but we do see each other when he's not working or doing his research. He's like a savior. I know that probably sounds corny, but he wants to save people. That's why he's here. To find a cure for malaria. I had no idea so many people in Italy suffer from malaria. I only remember Daisy Miller. Do you remember you read me the book?

He's very nice to me and he looks like an angel, like the ones you see in a painting by Raphael or Leonardo. He's funny, too. He makes me smile and laugh. You always told me that humor is much more important than looks. We have a good time together, and I just wanted you to know that.

How is New York? Tell me all your news. I'll write again soon, but I want to get this in the mail or it won't go out on the train. Love.

She licked the envelope, put a stamp on it, and decided it was time to raid the mission's icebox.

CHAPTER 24

In August, a group of American engineers came to Addis. They had been sent to survey a possible site for a much awaited dam on the Blue Nile as it issued from Lake Tana. The group had traveled into Lake Tana from Khartoum in the Sudan, then nine hundred miles along the river and then come down from Lake Tana to Addis by pack mule.

"Don't get overly optimistic," Rutherford told Ceseli and Standish before the three men arrived. "I have been working on this dam project ever since I got here. In 1933, they were already projecting a cost of twenty million dollars. I have no idea what that would be today."

Ceseli had flown over Lake Tana on the return trip from Axum. The lake covered one thousand four hundred square miles and formed the headwaters of the Blue Nile, or the Abbay, as the Ethiopians called it. The river ran for five hundred miles in Ethiopia, most of it through one of the world's deepest and most dramatic gorges, before it joined the White Nile at its junction near Khartoum.

The three Americans were welcome company. Robert Evans was the leader of the group. He was a big hardy man with a fanatical memory for facts and figures. His two assistants, Larry Peters and John Connolly, were both young and both from New Jersey where the company's headquarters were. This was their first trip so far from home, let alone Africa, and they were happy to be back to civilization, even if it was only Addis. A hot shower and a cup of coffee had done wonders for their spirits. It had been refreshingly American to see them playing touch football in the garden.

The evening was cool as Ceseli walked up from her tukul. She was wearing a black cotton skirt with a man's white shirt belted by a piece of Ethiopian cotton cloth that doubled as a headscarf. Her hair was combed loosely down her back and she wore soft leather boots made for her at the market.

The table was nicely set with tall white candles, and incense was burning in small earthenware holders. In the background, Ella Fitzgerald sang from the Victrola. The meal was American with some Ethiopian innovations. According to the chef's preference for roast beef, it was nearly raw, the potatoes were tiny and mixed with baked eggplant and the tomatoes cut in slivers and served with ground teff.

"The Blue Nile begins in Lake Tana," Evans said between mouthfuls. "It's a very rich agricultural area. The land bordering the lake has oranges, lemons, limes, citrons, and bananas. The lower valleys produce corn, teff, indigo, and doura. Barley and wheat flax grow on the highest plateau."

"What will the British say to this dam?" Ceseli asked.

"I understand they didn't have any objection when the idea was broached several years ago," Evans answered.

"It was at least three years ago," Rutherford corrected.

"Is it that much?" Evans questioned. "But the situation has not changed. If the Americans are going to build this dam, the British will lose out. We'll build the dam and may or may not find a way to sell the water. I don't think the British will object because I doubt they have the money or the inclination to follow up on the plan."

"We've seen a copy of the recent report from the U.K.," Standish intervened. "The British are saying that they have no economic interest in Ethiopia, other than the area of Lake Tana."

"That is to guarantee that the water continues to reach Egypt," Evans said. "Don't forget that Egypt's agriculture, for thousands of years, has come from the silt carried by the Nile. That's what protects their cotton production."

"What was the name of that report, Standish?" Rutherford asked. "By the way, do try the Ethiopian wine. It's very light."

"The Maffey Report. Secret and confidential," Standish smiled.

"Standish, can you tell Evans what it says. And please have some more meat. It's not as raw now."

"The gist," Standish began, "is that, besides the importance of the Blue Nile to the British controlled White Nile, Great Britain has no vital interests in Ethiopia which would oblige His Majesty's government to resist an Italian conquest. For the British, it is a matter of indifference whether Ethiopia remains independent or is absorbed by Italy."

"From some points of view, it might be better if Ethiopia were to be absorbed by Italy," Rutherford interrupted. "England and France will go to great lengths to appease Mussolini. He's like a child throwing a temper tantrum. He struts, thrusts out his jaw, yells, and they cave in. If it works the first time, it's learned behavior. He'll keep at it."

The men looked at Rutherford for guidance. "Maffey says that the British have no interest in Ethiopia. Which, of course, will be true, until they do. I believe there's another thing to be considered. It would not help the interests of the British Empire if a non-white civilization were to prevail against a white one. If you see what I mean," Rutherford said, smiling at his own acumen.

"Do you really think that's the way the British are thinking?" Ceseli asked, incredulous.

"I'm sure that is exactly what they are thinking, my dear. What Mussolini is attempting to do is precisely what the British have done to acquire their own empire. And the French, Belgians, Dutch, Germans, Spanish and Portuguese as well. Empire-building has gone out of style, but that doesn't mean that England and France aren't going to hold on to their own empires and they don't need unrest among the subjugated."

Ceseli looked from one of them to the other. "You're not kidding, are you?"

"I wish I were" Rutherford smiled.

"That's what we had been told," Evans said, looking uncomfortable.

To end the conversation, Rutherford pushed back his chair and walked to the verandah where Hilina was preparing coffee. They didn't have coffee served every night in this traditional Ethiopian ceremony, but Rutherford had arranged it for their guests.

"Coffee originated in the Kaffa province, to the south," Ceseli told them remembering her first taste of Ethiopian coffee on the train with Yifru. "The Ethiopians call it *buna*. There is an old Ethiopian legend about a young goat herder who noticed his herd becoming unusually frisky after nibbling the berries of a tree. After trying some himself, he found that the berries had a stimulating effect. A monk from a neighboring monastery decided to try the berries and to his amazement, he also found that the berries helped keep him alert during his late night prayers. Soon all the monks in the area were chewing the berries."

"You will find that Ceseli has a suitable legend or explanation for everything," Rutherford smiled.

"Warren!" she protested.

"She's got this little book. Ceseli's Bible. It contains everything you can imagine about Ethiopia. It's sort of an encyclopedia, journal, and scrapbook. Everything boils down to Solomon and Sheba, even the coffee."

Ceseli joined in the laughter.

"Well, almost everything. She's been a most welcome addition to our household," Rutherford continued. "She claims to be an archaeologist, but I fear that she is here to write her autobiography and needed some interesting material. Standish and I are only the background to the emperor." The three newcomers laughed appreciatively.

"Does that mean you don't want me to explain the coffee ceremony?" Ceseli teased.

"By all means, do. The coffee is nothing without knowing the ceremony behind it."

In the meantime, Hilina had spread a pale blue rug on the floor of the verandah. Sitting back on her heels behind the rug, she took fresh, long, green grass and wild flowers and scattered them on the rug. The girl was slender, with giant almond-shaped eyes and tonight wore a shimmering fuchsia shamma with embroidered purple flowers along one side. The pale blue, bright pink, and purple might have seemed like a strange combination, but they blended perfectly, making her look like a bouquet.

"The rug marks the borders of a sacred space," Ceseli explained. "The flowers and grass are reminiscent of our connection to nature and the earth. You'll have to be patient. Waiting for the coffee is an essential part of this ceremony."

Rutherford took his pipe and settled down into his comfortable chair, while the other men sat on upright wicker ones.

Hilina had taken the coffee beans and was roasting them on a tiny charcoal burner. It was of the same black-fired clay as the coffee pot that held the water that she was heating.

"Incense is placed on the little clay holder," Ceseli continued. "It is believed that this holy smell transports us into a deeper realm of being. In some areas of Ethiopia, it is believed that the smoke of the incense will carry any bad spirits out of the home." She paused, glancing at Evans, who was winking at her. "Each crackling noise is a bean opening itself up to release its rich provocative essence to tantalize our senses," Ceseli said, her voice low enough not to disturb Hilina's traditional movements.

"When the beans have been roasted to a dark chocolate color, the coffee maker takes the roaster and moves around the room, inviting us to gently coax the smoke toward us with our hands and become one with its enticing aroma."

As if on cue, Hilina stood up, going first to Rutherford, who passed his hands over the burner, wafting the smell toward him. His guests followed suit.

"Then she will crush the beans into fine grains with a mortar and pestle and sacrifice them in the boiling water of the coffee pot. She can choose to add a pinch of cinnamon, cloves, or cardamom, which will produce their own flavor."

"You can add sugar if you want," Ceseli said, passing the raw brown sugar. She noticed that the men had taken the tiny thimble-like cups and were holding them nimbly. They were smiling at Hilina as she passed again to refill their cups.

"If you want to go back to the states with us, Ceseli, we'd be glad to have you," Evans said later as he walked her back to her tukul.

"When are you going?"

"Next week. We've still got to write out a report for the emperor and hold a few meetings."

"I thank you for the offer, but I'm not going yet. I've still got a lot I want to accomplish."

"The atmosphere is not looking bright," he said, stopping at her verandah.

"I know, but I'm perfectly safe for now. Thank you anyhow."

"You're sure about that, Ceseli?" Evans asked again, taking her hand.

"I'm very sure, but thank you."

"All right. Look me up when you get stateside."

"I promise I'll do that, and thank you again," she said, going up the steps. "I appreciate your concern."

CHAPTER 25

"Do you want to come and listen to the emperor's speech?" Ceseli asked Marco on the telephone. "I'm sure there'd be no objection."

"I'd like that."

"Come on in," Ceseli greeted him the next afternoon as she led him to Warren Rutherford's office.

"Welcome, young man. Nice to see you," Rutherford said while shaking his hand. "Sit over here," he said, motioning to the couch. "It's almost time."

Rutherford turned on the radio and they sat in silence waiting for it to crackle into life. It was September 11, 1935 and according to the agricultural based Ethiopian calendar, the New Year was about to begin.

The emperor was addressing the world: "At this time, when according to the Ethiopian calendar, the year 1935/36 begins, we wish that this New Year may bring the peace which is essential, and which our people and the world desire with a warm heart. It appears to us right to recall the principal events which have occurred in the past year.

"This WalWal clash, which we demanded be settled by arbitration, was finally adjudicated on the 3rd of September. The five arbitrators reached the unanimous verdict that neither Ethiopia, nor Italy, was responsible for the attack. As Italy has made WalWal the pretext to wage war upon Ethiopia, Italy is now somewhat short of reasons to make war."

Ceseli looked across at Marco who was having trouble understanding the emperor's English accent.

"History will judge Italy's behavior. While Italy claims to be the very essence of civilization, she is making unjust war upon a people that is peaceful, that has been prevented from obtaining military equipment, and which lives still trusting a treaty which Italy publicly signed in August, 1928, so that peace and friendship would persist.

"The Ethiopian people emphatically seek peace and, moreover, loves its country dearly. It will resist by defending itself against the enemy and protecting its chest in which there is a proud heart burning with love of country.

"Our peasants, who live tilling their land in peace, whose arm is strong and who are jealous of their freedom, will rise up with their spades and lances to wield them quickly, overturning their ploughs to stop the enemy from invading their land.

"We do not like war. But we shall not let our enemy pass without defending ourselves fiercely. As Ethiopia's faith reposes in God, she knows that God's judgment will prevail over that of man. New weapons and guns which man has devised to destroy his kind, are not a measure of civilization.

"Finally, Ethiopia desires and hopes that with the assistance of the League of Nations, the quarrel which has broken out between Ethiopia and Italy may be resolved by law and proper judgment in consonance with the Covenant of the League of Nations."

As the radio crackling faded into silence, Minister Rutherford tapped the ashes from his pipe into a nearby ashtray. He looked at each one of them. "So?"

"I hope the American people were listening," Standish said. "If not the President."

"Does the emperor know that war is here?" Ceseli asked.

"He still has faith in the League," Standish replied. "It's hard to understand why."

"Because he signed a treaty to avoid war. He committed his name and that of his country," she answered, looking at him.

"Of course," Rutherford said, interrupting. "But Standish is right. He's been given no reason to think the members of the League will defend him."

"Isn't that what the Covenant says?" Ceseli asked.

"Yes," Rutherford added. "President Roosevelt refuses to get involved. Unfortunately, this is the war staring us in the face."

"Africa is very far from America. Not only in distance," Standish added.

"I'm afraid there is one point which is very clear," Rutherford remarked. "The majority of the American people agree that Mussolini is a dreadful fellow and they would be happy if someone were to stop him. But it should be someone else."

Marco looked at the others knowing that he, at least, was already committed.

"Thank you for letting me share this with you," he said. "I'd better get back to the hospital."

"It will be hard on you," Rutherford said. "If there's anything we can do, please don't hesitate to ask."

"Thank you, sir."

As they walked hand-in-hand to the entrance, Marco drew her to the side. "Ceseli, you need to leave."

"Maybe."

"No maybes about it. You need to go."

"You know, Marco, I'm really happy here. For the first time since Daddy's death, I feel that I am doing something I want to do. And I'm getting a lot accomplished. This is wonderful material for my thesis."

"That isn't the issue and you know it! It's time to go. You know that."

"You too," she said defiantly.

"I'm a doctor. I can treat the wounded."

"Not as well as you, but so could I."

"Get on that train, Ceseli. Please."

"I can't," she said. Marco took her hand and held it tightly. She looked up at him moving into his embrace. Not wanting him to leave her and not wanting to leave him, they stood there, together, her cheek on his chin for a long time. Then he broke away and was gone.

Later that evening, she sat on her bed and looked around her. The room had changed since she first moved in. It was more personal. Her own photos were on the walls and she had a small table in the bathroom to hold her developing equipment.

Was he right? Should she get out now? She felt like a child again, sitting in her bedroom at her grandmother's apartment in New York when she needed to make big decisions. None of them had been very big, but at the time they seemed so. She knew it was very important to her not to leave Marco. To be where he was. She looked over at the smiling photo of her father. She had become more confident about her own decisions.

CHAPTER 26

AUGUST WAS UNEVENTFUL EXCEPT for the knowledge that more and more troops were being sent to Eritrea and Italian Somaliland. But as the heavy rains began to peter out, the single most important subject of discussion in bars, hotels, and whorehouses was whether Mussolini was going to bomb Addis and what provisions should be taken for protection. Some people thought of seeking refuge on Mount Entoto, others rented safe houses near the Italian compound. Rutherford sent Daniele up to the roof to paint a huge American flag on it.

"Make sure it very big and very bright," Rutherford ordered. "Or we'll all be cooked duck."

The emperor set up a warning system: three shots fired from an old cannon at the Ghibbi Palace. If the people heard the cannon, they were ordered to leave town, or to take refuge in the shelters they had constructed. During the practice, the cannon exploded. As there is no word for "practice" in Amharic, the whole town panicked. Even though they heard no bombs and saw no planes, people ran to the hills and stayed there.

The foreigners were leaving. The train station at Akashi was flooded by those seeking to get out while they still could. The gay brown ladies of the night were ordered to prepare to accompany the soldiers to the front, or, if they declined, they could help the war effort by paying a fine of five silver *Thalers* to the imperial war chest. Most paid and stayed.

Bill, with his harmonica in his pocket, stopped by the legation to say goodbye. "I'm sorry to have to go, Miss Larson, but there won't be much mule breeding for a long time. Time to get back to Kansas."

"I'm sorry you're leaving, Bill." Ceseli smiled, holding out her hand to shake his. "Have a safe trip back, and thanks for stopping by," she said.

Several days later, Bruno Zeri, too, was leaving. "I have some new ideas for your bible," he said, coming abruptly into her office.

"About the Falasha Jews. You found them?"

"Finding them wasn't the problem. There are three communities up there. They do live on land rented from other landowners. That's true. The center of their religious life is the synagogue. The high priest is the head in each village. He is helped by lower priests. Falasha monks live alone, or in monasteries. There are no rabbis. That's different because the rabbi is a very important person in most Jewish communities in Europe. Also, the Sabbath requirements are rigid. They observe biblical dietary laws. And the part about animal sacrifice is true. You might want to add that to your bible."

"I will. So you're going to write about them?"

"No, I'm not."

"I thought that was the whole point of your trip?"

"I went there with that intention. They believe that they are descendants of Solomon and Sheba. They may even be the lost tribe of Dan, one of the ten lost tribes of Israel. One monk told me he thought that when the Red Sea opened not all the Jews crossed in time. They escaped from Egypt by going south and ended up here in Ethiopia."

"An interesting thought."

"But since I've met these people, I've changed my mind. If I write about them, they'll look like something out of a circus. They are what I see as a unique tribe of Jews. History has just passed them by. I don't want them subjected to ridicule because of me."

Ceseli listened to what he was saying, not passing judgment, one way or the other.

"You don't like me very much, do you, Miss Larson?"

"No," Ceseli admitted.

"Is it because I'm a journalist or because I'm Italian? Or because I'm a Jew?"

"I don't know."

"You think I'm a brainwashed journalist?"

"I'm not sure."

"But you're not willing to give me the benefit of the doubt. You might be pleasantly surprised. Maybe you have a glorified idea of what I actually do. It's very simple. I report what happens. The man walked down the street. The dog was shot."

"I guess I feel that you have to do more than that."

"What do you mean?"

"I feel that in a war you have to take sides."

Bruno Zeri hesitated, looking at the photo of the obelisk on the wall. "You mean like the Greek gods did. Zeus. Hera. Troy."

"The Gods decided the wars because of their petty differences. I can almost see them up on Mt. Olympus deciding the fate of the world."

"I can see them in Geneva," Zeri smiled. "Do you know the book, *A Tale of Two Cities*? Dickens?"

"It was the best of times, it was the worst of times . . . It was my father's favorite book."

"Your father was an intelligent man. Very true to his beliefs. I liked him for that."

"You never said you knew him."

"Mostly of him. He was a very respected man. I was in the Assembly Hall when he collapsed."

"He didn't suffer?" she blurted out.

"I think he was dead immediately. I'm sorry if I have made you relive memories," Zeri said. Ceseli could not help noticing that there was kindness in his voice.

"A day doesn't go by that I don't think of it, but thank you in any case."

"You remember Madame De Farge?" Zeri asked.

"Knitting her shawl."

"It wasn't a shawl, was it? It was a list of names. Those who had been executed."

"I stand corrected. But I don't understand the connection."

"Someday I'll tell you. But that wasn't the purpose of my visit. I'm leaving tomorrow. My paper needs me elsewhere."

"Eritrea?" she asked, thinking he would lie.

"That's right. I stopped by to thank you for your help. About the Falashas."

"But I didn't do anything, but give you some facts."

"That's what a journalist needs," he said, taking her hand and kissing the back of it. "It'll be a dreadful war," he said. "You should get out now."

"I will. When the time comes."

"Will you still go to Rome? I'm from Rome, you know. My house is near Torre Argentina. Next to the Jewish ghetto."

"I remember where that is. The Roman columns and the stray cats."

"The cats of Rome. That's right. If you get to Rome, give me a call."

"Maybe."

"I'm not asking for it carved in stone. Just maybe."

When he had gone, she tried to analyze what she did feel. Maybe, he was a modern gladiator. She felt that he was baiting her or perhaps even sparring with her. The fact was he made her uncomfortable.

As Bruno walked back to the Imperial Hotel, he wondered why it mattered that Ceseli Larson should like him. At least respect him.

CHAPTER 27

The situation in Ethiopia was growing more and more ominous by the time that Rutherford received a disquieting telegram from Washington. He hurried to Standish's office waving it in front of him.

"Standish, I think you better go see Yifru, immediately. I'd like him to hear this from us rather than our close allies," he said, handing Standish a telegram on the coarse yellowed paper.

"What is it?"

"Congress passed the Neutrality Act on August 31. Goddamn those bastards! That means no help for Ethiopia. We will be neutral to every country in war. Just that this is the only one staring us in the face. And we are utterly involved in it. The president has signed it."

Standish looked at Rutherford in utter disbelief. "How could he do this?"

"There's also a message from President Roosevelt. Look at it so you know what to answer if there are questions. I'm sure there will be. You can give the emperor the full text, if you want. It's public property."

Standish took the telegram and began to read it as Rutherford left. "I have given my approval to Resolution 173, the Neutrality Legislation, which passed the Congress last week." President Roosevelt had written.

Standish picked up his jacket and ran toward the entrance to the legation yelling for Daniele as he did so. It took them ten minutes to reach the palace. The lower floor was crowded like almost any day at the Ghibbi. There were about three hundred people lounging in the courtyard, waiting to see or to talk with the emperor.

"Hey, stranger. You must have something pretty important to bring you over here," Ceseli said as Standish came abruptly into her office.

"Know where Yifru is? He's not in his office."

"Probably with the emperor."

Standish looked at his watch.

"What's the matter?" Ceseli asked. "You look worried."

"Congress has signed the Neutrality Act. And Roosevelt signed it. That's what."

"What does that mean?"

"We can't sell arms to Ethiopia. God, what do they think they're doing? Assholes."

"Now what?" Ceseli asked, her voice quavering.

"The guard said you were looking for me." Yifru said, abruptly opening the door.

"Rutherford thought you should see this from us directly. It couldn't come at a worse time."

Yifru took the text of the President's message and skimmed it. Then he reread it more carefully. "Let me see. This resolution provides for a licensing system for the control of carrying arms by American vessels. For the control of the use of American waters by foreign submarines. For the restriction of travel by American citizens on vessels of belligerent nations, and for the embargo of the export of arms to all belligerent nations."

"Here again," President Roosevelt had written, "the policy of this government is definitely committed to the maintenance of peace and the avoidance of any entanglements that would lead us into conflict. At the same time, it is the policy of the government by every peaceful means and without entanglement to cooperate with other similarly minded governments to promote peace."

Yifru drew in his breath. "This is something we didn't need. I guess we knew it might happen, but now it's a fact. We need to look elsewhere for help."

"I'm sorry," Standish said, earnestly shaking Yifru's hand.

All of a sudden Ceseli felt physically sick to her stomach. "It does say that the U.S. will cooperate with other peace wanting nations. Does that include the League?"

"It does imply that," Standish said. "Let's hope so."

"Thank Rutherford for me." Yifru said, still looking at the text. "I think I need to interrupt the emperor."

When he had gone, Ceseli looked at Standish. "Is this it?"

"I'm afraid so."

Alone, Ceseli walked to her window. Outside, there was no sense of panic as the home guard drilled in the garden. She looked at the young boys who were smiling as she heard the bare feet padding rhythmically. *Gra-Gra-Gra-Ken-Gra. Gra-Gra-Gra-Ken-Gra.* Tears began to form in her eyes and she didn't stop them as she continued to hear the *Gra-Gra-Gra-Ken-Gra. Gra-Gra-Gra-Ken-Gra.*

CHAPTER 28

ON SEPTEMBER 23 CAME the King's *Maskal*, or the Dance of the Priests. The dim *gebir* hall of the great palace was opened to foreigners. It is at this festival that the emperor appears to his chiefs and priesthood, and acknowledges the triumph of the Ethiopian Coptic Christian Church over African paganism and popular beliefs.

The windows and immense doors of the hall were covered with strips of orange silk, and the floor was strewn with reeds and strong-smelling mint leaves. Haile Sellassie on his bed throne, escorted by two of his battle impersonators and surrounded by the Diplomatic Corps, presided over the ceremony. Bouquets of spring iris and marigolds from the school gardens were presented to the emperor and the members of the Diplomatic Corps. All the diplomats, including the Italian Ambassador, kissed his hand.

The palace servants in shimmering chartreuse satin coats and jodhpurs, carrying their whipping wands and long red swords, ushered in a hundred priests. Under the faded Ethiopian flags and fringed silk umbrellas, the priests sang in a chorus to five choirboy altos dressed in white robes and two tenors, whose solos were part of a composition in praise of the emperor.

When the songs were over, the priests advanced toward a table in the middle of the hall, on which lay the Ge'ez bible. Slowly dancing and swaying rhythmically, crossing their silver-topped staves and shaking copper rattles to the accompaniment of two sweetly toned leather drums, they showed no emotion, for their eyes were lost in a measureless profundity. As a token of his loyalty to the Ethiopian Coptic Church, the emperor kissed the Bible.

Four days later, it was the first day of the Feast of Maskal, celebrating the end of the rainy season and the beginning of the new agricultural year. The large yellow Maskal daisies erupted in millions over the fields around the city, carpeting them in astounding golden colors framed by the blue Eucalyptus forests. The end of the rains brought festive religious holidays.

"We'll go together," Marco said. "Maskal commemorates the finding of what was believed to be the True Cross of Christ. The one he was crucified on."

By the time Ceseli and Marco walked into the square, the closely packed crowd was so dense it looked like everyone in Addis was there. Thousands of people held up long poles from which dangled the Maskal daisies.

A colorful procession of priests in scarlet and magenta, deacons, and choirboys and girls wearing embroidered robes were walking around a huge pyre. They held ceremonial crosses and wooden torches decorated with olive leaves.

Warriors had come wearing colorful costumes to posture and swing their swords, fire their guns and boast of their exploits in front of their emperor. Jousting, cavorting and slicing open ghostly enemies, they told their emperor that it was high time he did the same.

"At the Maskal, everyone gives advice to the emperor," Marco said. "They're begging him for rifles instead of spears."

"The other day there were thousands at the palace screaming for guns, not sticks. It's pathetic," she said, squeezing his hand.

As the sun began to set, the torchbearers lit the slender pyramid-shaped structure. On top was a cross that was made from the yellow daisies. The sky opened, in a final deluge, drowning the holidaymakers and the flowers.

But in the North, in Tigre, the earth was already dry. Yifru knew that the emperor was upset. These same Maskal daisies that now heralded the end of the rainy season, would also signal the beginning of war.

Since May, sitting in his large office, the emperor had studied his options and knew they weren't good. He knew all too well that Ethiopia was pitifully short of everything it needed to survive. Yet, despite the gravity of the situation, he remained adamant that he would not make any concessions that would damage the integrity and sovereignty of his country.

He was now focusing all of his attention on Geneva hoping that the League would somehow step in to keep his nation free. He followed closely the positions of the League's most powerful members: Britain and France. He was acutely aware of the fact that, unfortunate as it was for Ethiopia, the English and French ruling classes, both with their own empires in Africa, shared more in common with white Europeans, even the Italians, than with black Africans.

In March, the emperor had gratefully accepted the Fuhrer's secret offer to let him purchase German weapons. In April, while the Italians were hosting the leaders of Great Britain and France and sealing Ethiopia's fate at the lovely Italian resort at Stresa, he sent Yifru to Berlin to arrange payment for the arms and their transfer to Ethiopia. The armaments had been ingeniously smuggled into Ethiopia in the piano crates on the same train as Ceseli. Their pitifully small numbers only reminded him of his huge lack of armaments.

But everything deteriorated over the summer. Just the day before, the emperor had received a telegram from his ambassador in Geneva informing him for the first time that within the League, everyone now agreed that war was not only inevitable, but imminent.

The next day, September 28, Haile Sellassie wrote the orders for the general mobilization of his people and put it into the drawer of his desk. Then Yifru prepared for him a telegram to Geneva.

"We must obey the League and keep the thirty kilometer neutral zone," he said, while dictating the telegram.

"Earnestly beg Council to take as soon as possible all precautions against Italian aggression since circumstances have become such that we should fail in our duty if we delayed any longer the general mobilization necessary to ensure defense of our country. Our contemplated mobilization will not affect your previous orders to keep our troops at a distance from the frontier and we confirm our resolution to cooperate closely with the League of Nations in all circumstances."

Geneva did not reply.

To the north, in Eritrea, the land was already dry. In Asmara, the capitol of the Italian colony of Eritrea, Bruno Zeri looked out over the yellow Maskal daisies. The Eritreans, who shared the same traditions as the Ethiopians, were celebrating the second day of Maskal. War whoops, tom-toms, rifle shots and shouting filled the air. The Italian colonial native soldiers, known as *Askari*, in their khaki uniforms with their cheeks and foreheads painted with their battalion colors, waved flaming branches above their heads and the hot embers rained down on the crowd.

Zeri flinched as hundreds of the soldiers ran barefoot over a bed of live coals. Others danced with their spears overhead making mock charges against the enemy, be it lion or man.

In 1869, the Italian Rubattino Steamship Company, needing a coaling station in the Red Sea, bought the Bay of Assab and its miserable oasis from the local sultan. On January 1, 1890, the Italian government christened the new colony Eritrea in remembrance of the Erythraean Sea as the ancient Romans had called this sea. Now, the red, white and green Italian flag flew over a strip of torrid, barren and fever-ridden Red Sea Coast six hundred seventy miles long.

The Italian Consulate now dominated the port where seagulls floated like clouds over the Regina Margherita dock and as many as forty ships were in the bay waiting to unload.

In this Italian colony, it was General Emilio De Bono, who was presiding over the festivities. Bald and frail looking at sixty-nine, De Bono, with his white goatee, was the oldest of the original Fascist leaders and a devoted follower of Mussolini. The Minister of the Italian Colonies as well as the Italian Commanding General, De Bono had spent the last ten months in Asmara preparing for the invasion.

Arriving in Eritrea the week before, Zeri found De Bono tired, nervous, and upset. As the time for invasion neared, he was overwhelmed by doubts that the army was still not ready.

In his spare time, Zeri explored Asmara. Most of the city looked like a construction site, as under De Bono's orders new buildings, hangars, and airports were built, joined by warehouses, arsenals, offices, barracks, and repair shops. Three new state-controlled brothels were opened and a Fascist clubhouse added.

On the evening of the second day, he came upon a small garage sandwiched between two parking lots. There was a sign above the door: the Office for Gas. In the few minutes before he was expelled, he saw the canisters clearly marked "Yperite". Yperite—mustard gas—dichlorodiethyl sulfide $S(CH_2\ CH2Cl)_2$. Later, he learned that the warehouse already contained one hundred thirty tons of mustard gas in well-marked containers and that there were some one hundred fifty thousand gas masks.

That evening Zeri sat deep in thought. Here he was, in Eritrea, about to write about a war. He would be participating in a war. He thought back on his conversation with Ceseli. Zeus or Hera?

He was extremely upset. The Geneva Convention of 1926, signed to avoid a repetition of such barbarity as the Germans had perpetrated during World War I, specifically forbade the use of mustard gas or any other poisonous gas. What was Mussolini thinking? Who would know better than he what destruction Yperite would cause? The Italian army, when commanded by General Pietro Badoglio, was gassed by the

Germans during World War I at the Isonzo River. Zeri, then a conscript, spent months recovering in a military sanitarium. Hundreds died.

War was imminent, and hundreds of thousands of Ethiopians would die. Italians too would die for this futile gesture. The question was when?

The answer came the following night, September 29, 1935, when General De Bono received the telegram for which he was both waiting and in dread.

"No message of war at the beginning. It is absolutely necessary to put an end to all delays. I order you to initiate advance in the early hours in the early hours of three, I say, three October. I await an immediate confirmation. Mussolini."

CHAPTER 29

The pre-dawn light was teeming with waiting troops. The day had come. It was 4:45 a.m. on October 3, 1935. Some one hundred thousand Italian soldiers were ready for the invasion of Ethiopia. Each man had been issued one hundred and ten rounds of ammunition, four days rations, and a quart of water.

General Emilio De Bono's headquarters was on the brow of the Coatit Mountain, eight miles from the Abyssinian border. The maps on the table were just visible as his staff conferred, the gray-green of their uniforms barely distinguishable in the subdued light.

Nearby a small group of war correspondents set up their typewriters on a sandbagged parapet. It was 4:50 a.m. Bruno Zeri looked out over the Asmara plain half a mile below. He could just discern the shallow waters of the Mareb River, the border between Abyssinia and Eritrea. Feeling that he was as ready as he ever would be, he lit one of his precious Tuscan cigars.

Zeri knew that this stream of water, which flowed between bare foothills, could hardly be called an obstacle, but to the one hundred thousand men who would cross it that morning, it had a shameful significance. It was the border imposed by the Ethiopian Emperor, Menilek II after the shattering defeat of the Italians at Adowa in which thousands of Italian and Eritrean soldiers were killed, and thousands more taken prisoner.

For these young conscripts, crossing the Mareb River was symbolic. They were proving to the world that they were avenging their dead, hurling defiance at the colonial powers that opposed this war, and showing the whole world that a new generation of Italians were soldiers in the tradition of the Roman Empire.

Slowly, to the east, melon turned to peach and deepened to rose. Now the muted silhouette of the Danakil Mountains appeared. Apart from the subdued clicking of telegraph instruments, there was total silence. As the minutes ticked away, the war correspondents realized that the bluffing and the daydream diplomacy were over. A huge war machine was now ready and waiting only for the appointed minute. The correspondent of the Associated Press punched out the first bulletin that would headline the newspapers of the world: Italians commenced the invasion of Abyssinia at 5 a.m.

At exactly five, the time Mussolini had chosen, the Eritrean cavalry units nudged their horses into the shallow water, emerged on the other bank, and rode southward through the wide Hasamo plain into a largely treeless, broken, difficult countryside.

De Bono and his chief of staff paced back and forth on the plateau. Through field glasses they watched the endless lines of men wading across the wide river, their rifles held high over their heads, their banners waving, trumpets blaring, and soldiers singing. They marched to "Youth," the lightly played Fascist marching anthem. The veterans in this endless human chain could think with nostalgia of a day in 1922 when they had marched on the Eternal City of Rome to make Fascism the party of the state.

After the cavalry came the Italian light tanks, then the infantry, many of them blond-haired teenagers from the northern Italian provinces. Attached to their Panama style sun helmets and sticking from the barrels of their guns were freshly picked yellow Maskal daisies. Behind them were the mule trains of the supply corps, miles of heavily burdened animals carrying ammunition, rifles, machine guns, food, and water.

By nightfall, the three Italian columns had seized two thousand square miles of Abyssinia. Not a shot had been fired.

CHAPTER 30

LATER THAT MORNING, FIVE thousand faithful subjects crowded into the square in front of Menilek's imperial palace. They had been there since dawn waiting for confirmation of the rumor that most of them already believed.

Ceseli and Marco watched from her office window as five servants emerged from the palace carrying the great lion-skinned war drum of the empire and the heavy, crooked club. The drummer began a series of deep, powerful single thuds that could be heard for miles.

The people of Addis Ababa knew what it must mean. They hurried through the palace gates to the imperial residence, where the royal family and important government officials were standing on the second floor balcony.

In the emperor's office, Yifru stood behind him as he took from his desk the mobilization decree he had written on September 28.

At a few minutes before 11 a.m., court dignitaries and military chiefs gathered around the drum. As the drumbeats stopped, the soldiers rose in one wave. Silence descended as the court chamberlain mounted a wooden chair and began to read the emperor's proclamation.

"Listen! Listen! Open your ears!

The Lion of Judah has prevailed.

Haile Sellassie I, Elect of God,

King of Kings of all Ethiopia.

"People of my country Ethiopia! You know of Ethiopia's ancient tradition since the days of Menilek and that she is well known and honored for her independence.

"Some forty years ago today, Italy, boasting of her ability and strength, wanted to acquire our people as slaves after destroying Ethiopia's independence. When she came into our country to fight us, our God, who does not like violence, helped us, and when he gave us victory we did not seek to recover our land that had been taken. Your eyes can see and your ears can hear the yoke of serfdom that our brothers, who live in the areas Italy has usurped, have had to bear.

"We for our part entered a League of Nations that was established for the sake of world peace. We informed the League so that the offender be identified once the WalWal conflict had been looked into by the arbitrators, according to the law. When these men investigated the matter, they found in our favor, determining that the Ethiopian government had done no wrong and carried no responsibility for the attack which had taken place at WalWal."

"That was the verdict," Marco whispered.

"Shh . . . I can't hear."

"While the arbitration was going on, Italy did not abandon its warlike activities. She was meaning to deprive Ethiopia of her liberty and to destroy her. A nation without freedom is tantamount to a people driven from its land, being pushed like cattle by the hand of the enemy. A nation thus becomes one that lives in bitter affliction, and in humiliation, as a tenant watching its inheritance in its own country in the hands of other men. It becomes a country that has no control over its possessions, nor its livelihood, not even over the soil of its grave, one that exists by inheriting serfdom that passes on to the next generation.

"With other people, when a king or a bishop dies, his descendant is substituted for him. But when a country's independence is extinguished, there is no replacement. While serfdom passes on from one generation to the next, it is an eternal prisoner living with a name that does not die. However proud Italy may be of her arms, she, too, is known to share in death."

After the chamberlain finished, the cheering continued unabated. "Long live the emperor! Death to the Italians!"

Imperceptibly, the crowd swung around to face the balcony, where the emperor was standing. With the great dignity that surrounded all his dealings, he bowed to them.

"I am happy to see you before me with knives, swords, and rifles. But it is not I alone who knows, it is the whole world that knows that our Ethiopian soldiers will die for their freedom.

"Soldiers, I give you this advice: Be cunning, be savage, face the enemy one by one, two by two, five by five, in the fields and in the mountains. Hide, strike suddenly, fight the nomad war, snipe and kill. Today the war has begun, now scatter and advance to victory."

Ceseli and Marco watched as the emperor finished while the cheering crowd of soldiers and people yelled.

"So it's here," Marco said. "I was hoping that I was wrong. That something, some country would intervene. Or Italy would stop."

"I never thought it would come to this," Ceseli whispered. "I believed in the League."

"I'll leave you now. I know I should tell you to leave, but I know you won't listen to me. There's something very important I need to do," Marco said, gently kissing her on the top of her head. "Take care. I love you."

CHAPTER 31

In Rome, on the morning of October 3, the people were still sleeping after the compulsory Fascist celebration the previous evening. Mussolini had decided to proclaim the invasion before it happened and had planned a Fascist mobilization. Restaurants and shops throughout the country were closed so that people in every community could assemble in the public squares to hear Mussolini's speech.

Mussolini had spoken from his own balcony hanging over the crowded Piazza Venezia, the huge piazza in downtown Rome, down the street from the Forum and the Coliseum. Pope Paul II built the Palazzo Venezia in the fifteenth century so that he could watch the excitement of elaborate carnival celebrations a custom he had brought with him from his native Venice and there was surely something carnivalesque about the meeting of October 2, 1935.

Il Duce had thought of summoning the crowds by having all the church bells in Rome toll at the same time, but the church bells in Rome all toll together only when a pope dies, and the present Pope, Pius XI, said it was inappropriate. Mussolini used whistles.

The focal point of the celebration was the balcony of the Palazzo Venezia that adjoined the Duce's office. By the time Mussolini was ready to appear on his balcony, the Piazza Venezia and all the streets leading to it were packed. After the cheering diminished, after he had satisfied the cameras with his posturing, he began shouting into the microphones:

"Black Shirts of the Revolution! Men and women of all Italy! Italians scattered the world over, beyond the mountains and beyond the seas, listen!

"A solemn hour is about to strike in the history of the Fatherland. Some twenty million men at this moment fill the public squares of Italy. Never was there beheld in the history of mankind a more gigantic spectacle. The twenty million men: one heart, one will, one decision. Their demonstration must show and does show the world that Italy and Fascism are one and a perfect, absolute, unalterable whole . . .

"For many months the wheels of destiny moved toward this goal: Now their movement becomes swifter and can no longer be stayed!

"It is not just an army that strains toward its objectives, but an entire people of forty-four million souls, against whom an attempt is made to perform the most hideous of injustices: that of snatching from us a small place in the sun.

"To economic sanctions we shall oppose our discipline, our sobriety, our spirit of sacrifice.

"To military sanctions we shall reply with military measures.

"To acts of war we shall reply with acts of war!

"Let no one think of subduing us without a hard fight. . . .

"Proletariat and Fascist Italy! Let the shout of your decision fill the heavens and bear solace to the soldiers waiting in Africa, an incitement to friends and a warning to enemies in every part of the world. A cry of justice, a cry of victory!"

As he finished, there was none of the earth-shattering din of applause, none of the mob's unlimited enthusiasm. The three hundred thousand people in the square were not impressed. Those he called 'one heart, one will, one decision' left the square immediately, disdaining the remainder of the four hour program.

At this critical moment, while Il Duce's exhortations on the valor of the Italian Fascist army may have impressed the British and French, they did not convince the Italians. They were certainly far less united than Mussolini would like to admit, but these forty-four million people had given Mussolini absolute power and whether they liked his war or not, they were in it.

CHAPTER 32

"I WOULD BE VERY honored if you would allow me to join the Ethiopian Red Cross," Marco said, coming right to the point. Looking around him, he was surprised by the austerity of the small room: two straight backed chairs in front of a monastic style desk, a small copper lamp a desk calendar, and the holder for his silver pen. He wondered why he had assumed that this inner sanctum would be more luxurious and more in keeping with the power that the Keeper of the Pen actually wielded.

"I thought . . ."

"That I would serve with Italy? No," Marco said, interrupting. "I am ashamed of my country. I have been working here for more than two years. This is just not right. As for me, I know enough of the language to make a substantial contribution. Or, at least I think I could. Let me go with one of the Red Cross units."

Yifru studied the earnest young man in front of him. He remembered the train ride. He didn't know him at all, but Ceseli did and he respected her judgment. Ethiopia would need doctors and she was not going to get nearly enough of the good volunteers such as Marco would be. Ethiopia would be privileged to have him serve in the Red Cross. "There is a unit from the British and the Swedish Red Crosses. You know, of course, that in keeping with the rule of the International Red Cross, the units treat soldiers from both sides equally. You're ready to do that?"

"Yes, of course."

"Then I accept your generous offer. It won't be easy and it won't be fun. The Ethiopian Red Cross will be serving in the Tigre, Ogaden, and Sidamo. Do you have a choice?"

Marco hesitated. He had already been in the Ogaden in the south. He remembered Ceseli's vivid descriptions of Axum in the Tigre. "Tigre. If that's possible."

"There is a unit near Quoram. It will be under the supervision of a British doctor, but there are several small units near that one. He's flying up there tomorrow."

"Will there be room for me in the plane?"

"I'm sure that can be arranged."

"I know it's not going to change the course of history, but that's what I've decided to do," Marco smiled tenderly at Ceseli that evening. "I just finished a letter to my family. And I want to give you this," he said, taking a leather book and handing it to her. "It's the work I've been doing on epidemics. I'll be too busy up there on more menial tasks. I'm calling it Marco's bible," he joked. "It contains everything I've been able to find about tropical diseases, but so far I haven't been able to put it together. Some of this material tells of miracles that supposedly took place after some kind of emergency. Famine, for example."

"May I read it?" she asked, taking the book.

"I'd be very happy if you would."

"You'll be working with the Red Cross?"

"In Tigre."

"It's beautiful up there. There's no danger is there?"

"None at all. Red Cross hospitals are always considered neutral havens. So are their doctors. That's part of the Geneva Convention. And Italy was one of the five founding members."

"What will the Italians think?"

"I haven't told them and I don't think I will. There's going to be a lot of suffering. I'm going to do what I can."

"That's very brave of you."

"It's what I need to do."

"There's no real danger? You're sure?"

"Positive. I could get myself killed, as you know, just walking across the street. I don't have to tell you that. A caparisoned mule, for example. But pamper me. Should anything happen. Send the book to my father in Florence."

"I will."

His brightly shining eyes looked back at her. "You'll take care of yourself?"

"I will. I'm going to volunteer at the American hospital here in Addis."

"You should get on the next train, you know that?"

"But you know I'm not going to do that."

Marco looked at her knowing it was senseless to insist. "One more thing. Would you let me take that photo? The one with you and the Afar girl. I'd like to remember what I'm doing this for."

"Yes," she said, turning to the photo propped against the one of her father on the bureau. She turned back to him searching his eyes and trying to see how he felt.

"I'll take good care of it and I'll see you sooner than you think."

"You know something, Marco. You look like an angel. I thought of that the first time I saw you sleeping on the train. A curly-headed Renaissance angel. Take care of that head of hair," she said, as she tiptoed and kissed him on both cheeks. "Isn't this the way the Italians do it?"

He looked at her, his eyes twinkling mischievously. "No. This is the way Italians do it," he said, lifting up her face to him and then kissing her deeply. "Don't forget it. Will you wait for me?"

"You know I will."

"I love you, Ceseli. Take care of yourself. We'll be together very soon." He held her hand tightly before releasing it, then stood back from her. Tearing himself away, he pinched her elbow and was gone.

Turning from the door, she sat on her bed. She would miss him terribly. Being with him was the best thing that had ever happened to her, and also the most confusing. It had been wonderful talking with him, sharing their thoughts, confiding in him, making plans for the future. Now she was alone again. Her father was gone, and now Marco. Even though she understood completely his need to go, she felt so lonely, and so hurt and so starved. Completely deserted.

CHAPTER 33

On October 14, De Bono decided to enjoy some of the glory his quick success had earned him and traveled to Adowa for a triumphal ceremony of conquest and submission planned for the next morning.

He expected the trip from his headquarters at Coatit to include at least six hours on mule back over the rugged mountain trail and was surprised and gratified to learn that after only one week's work, his labor battalions had proven again the renowned Italian skill in building roads. The trail was already in such excellent condition he was able to make the entire journey in his black FIAT Balilla motorcar.

The small town of Adowa, only twenty miles south of the frontier with Eritrea, had always been an important trading center on the routes from the Red Sea to central Ethiopia and was for this reason the scene of the devastating defeat of the Italian army in 1896.

Like most Ethiopian towns, there were clusters of the beehive tukuls nestling around the round Coptic Church. The squalid little town, now damaged by the bombs from the Royal Italian Air Force's Caproni bombers, was nevertheless bedecked with flags. Flowers lined the streets and several triumphal arches had been erected in accordance with De Bono's instructions, although they were made from wood and not marble. Sure of the impending Italian invasion, De Bono had commissioned in Italy a large stone statue to honor the Italians who had died at the Battle of Adowa and had brought it to the town. Surrounded by his troops standing at attention in the seething heat in the dusty main square, while the band played the Fascist anthem, *Giovanezza,* De Bono with great fanfare unveiled the statue by pulling from it the green, white, and red Italian flag.

Zeri, hot beyond means and thirsty, was not in the mood for such shows of patriotism. He coughed and moved off to one side.

De Bono's second official act on this October day was the issuance of a proclamation to the people of Tigre:

"Concerning the Assumption of Government Beyond the Frontier." The proclamation declared:

"In the name of His Majesty the King of Italy, I assume the government of the country. From today, you, the people of Tigre, are subject to and under the protection of the Italian Flag.

"Those of you in local authority should remain in office and are responsible for the order and discipline of your respective districts. They will present themselves before the nearest military authority together with the clergy of the parish church to make the act of submission. Those who do not present themselves within ten days will be considered and treated as enemies.

"Let whosoever has suffered injury present himself to my generals and he will receive justice.

"Traders, continue to trade; husbandman, continue to till the soil."

At the same time, De Bono issued another directive, a kind of Fascist Emancipation Proclamation. "You know that where the flag of Italy flies," it declared, "there is liberty. Therefore, in your country, slavery under whatever form is suppressed. The slaves at present in Tigre are free and the sale or purchase of slaves is prohibited."

Zeri, thought this ironic. Why hadn't De Bono freed the slaves in Eritrea? He knew that a 1935 League of Nations report on slavery acknowledged its existence in Ethiopia, but praised Emperor Haile Sellassie's efforts to phase it out. Furthermore, Zeri noted that De Bono would have a problem that he should have foreseen. If the slave owners no longer fed their slaves, who would? The Italians!

CHAPTER 34

As far as eyes could see was a densely packed, living wall of men waiting for the ceremonial march. It was October 17, already two weeks after the invasion and only now was the Minister of War, Ras Mulugeta, ready to lead his seventy thousand soldiers north to meet the enemy.

In a huge open tent on a hill above the JanHoy Meda Imperial Parade Ground, Haile Sellassie, in his uniform of commander-in-chief, sat on his throne chair. The cabinet ministers squatted in front of him on the fine scarlet Persian rugs. The palace guards, with swords, rifles, and rhinoceros whips stood ready to maintain order.

In an area reserved for foreign dignitaries, Ceseli and Standish watched with fascination.

"Where do they all come from?" Ceseli asked.

"The emperor issued a *chitet*. That's the summons to arms. The men are recruited from the Shoa Province. They owe the emperor two months of military service in exchange for the use of his land."

Units of the Imperial Guard, in European uniforms though barefoot, marched with their heavy guns mounted on pack mules. There were fearsome war whoops as Mulugeta's troops approached the emperor's tent. Ceseli grabbed Standish's arm as the first swordsman drew his weapons in front of the emperor.

"Don't worry. They're showing him their techniques of attacking and dismembering an enemy. It's the way they show their bravery. You'll get used to it."

Indeed, such was the skill of these warriors that no blood was drawn during the entire review.

"Here's Mulugeta," Standish said just before noon, as fearsome yells and the beating of the *Negariat* War Drums announced his arrival.

A corps of horn blowers, in European dress, ran in front of him. Another corps of scarlet-turbaned drummers sat astride the hindquarters of the mules that carried the drums.

"He's the minister of war?" Ceseli asked, shading her eyes from the sun as she studied the legendary seventy-year old aristocrat. The towering, grizzled figure with the face of an eagle had replaced the silk jodhpurs and lion-trimmed cloak he wore in Addis with a khaki field uniform. His chest bristled with the war decorations of Adowa and of Ethiopian civil wars.

As Mulugeta approached, the emperor rose to salute him. Laying his sword on the ground as a gesture of fealty, Mulugeta began repeating to his ruler the advice he had given many times before.

"JanHoy," he shouted, using the emperor's Amharic name, "I killed Italians before you were born. I helped preserve the country of which you are now emperor. I am still a soldier. Our old enemies have forgotten Adowa. I go to battle again, perhaps never to return. I await you in battle, O King." Then the old warrior, using both arms, brandished his great sword above his head.

"Do not interest yourself overmuch in politics. Your weakness is that you trust foreigners too much. I am ready to die for my country and so are you. War is now the thing. But to conduct it you had better remain in Addis. I swear to you complete loyalty."

Hearing this, Ceseli and Standish noticed that the emperor made no attempt to reply. What was he to answer to the general who intended to await him in battle, but at the same time advised him to stay in Addis?

The emperor watched the remainder of his troops make a turn around the parade ground. Hundreds of times in those four hours, he listened to the pleading of these men, who wanted rifles instead of spears and sticks.

Standish and Ceseli were not certain, but it seemed to them that at one point the emperor wept as he watched the stragglers pass by on their way north. He certainly knew better than anyone the fate to which he was forced to send these soldiers.

"It makes me sick to think how these people will be slaughtered," Standish said. "Imagine what modern weapons will do to them."

Ceseli thought of Marco, already in the Tigre, and wondered what he was doing. She missed him, but she also knew that going to help was something he needed very much to do. "Can I ask you something?"

"Shoot."

"The emperor has been telling his soldiers to creep up behind the Italians and take them by surprise. Am I right?"

"You are. He understands that if he could persuade his chiefs and warriors to concentrate on guerrilla warfare, they might have at least a slim chance, but he also knows how proud his people are. He's telling them to be cautious," Standish said as they watched the straggling line leave the parade grounds. "But the total destruction of an enemy force, which is a basic concept in European military strategy, has never been part of the Ethiopian tradition. Here, a war is a series of battles or one climactic battle. Each battle should be fought in a single day, and if possible, in an open field where one side marches directly against the other. That's how the Romans fought and nothing has changed."

"And the winner?"

"Both sides agree that the winner of the last battle is the winner of the war. That's how the Ethiopians defeated the Italians at Adowa, but that doesn't mean the Ethiopians could win today, with these odds and with these arms."

"There's something else. The emperor has been telling his soldiers that they must not stop if their leader is killed."

"Right. That's because the Ethiopian soldier is totally loyal to his leader. But if that leader is killed, he won't automatically obey orders from another person. He may even decide to go home."

"Desert?"

"No. Although that may be the end result. Just that they have followed a beloved leader into battle and now, if he's dead, the battle is over. They have to carry his body home and bury him in a consecrated place."

"And the League? You believed in that?"

"I used to," Standish said. "But it's looking more and more like daydream diplomacy."

By late that day, the line of soldiers heading north to Dessie was almost twenty miles long. They would take two weeks to reach Dessie, where half of them would stay with the nineteen year old Crown Prince, Asfa Wossen, while the others followed Mulugeta north to Makallé.

The day after Mulugeta and his army left for the north, Standish looked up from the paper Rutherford had asked him to draft to find Yifru standing near his desk. "I guess I was expecting you. You have a copy of the sanctions?"

"The communiqué has finally come from Geneva. It's dated October 11, 1935. They took eight days to consider this an invasion."

"What was the vote?"

"It was fifty to one. Italy, of course, voted against. Austria, Hungary and Albania all abstained."

"Of course, they're all Italian allies."

"They established a committee to consider the imposition of sanctions. The sanctions are to begin on November 18. You've read them?"

"Yes."

Standish knew that the sanctions were ridiculous. They would not paralyze any aggressor. They were merely what Italy would be willing to tolerate without withdrawing from the League.

The official communiqué from Washington, which were Standish's orders, added some highlights on the absurdity of these exclusions. Aluminum was a perfect example. Washington quoted Britain's Winston Churchill as saying that the export of aluminum to Italy was strictly forbidden. Yet aluminum was almost the only metal that Italy produced in quantities beyond her own needs. The importation of scrap iron and iron ore was sternly vetoed in the name of public justice. But the Italian metallurgical industry made very little use of them, and as steel billets and pig iron were not interfered with, Italy would not suffer from these sanctions.

"The emperor is disappointed, I know."

"He has believed in the League with all his heart. That joining it was important for Ethiopia. That membership in the League would protect small countries like ours. The principle of collective security was visionary, you've agreed with me on that."

"I have, yes," Standish nodded.

"And that the League should take action. Some action. Any action. Perhaps if oil had been included in the sanctions, it could have had some real effect. But it isn't."

Standish looked at his friend. "I'm very sorry, Yifru."

"I wish that were the official line," Yifru replied. "But thank you anyhow."

There would have been no way for either Standish or Yifru to estimate at that time what effect sanctions would have on the outcome of the war. Although the sanctions would not halt the aggressor, they were to have considerable effect on the Italian economy. The discontent of the Italian people had increased with the onset of the war, but when the sanctions were put in place in November, the Italian people rallied to their cause and to their leader. The response was electric. Poverty-stricken peasants, given a chance to join the army, walked hundreds of miles to enlist for wages far superior to what they might earn at home.

Mussolini set up his own restrictions on the consumption of meat, gas, wool, and electricity. New materials were used such as synthetics made from linen, and other natural fibers, and a campaign was launched to recycle metals. On meatless Fridays, restaurants served "sanctions soup" and although Michelangelo would have turned over in his grave, Rome's elegant Piazza di Spagna was renamed for General Emilio De Bono.

Later that day, Yifru was sitting in the penumbra of his office as Ceseli knocked and then entered. She looked at him and turned to leave. "He wouldn't believe me," Yifru said, holding his head in his hands. "But I was right. Gugsa has gone over to the enemy, with more than a thousand men."

"Gugsa? The emperor's son-in-law?"

"How can a descendent of Emperor Yohannes become a traitor to Ethiopia?"

"When?" she asked.

"On October 11, I'm told. The same day the League decreed that there was a war going on. Imagine needing eight days to declare an invasion."

"I thought he had more than ten thousand men?"

"But only twelve hundred went with him. The Italians are saying ten thousand, but Ras Seyoum says that it's not true. The others have stayed loyal to the emperor. This will not be good for the morale of our soldiers. He is, after all, the emperor's son-in-law. The Italians have instated him as the Ras of Tigre. He will need to look over his shoulder for the rest of his life."

Ceseli had nothing to say.

CHAPTER 35

CESELI LOOKED AT HER favorite tree in the compound garden. The cat's cradle-like spidery needle branches of the Acacia were perfectly symmetrical in their asymmetry. She reminded herself to paint it.

It was November 11, the anniversary of Armistice Day of World War I, and a month since Ras Mulugeta, the Minister of War, led his army north. The small Anglo-American colony was joined by journalists of the *London Times* and *Reuters*. They were sitting in the garden after the Padré's tedious sermon on the lessons learned from the war. Even Rutherford had been forced, grudgingly, to say a few inanities on hopes for world peace.

"Oh, by the way, Ceseli," Standish said as the others were leaving, "you remember what I said about Mussolini getting the blessing of the Catholic Church?"

"Yes. That it would give him a sacred mission. To civilize the Ethiopians."

"Well, it's now official. The Bishop of Milan has declared his full approval."

After dinner, they learned that the Ethiopians had ambushed an Italian motorized column in the south along the border with Italian Somaliland.

"Wonderful news! That calls for a drink! After Gugsa, they needed a morale booster. You're sure it's true?" Rutherford asked.

"I'm reading from a dispatch that Yifru just sent over."

"Can you read it out loud, please?" Ceseli asked.

"It's from the Ogaden. In Italian Somaliland. When the Italians took the last Ethiopian outpost of Gorahai, the Ethiopians fled north. General Rudolfo Graziani, the Italian commander in the south, sent bombers after them. The Ethiopians soldiers stopped for water at a watering place named Anale. Their tires were flat and radiators were steaming. They took their wounded off the trucks and put them on the ground. When the Ethiopian commanding officer heard gunfire he ordered his troops to seek refuge in the bush. The Italian tanks pursued them. One of the tanks ran over their wounded men."

"Ran over the wounded men?" Ceseli asked incredulous. "With a tank?"

"The Italians are following orders," Rutherford said calmly, "and I'm sure they're not pretty ones."

"But running over wounded soldiers with a tank!" She could picture the tanks moving forward, tilting back and forth, like a giant Praying Mantis, as they ran over the bodies and she could hear the screams of the wounded soldiers.

"It's war, Ceseli, not a sewing bee."

Ceseli looked at Warren, speechless, as she rubbed her father's dog tag. "I don't care what it is. That's no longer human, or humane."

"I suspect the tankers couldn't see very much."

"Are you justifying running over the wounded?" Ceseli was incensed.

"Certainly not! Just stating a fact," Standish replied. "The tank's portholes are pretty small, and if it's a regular day in the Ogaden, it must have been a furnace. The Italians stopped and must have come out of the tank not knowing that the Ethiopians were hiding in the bush."

"So?" Ceseli and Rutherford asked together.

"They killed the tanker and the gunner. Altogether, they took over three tanks. The rest of the Italians turned and fled."

"That's too bad," Ceseli quipped. "They should have got them all. I'm tired of hearing what great soldiers the Italians are."

"I don't think anybody ever said they were great soldiers. With the possible exception of Il Duce," Rutherford added.

When Ceseli got back to her tukul that evening, she noticed a letter sitting on the table on the porch. There was no stamp, and the envelope was creased and dirty.

My beloved Ceseli,

How are things in Addis?

I hope this finds you at work on your Bible.

I think of you all the time, Ceseli, and of how I would like to grow old with you. How do you think you'd feel about living in Florence? It's a wonderful city.

I would like to ask you to write to me, but there is no chance that I would receive your letters. Keep them in your Bible, and I will read them when this hell on earth is over.

Be well, my darling. It won't be forever.

Marco

Ceseli reread the letter, then folded it and put it in her pocket. What had happened to her letters? She rubbed her forehead hard trying to straighten her thoughts. This war was out of all proportions. Did civilized nations run over the barefoot enemy in tanks? Her whole concept of humanity had changed dramatically in the last few hours. There must be some way to help these people. She thought of Marco. He had the answer. Saving lives was important. Was there something she could do?

CHAPTER 36

WHILE CESELI WAS THINKING of ways to help the Ethiopians, Bruno Zeri nudged his mule forward. He did not suffer from vertigo, or at least he never had, but he was reluctant to look down at the steep gorge below. The narrow path appeared to be non-existent, but the mule didn't seem to mind.

After the invasion, Zeri had gone with General Oreste Mariotti. Zeri respected Mariotti as a bold and fearless officer. They were now less than fifty miles northeast of their destination of Makalle.

It was about 9:30 in the morning, when the Italian column entered the Ende Gorge, a narrow, east-west ravine about half a mile long. The stiff-*fezzed* Eritrean Askaris were in the front followed by recently recruited and undrilled Danakil tribesmen who were watching for the enemy. Flanking parties marched on each side of the column. Then came the mules carrying Mariotti, his staff, and finally Zeri. A long supply train followed.

Despite the peacefulness of the morning, Mariotti was worried. Something didn't jibe with the birds chirping and twittering in the bushes. As the column moved forward, he noticed a ridge right in front of him and straight across the path his army must take.

"Mount the heavy guns," he ordered, blowing his whistle, never changing his stern expression.

Hurrying to obey the order, a non-commissioned officer had taken only three steps before a burst of rifle fire hit him in the groin and right knee. Zeri's orderly was hit in the ankle and grabbed the mule's neck to stop his fall. Zeri jumped off the mule and using it as a shield, held tightly to the reins.

"*Avanti!* Take cover!"

Machine gun fire started, but it was difficult to locate its source. The tree covered walls of the gorge were so steep and so narrow that echoes distorted the direction of the sound.

The Ethiopians had chosen an excellent position from which to close off the gorge at both ends and obliterate the Italian column, almost at their leisure.

Zeri watched as waves of Ethiopians, whooping and yelling, came storming down the hillsides, like an angry sea crashing against a rocky headland. They rushed forward, their white and angry eyes glaring as they yelled in unison:

"Adowa!"

"Adowa!"

"Adowa!"

The Italian guns were drowned out by the crescendo of their war cries. Bullets made no impression on the densely packed ranks. The blood splattered against their white shammas, but as soon as one wave fell, another began.

Seeing this massacre, some of the Danakil tribesmen, who were part of the Italian column, bolted toward the rear, throwing down their rifles and running helter-skelter, trying to escape from the brutal assaults and the gorge.

Zeri watched as the white Italian officers stepped into line across the gorge cutting off their escape. Seeing this, Zeri wasn't sure whether the Danakils were trying to avoid fighting their brother Africans, or trying to escape. Firing directly into these soldiers, the Italian officers forced them back to their fighting positions.

When the fighting stopped soon after nightfall, the Italians knew that their prospects were bleak. Escape was impossible. There were probably more than five thousand Ethiopians poised on the parapets with nothing stopping them from continuing their slaughter until the entire Italian column was wiped out.

"It's hopeless," Mariotti said. "Let's pray God won't abandon us." Then, he turned and took a Beretta from his saddlebag. "I think you should have this," he said.

"I'm not any good," Zeri said, looking at the pistol.

"If you had said that earlier, I would have found someone to teach you. But it's not against the enemy. It's for you. Put the barrel in your mouth and pull the trigger. The Ethiopians are said to emasculate their prisoners," Mariotti said. "I can't imagine that would be much fun."

The emasculation bit was in the propaganda booklets distributed to the Italian troops. Zeri doubted its veracity, but took the Beretta.

"And now get some sleep and hope you can give it back to me tomorrow."

As the first light began to filter into the narrow gorge, Zeri woke from a troubled doze. He felt himself nervously waiting for the outcry that would signal the new assault. He watched the desperate men all around him looking up toward the heights of the gorge. As they cocked their rifles they were tense and agitated. Were they all thinking the same thoughts, Zeri wondered? Was he ready to die? Is anyone ever ready to die alone in a foreign land? To die for what was another man's dream, another man's madness?

As the light increased, the silence continued. Zeri began to realize that there would be no fighting. They had been released from death. He knew that the Ethiopians were no longer on their ramparts. With victory in their grasp, they had withdrawn during the night. In their minds, they knew that there was no reason to fight: They had already won.

CHAPTER 37

As the war progressed, there was bad news every day. Ceseli was feeling more and more useless and depressed, and there was no recent news of Marco. She had been volunteering at the hospital and she was learning a lot. She knew how to suture and other basic first aid measures. That was helpful, but it wasn't the war. What could she do to help? She wondered when she had begun to think like this and pinpointed it to the tanks. She had reviewed several options at length before making her decision.

She walked out of the small office where she had been working for the last five months. She liked the work and being able to consult the emperor's personal library was adding enormously to her study. She had also photographed and made rubbings of all the coins in the collection including the thirty rare ones she had found at Axum. She had not found out why the obelisks fell.

She read and reread Marco's last letter.

The pain I feel for these people is unbearable. I am so ashamed of being Italian. It is not only the wounds from battle that I am treating, but the horrifying pain brought on by the mustard gas. The Italian bombers come daily and spray not only the armies, but also the local villages. Worst still, they spray the fields so the people can't eat, and the lakes so they can't drink. All the people of Ethiopia have become victims. I treated one old man who looked liked someone had tried to skin him alive. He had only giant red cauldrons as eyes. So many of my patients are children.

I miss you so much, Ceseli. So, so much.

She folded the letter and tucked it into her pocket. As she walked toward Yifru's office she reviewed her plans and still finding them acceptable, knocked on his door. He raised his eyes and smiled as she entered. "This is a pleasant surprise. How is the work going?"

"It's fine. Everything is fine. I'd like to talk to you," she said, taking the seat in front of him. "Yifru. I want to go to Dessie with the Emperor's hospital unit."

"Do you know what it will be like?" he asked.

"I've given it a great deal of thought. I don't have a great deal of training, but I can help and goodness knows you do need that. You won't regret letting me go."

He looked at her for a long time before speaking, knowing that he needed to find some convincing argument that would dissuade her. "Ceseli," he started to say, "do you have any idea of what you'd be getting yourself into? This is not what women do."

"Lots of Ethiopian women follow their men to war. And women are nurses."

"Yes of course they do; but they are Ethiopian. This is their war."

"I'm very committed to this. I know you have the power to say no, but I'm hoping you won't use it."

"You'd be in constant danger."

"I can't just sit around doing nothing. This means a lot to me. I care deeply about what will happen. I want to help."

He looked into her supplicating eyes. "I'd need to assign someone to take care of you."

"No you won't. I know the language and there's lots I can do at the hospital up there. And I know I wouldn't be the only white person there. There are several other nurses and plenty of journalists. That's not an excuse either."

"That's true, but I don't feel responsible for them. I would for you."

"Yifru, it's something I very much need to do."

Yifru studied her. He couldn't help remembering Debra. He'd known Ceseli for months. *I've been taking her for grante*d, he thought, *like someone you see every day and never really look at*. Yifru looked at her now knowing that part of her desire to go must be connected to Marco. But the truth at hand was that Ceseli could be of help. Did he have the luxury of using her? Was she expendable? Not to him she wasn't, but could he put his feelings before hers?

"On one condition. No, actually two. If it gets very bad, you will obey my orders. I will evacuate you."

She pondered this for a moment. "That's perfectly acceptable. And the second?"

"I want Warren Rutherford's permission."

"Warren Rutherford is my godfather."

"I know that. And the highest ranking American in Ethiopia. I know the emperor would want to know that he's not going against Rutherford's private wishes."

"If I get his permission, when can I leave?"

"With the emperor's honor guard. That will be soon. There is an American mission hospital in Dessie run by the Seventh-Day Adventists. My nephew, Yohannes, is with the guard. You know him, don't you?"

"He flew us to Axum."

"He would be flying now if we had any planes worth flying. I will tell him to take care of you on the trip."

Ceseli was so overjoyed she grabbed his hand on the desk, smiling. "You don't know what this means to me. You won't regret this, Yifru. I promise."

"I pray to God you're right." Yifru bent over and took from his side desk drawer a Luger pistol.

"German?"

"The only ones we could get," he said as he fished around for a box of bullets.

Ceseli wondered whether she could ask and decided in the affirmative. "Guns from Hitler?"

"Yes, and on very favorable terms."

"The piano crates?" she asked, now understanding.

"Rifles and ammunition."

"Ingenious," she smiled, holding the heavy pistol. "But why would Hitler want to sell arms to Ethiopia?"

"He didn't whisper in my ear, but if I were to guess, I would have to think that if Mussolini's army was involved in a protracted war in Ethiopia, he, Hitler, would have a more open hand in Europe. Austria and Czechoslovakia I should say." Yifru smiled at her, "But that is my supposition. You'll need to learn how to use it," he added, nodding at the pistol.

"I know how to use it. My father taught me."

Minister Warren Rutherford stood up as soon as she walked into his office. Ceseli was not surprised by his agitations, but neither did she intend to be dissuaded. She walked over and kissed him on the cheek.

"Ceseli, I will not permit this," Rutherford said, holding both her hands. "For all the friendship I had for your father, I will not send you up there to die."

"I'm not going up there to be killed."

"I can forbid this, you know. I am the American Minister."

"But I hope you won't," she said, still holding his hands.

"You're about the age of my daughter. You don't have to be Joan of Arc."

"I'm not thinking of Joan of Arc and I'll be as safe as the emperor." Ceseli said, determined not to get sidetracked.

"That is certainly not saying much."

Ceseli turned as Standish entered the room. She turned back to the friendly, but stoic American Minister she had come to know and respect. She felt sure that her admiration for him would not be diminished. "I'm sorry if you don't approve. I probably would not either. But my father always taught me to make my own decisions. To follow my head. But, when necessary, to follow my heart. This is very important for me." She looked at him. And then at Standish.

Rutherford turned to Standish. "I forbid it. You agree with me don't you, Standish?"

"If I could do it myself, I would," Standish answered. "But there's a condition I think you should hear about. If Yifru tells her to return, he will see to it she gets back to Addis."

"How, pray tell, can he guarantee that?" Rutherford asked, looking from one of them to the other. "As this war progresses, the emperor himself will become the prey. He already is."

Standish looked at Ceseli. "I will," Standish said.

"Uncle Warren," Ceseli spoke quietly, "if Daddy could tell you what he thought, you know what he would say."

"I do know that, Ceseli, my dear. I know very well."

After a prolonged discussion at dinner, Ceseli walked back down the dark path to her tukul. She lit a candle and sat undecided as to what to do next. Then she got up picked up a pad of paper and sat down at the small table.

November 23, 1935

Dear Sotzy,

Everything is not fine in Ethiopia. I'm sure you are keeping up with the events even better than I am. It is so hard to find out what is going on in the rest of the world. I have been volunteering at the hospital as I've told you, but somehow it's not really like being part of the war. Everything is happening a long way away.

I need to tell you something, and I have no doubts on how you will accept this. My work at the hospital is dandy. You know, Sotzy, that's the best expression I can find for it. Almost as if I'm spending my time dividing the right socks from the left ones. So I have decided to volunteer with the Emperor's Hospital unit. Guess what? They said yes. Or Yifru said yes and he's the only one who counts. Except the emperor of course, who would never be involved in such a humble decision.

Warren Rutherford is not pleased, but he has not forbidden me. So I'm going to leave Addis in five days' time.

I know you will understand me, and you know how much your love and opinion mean to me, Sotzy. However, I'm sure that it will be quite some time before you will get any letters from me. I'll write when I can. Just believe in me. Happy Thanksgiving!

My love to you always.

Mrs. Frances Sheraton
290 Park Avenue
New York, NY

CHAPTER 38

On November 28, the same day that the emperor began to move his headquarters forward to Dessie, General Pietro Badoglio succeeded General Emilio De Bono as the new High Commissioner of the Italian Expeditionary Forces. Mussolini sent De Bono word of his dismissal by a secret and personal telegram read by everyone. The dismissal was not surprising. De Bono was not moving fast enough and it was ludicrous to think of the massive Italian army at a standstill in front of a virtually unarmed, barefoot army.

Two weeks later, General Badoglio reached the general headquarters now at Adigrat. One of his first official duties was to call an impromptu press conference.

Badoglio stood at attention as the journalists walked into his large square tent. He wore a beret over his thick white hair, a flannel-lined cape, and the thick socks and heavy boots of an Italian mountaineer. His hands, feet, shoulders, and neck were reminiscent of Mother Earth.

Bruno Zeri studied his wide, wrinkled forehead, his flat, pugilist's nose, his trim, solid physique maintained, despite his sixty-four years, by rigorous daily exercise.

"I will give you a general plan of where the enemy is," Badoglio began in his gravelly voice as he turned to the map propped up against a folding chair.

"On the general line between Dessie and Makalle, a body of troops under the command of Ras Kassa, estimated according to our information at about fifty thousand armed men, has reached the area of Lake Ashanghi. Here," he said, pointing to the map, "another of about equal strength, under Ras Mulugeta, has come up from Dessie to join them." Badoglio hit his rhinoceros tail fly-switch on his boot as he moved to the other side of the map.

Zeri knew that Badoglio, once a royalist opponent of Fascism, was regarded in Fascist circles as a political ignoramus with the limited mentality of a soldier and virtually no understanding of the grand concept of Fascism. He was, however, a good soldier. Zeri, taking notes as the general continued, could not help admiring Badoglio's precision and detail.

"As we began to make plans for this campaign, I calculated that Abyssinia could put in the field, to start with, from two hundred thousand to two hundred fifty thousand men in the northern districts, and from eighty thousand to one hundred thousand men in the southern districts. For historical, ethnical, and political reasons, and in view of supply considerations, I calculated they would certainly be massed in two bodies and would operate in this way in the two different theatres of war."

Zeri stopped writing as his mind wandered. He put his notebook aside. He had not seen at first hand the use of mustard gas, but he was convinced Badoglio would use it. He knew the army would not transport one hundred thirty tons of it to Eritrea just for fun.

Later that evening, he looked at his harmonica. It had ten holes above and ten below. He thought about how the code could be used. He started with the Italian alphabet, which has twenty-one letters. He needed twenty. He subtracted the "H", so that he could divide the higher level of the harmonica and the lower one. But he needed a way to show that he was changing from letters to numbers. Bruno spent some time debating before eliminating "z," not often used in any case and he could substitute with an "s."

He sat there studying the situation. He could now use ten letters in the G Clef and ten letters in the F Clef to signify the twenty letters in the Italian alphabet. Middle C could be used to signify switching from letters to numbers, or vice versa. A single letter "C" indicated that letters followed, two middle "C's" indicated that the next ten notes in the "G" Clef would be numbers. The end of a number or of a single word was indicated by a bar line. His fingers faltered. He wrote the music. To his surprise, the code worked. He looked at the tune he had composed: MUSTARD GAS.

Ceseli found the trip north with the Imperial Guard depressing after the mood of the same itinerary eight months before. The road was so heavily trafficked that it was difficult to make much headway. She had been assigned her own chocolate brown mule and it was young and a bit skittish. She named him Don Quichotte.

"How do you speak such good French?" Ceseli asked Yohannes as they rode side by side.

"I studied at St. Cyr," Yohannes replied. "You know it?"

"Only that it's a well-known French Military Academy."

"It's the best. You noticed my French accent?"

"Not much of an accent, but the way you pronounce my name is clearly French," she said, imitating his accent on the last letter. "Ceselí. That's cute. I guess I think the French are often cute. How did you get to St. Cyr?"

"The emperor sent me."

"Like your uncle? Studying at Columbia?"

"The emperor has been very good to my family. He has promoted many of us even though we are not noble by birth. My father died when I was seven and Yifru has been like a father. My uncle was one of the first to study abroad," he paused, kicking his mule to move over toward Ceseli.

"My grandfather worked in Harar for the emperor's father. He was one of Governor Makonnen's closest advisers and responsible for Tafari's early schooling. When Makonnen died, Tafari was sent to the court of Menilek and my grandfather went with him. Both Tafari and my own uncle went to Menilek's school. When Tafari became the regent, he persuaded Queen Zauditu to send my uncle to study in America."

"He told me that. That's where he met Standish's father."

"And learned that American women can be very strong-willed."

"Which is probably why I'm here," Ceseli smiled.

"I don't doubt it, and why it's my duty to take care of you. I really can't understand why he let you come."

"I'm sorry you feel that way. But I'm glad he did. In the future, I'll be sure to make that as light an assignment as I can," she said, and then kicked her mule and rode forward.

CHAPTER 39

Dessie, near the eastern rim of the Ethiopian high plateau in north central Ethiopia, was a market town of twenty thousand people. In 1882, while camping in the area, Emperor Yohannes IV saw a comet that he believed signified an important omen. He decided to found a city there and named it Dessie for the Amharic meaning of "My Joy."

In 1935, it had a sizable cluster of Ethiopian tukuls with an occasional European style building among them. The town was scattered at the bottom of a cup, irregularly formed by the surrounding three thousand foot yellow bluffs. Through a deep breach in the mountain wall to the southeast, the Borkenna River cascaded away to the landing strip and the far away Danakil Desert.

On one of Dessie's small hills was the rambling Ghibbi, or palace of Crown Prince, Asfa Wossen. On another, the house of the local chief. On the west lay a long ledge of mountain and on its extreme slope, the Italian commercial agency. The Italian building, a handsome stone structure with a porch in the front, was undoubtedly Dessie's finest building and now the emperor's field headquarters.

Not far away, housed in a new stone building with a corrugated iron roof and a huge red cross painted on it, was the American Seventh-Day Adventists Mission Hospital where Ceseli was working.

With the arrival of the emperor, Dessie was swelled to overflowing not only by the recruited army, but also by the numerous camp followers, the women and children, who accompany their fighting men.

At Dessie, Haile Sellassie maintained his peacetime lifestyle. He dined with guests on both European food and choice Ethiopian ones like wot, chicken served with chili peppers washed down with bottles brought from his wine cellar in Addis. He had his Arab race horses brought up to Dessie and stabled them in the grounds next to his only Oerikion antiaircraft gun.

It was shortly after 8 a.m. on Friday December 6, 1935, one week after Badoglio assumed command, when the distant hum of airplanes became audible. If the Italians were coming to bomb, it was because they had learned of the emperor's presence. He was certainly a legitimate target and Badoglio intended to win this war as soon as possible.

When Haile Sellassie heard the approaching airplanes, he ran into the garden where his antiaircraft gun was already installed. As the planes neared, he could count nine white Italian Caproni bombers. These CA.133 three-engine monoplanes could carry two tons of high explosive and poison gas a range of nine hundred miles. The emperor, who knew how to use the antiaircraft gun, pushed aside the fumbling frightened soldiers and began shooting at the planes.

The noise of the planes and the crashing of the bombs was deafening as if the mountains themselves were protesting. The whole earth heaved under the thunderous explosions. As the incendiary bombs dropped, fires sprang up and began to eat up the straw-roofed tukuls. Women and children, who had never seen a plane, were fleeing from the fires. Thinking this was a game, the children were laughing as they ran from the bombs. Yifru saw one woman and her two children all hit by a bomb as they tried to cross the narrow mud road.

The Seventh-Day Adventist Hospital was hit in rapid succession by five high explosive bombs. One bomb went directly through the hospital building, tearing off the roof of the surgery, destroying two wards and the instrument room. Then, as it had started, seventeen minutes later it was over.

"Ceseli, Ceseli . . .," Yifru hollered, looking inside the building. His eyes were burning from the smoke. He looked around to see whole clusters of Ethiopian tukuls burning. He spotted her crawling out of the wrecked building.

"Are you all right?"

"Fine," she said, wiping the tears from her smarting eyes. "I'm not crying. It's just the smoke."

Yifru looked at her. Her hair was singed at the back and dark spots of soot covered her face and hands. "Ceseli, I think it's time you went home."

"No. It isn't. Don't change your mind the first time something goes wrong."

Yifru, not answering, studied her determined expression. Then he noticed the small boy who came up to her and put his hand into hers.

Kneeling she smiled at the child. "Don't be afraid."

The little boy began a tentative smile that soon widened to reveal his irregularly shaped teeth. He was tiny, Yifru noticed, but seemed to have considerable courage for his eight or nine years. He stayed with her holding her hand reassuringly.

Yifru looked at her. "You've made a friend for life," he said, turning to the child. "What's your name?"

"Habtu," the boy answered shyly.

"Where do you live?"

"In that cave," the boy said, pointing toward the far ridge.

"You see, I'm in good hands," Ceseli smiled at Yifru. "What does Habtu mean?"

Yifru paused for a moment. "It's the kind of feeling you get when you have your first child."

Ceseli frowned trying to capture the feeling. "He comes here every day. One day, he even brought one of his sheep to show me and I think he wants to take me home to meet his mother. We'll see. We're pretty busy right here for now."

After the planes withdrew, the emperor abandoned his overheated gun to return inside and draft a letter of protest to the League against the bombing of civilians. Then, donning a cloak and selecting a stick, he walked through the town visiting the wounded. Yifru, walking with him, counted fifty-three people dead and about two hundred injured. These were not the cheap fragmentation bombs of other Italian air raids. Two unexploded two hundred pounders were taken to the emperor's garden where Haile Sellassie and his twelve-year-old son, Ras Makonnen, posed for photographers.

There were many war correspondents at Dessie camped in the grounds of the American Advent Hospital. Each one of them would have his story, if the same story. One was evacuated to Addis by plane along with a Red Cross nurse who had broken her leg jumping into a ditch to avoid the bombs. Their dispatches about the bombing of a hospital and civilians raised outrage in the capitals of the world.

As soon as the surgical unit could be set up in the last remaining tent, the doctors began the heart-rending job of amputation. Ceseli's heart pounded recklessly as one by one, the mutilated limbs were hacked away from their bodies with no anesthesia. These were the first amputations she had ever assisted with. The last one was a girl not more than four. It was her only chance to live, Ceseli knew, but still she felt sickened.

When it was over, she walked out to the edge of the compound and looked beyond the town. She felt ill and wondered if she would vomit.

She was used to blood by now, and the frequent smell of gangrene, the endless moaning of the living and sunken faces of coming death. But this little girl brought her pain beyond belief. Tears started to roll uncontrollably down her cheek. She made no effort to stem them. She sensed, rather than saw, Yifru standing not far away in case she needed protecting. After she recovered she turned to walk back. She knew he would not be there.

CHAPTER 40

ON DECEMBER 16, TEN days after the first bombing of Dessie, the emperor received a copy of the secret proposal to end the war. It was prepared by the British Foreign Secretary, Sir Samuel Hoare, and the Prime Minister of France, Pierre Laval and christened the Hoare-Laval Pact.

The next morning, the emperor summoned to a press conference the European and American journalists who were camped out in the compound of the hospital. Some already knew of the Hoare-Laval proposal and a few had even read its terms.

The emperor, dressed in his khaki commander-in-chief uniform, was on the porch waiting for them with a prepared statement:

"We desire to state, with all the solemnity and firmness that the situation demands today, that our willingness to facilitate any pacific solution of this conflict has not changed, but that the act by us of accepting even in principle the Hoare-Laval proposal, would be not only a cowardice toward our people, but also a betrayal of the League of Nations and of all the states that have shown that they could have confidence up to now in the system of collective security."

"Is that all you have to say, Your Majesty?" Granger Walker of the *New York Times* asked.

"At this time, yes. We are sending a reply to our ambassador in Geneva."

The emperor returned to his office and requested that Yifru draft a text to be given to the Ethiopian ambassador at the League.

"The government and people of Ethiopia do not ask any people in the world to come to Africa and shed their blood in defense of Ethiopia. The blood of Ethiopians will suffice for that."

Yifru paused looking out the windows at the towering mountains and thought about the statesmen in Geneva. He could not help wondering how futile was this attempt to try to persuade them that Ethiopia should not be thrown to the wolves. He started again.

"Is the victim of the aggression to be invited by the League to submit to the aggressor and, in the interests of world peace, to abandon the defense of its independence and integrity against its powerful enemy on the grounds that the latter's resolve to exterminate its victim is unshakable?

"Is the victim to be placed under the implicit threat of abandonment by the League and to be deprived of all hope of succor?

"This matter, which is the main problem for future international relations among peoples, whatever their appearance, their race, or their power may be, ought it not, first of all, to come up before the League, and be examined openly with full freedom and before the eyes of the whole world?"

As Yifru was finishing the communiqué, Ceseli came up beside him. He handed her the letter and she read it carefully. "He's not going to give in, is he?"

"No. He will send this to Geneva and protest the bombing of innocent civilians. He cannot surrender our country, which has remained free for over three thousand years, unless the League of Nations compels us to accept such a judgment."

"Which it can't?"

"Which it won't! The British and French seem to think they're doing us a favor. They think these are the best terms we could expect. I don't believe that. The best we could have gotten was the embargo on raw materials and the munitions loan the emperor asked for. I would like to know what Mussolini has said of this proposal. I don't suppose we will."

While the emperor was sending his protest to the League of Nations, Mussolini was in Rome toying with the Hoare-Laval appeasement proposal that he had received the week before. In the meantime, he had chosen to make no public mention of it. That was not because he was totally indifferent. The plan did have certain advantages. Foremost of which the fact that the League would probably not apply an oil embargo while the Hoare-Laval was under discussion. That alone would buy him time.

Early that morning, Il Duce was driven in his huge black FIAT *Balilla* through the area along the coast to the South of Rome known as the Pontine Marshes. He was on his way to attend the dedication of Pontinia, the latest of the towns reclaimed by draining the malaria infested swamps. The reclamation of these Pontine Marshes, begun in 1931, was one of the accomplishments for which Mussolini could not be criticized. His plans had provided homes and land for more than fifty thousand people.

Mussolini was going to Pontinia because it would provide the opportunity for an important speech he wanted to make. Without preamble he began:

"The Italian people are capable of resisting a very long siege, especially when it is certain in the clearness and tranquility of their conscience that right is on their side, while wrong is on the side of Europe, which in the present circumstances is dishonoring itself. The war we have begun on African soil is a war of civilization and liberation. It is the war of the poor, disinherited, proletarian Italian people. Against us are arrayed the forces of reaction, of selfishness, and hypocrisy. We have embraced a hard struggle against this front. We shall continue this struggle to the end. It will take time, but once a struggle is begun, it is not time that counts, but victory."

He waited while the cheering continued, then waved his hand to silence his audience. He needed to hurry back to Rome for an important and scenographic ritual.

For this important occasion, Mussolini chose an entirely black military uniform to set off his Fascist black shirt. It was already dark and cold on the evening of December 18 as Il Duce looked out at the huge square filled with women. GOLD FOR THE FATHERLAND was to be a propitious ceremony: a truly massive exchange of gold wedding rings for iron ones, each with the inscription Gold for the Fatherland.

The focal point this evening was the Altar of the Fatherland, the audacious white marble wedding cake monument at the side of Piazza Venezia built in memory of the unification of Italy and its first king, Vittorio Emanuele II. A huge flame rose from a giant crucible on the steps of the Tomb of the Unknown Warrior. The flame was meant to suggest that the gold began melting as soon as it fell into the crucible.

Now, as Mussolini watched, Queen Elena, tall and erect, began the procession and with great dignity dropping into the crucible not only her own, but also the King's ring. Then came Mussolini's own wife, Rachel, and the wives of other officials.

After the more celebrated wives had made their sacrifices, the ordinary women of Rome, at least two hundred fifty thousand, took part in the ritual in a seemingly endless procession walking up the steps of the monument to the flaming crucible. Like these women, were millions of other women with as much solemnity in every other Italian city or town.

Mussolini never disclosed how much gold he collected in the "Gold for the Fatherland" ceremonies, but whatever its monetary value, it was surpassed by the psychological benefit of winning over the Italian women who were now completely on his side.

CHAPTER 41

There were many war correspondents in Dessie camped out in the grounds of the Advent Hospital. Ceseli did not know them well, but she did know some of them on a first name basis. Harold Anderson was with the *Herald Tribune*, Granger Walker with the *New York Times*, Scott Ludlow, the *Associated Press*; David Park Jennings, the *London Times*; and Jacques La Housette, the *French Agence Havas*.

It seemed only logical to celebrate Christmas on Christmas Eve, as there would be no bombing that night. Ceseli was happy that there were two other nurses. One was from Sweden, the other from Great Britain. It made her feel less alone.

"You're coming, aren't you?" Walker asked, putting his head into the small room where they kept hospital supplies.

"Of course I am," she answered. "Who got us the chicken?"

"I think it was a gift from the emperor. It is certainly cooked like an Ethiopian chicken," he laughed. "I guess we're all getting used to wot."

"That's for sure." She smiled.

She liked Walker with his keen sense of humor, ruddy complexion, red hair and freckles. *He's probably in his early forties*, she thought, *but looked like a plump cherub.*

After dinner she decided to detour to her room by way of Yifru's office and she found him there, as she was sure she would. *I really have to wonder if this man ever sleeps*, she thought, *and if so, where.*

"Yifru. I have an idea."

"I'm sure you do," he smiled indulgently, "but the answer is no."

"You haven't even heard it."

"Ceseli, unless you consider me more of a moron than you let on—"

"I do not consider you a moron," she interrupted.

"Good. That testifies to your good judgment," he smiled. "Okay. You are not going to celebrate Timkat in Axum. I will send you back to Addis, but I will not risk your life, or that of any of my men, to go to Axum. Not even your mule. I hope that gets my point across."

"But . . ."

"There are no buts. Against my better judgment, I agreed to have you come with the hospital unit. We are very grateful for all your work. You've been more help than I could have imagined." He paused. "And I'll make you a promise. If we win this war, I will have you taken into the Holy of Holies to see the Ark for yourself."

"Really?"

"I promise, and I'm a good promiser."

"What does that mean?"

"That I keep my promises."

"It's a quaint way of putting it," she smiled, "but I get the meaning, and I accept."

"Good," he smiled again, concealing his mirth.

"You are very generous to me, Yifru. Thank you."

"I knew you were celebrating your Christmas and there is reason to celebrate. Sir Hoare has been forced to retire. The English people were appalled at his proposal. It seems they generally hate Mussolini. Hoare has been replaced by Sir Anthony Eden. Eden has not only been an excellent diplomat at the League, but a good friend to Ethiopia."

"He didn't do too well on the Zeila port deal!"

"Nobody could have succeeded. He tried to find a peaceful solution. We are grateful to him for that."

"Well, I'm glad Hoare was kicked out. Serves him right. Good Night, and thank you for your promise. Let's see if you are a good promiser."

"I am. Don't worry. I am." He smiled to himself as she left.

CHAPTER 42

"WELL GENTLEMEN, ARE YOU satisfied?" Badoglio asked as he smacked his fly swat against his boot. "You are watching a drama that will unfold in several acts. This is the prologue."

The war correspondents assigned to the Italian army listened while General Pietro Badoglio explained how he was going to liquidate the major obstacle blocking the way to Addis Ababa. Bruno Zeri knew that even Badoglio could not remove the nine thousand foot flattop mountain fortress of Amba Aradam twenty miles south of Makalle. He concluded that Badoglio was speaking of the army of the Minister of War, Ras Mulugeta, and his fifty thousand men dug into the peaks, caves, crevices and foothills on its heights.

Mulugeta had been told that he must occupy a powerful position and simply by sticking to it, keep the Italians in Makalle. He chose Amba Aradam. The great ras was known for his cunning and this was no exception. He sent search parties up the Amba to make sure there was plentiful water and they found five springs. Then slipping through the Italian outposts every night, in groups of fifty to one hundred, he sent his soldiers up the mountain.

Many of the correspondents had just arrived in Ethiopia and had been banished to Asmara since December. In that time, Badoglio had reinforced his positions, doubled the strength of his artillery and completed a network of roads to establish his supply lines and communications. Furthermore, under Mussolini's direct orders, the Royal Italian Air Force systematically tormented the Ethiopians, including civilians, with bombs and mustard gas on both the northern and southern fronts.

As the journalists listened with their notebooks in hand, Badoglio told them that numerically the two armies were about equal. Zeri knew he was lying. He also knew that in comparison to the Italian firepower and the Royal Air Force's one hundred seventy planes, the Ethiopians had almost nothing. Furthermore, when the planes were not on bombing missions they were used for reconnaissance. The aerial photographs of Amba Aradam showed that while Mulugeta could defend the mountain's impenetrable northern wall and its virtually impregnable east and west faces, his defenses could be penetrated behind from the Antalo Plain.

"Put away your notebooks," the General ordered. "Until further notice, no one will be allowed to send anything to his newspaper. Each man will be expected to maintain military discipline. I consider you soldiers."

That night, Zeri indulged in some soul searching. Most of the other journalists were sent to chronicle the campaign in exalted terms and after the war would write books glorifying the achievements of the Italian army. After weeks of self-analysis and long hours of introspection, he had decided that Ceseli Larson was right. You did need to take sides. The truth needed to be told. He now had a mission. So, although he followed Badoglio's orders not to write dispatches for the paper, he nevertheless, in his own De Farge style, composed his secret music.

Soon after, Badoglio lifted his orders and on the eve of the fortieth anniversary of the Italian defeat at Adowa in 1896, all the journalists were expected to write a patriotic dispatch. Zeri knew that if he refused, he would be sent home and never complete his own mission. He spread out his notes, lit his cigar, and began to write.

Special to Corriere della Sera by Bruno Zeri
29 February 1936, Tembien, Ethiopia–On the eve of the 40th Anniversary of the Battle of Adowa, a decisive victory today avenged the death of our proud martyrs.

As the ponderous roll of the great Negarait war drum started at dawn, wave after wave of Ethiopians in a seemingly uncoordinated mass left the cover of the woods on the slopes of Debra Ansa flinging themselves onto the Italian lines. With their white toga-like shammas floating on the wind, from eight in the morning until four this afternoon, armed for the most part only with swords and clubs, they tried to break through or get around the forward lines held by the mighty Alpines and Blackshirts.

Time and again, our forces were able to withstand the onslaught. The Ethiopian soldiers were mowed down and thwarted by our concentrated machine gun fire.

Zeri paused. He did not write that the Italians had dropped two hundred tons of high explosives on the Ethiopian forming up zones, nor that threatened with encirclement by Italy's advancing infantry, Ras Seyoum's warriors decided they had had enough.

"Finally, when the attacks seemed to be less frequent and less fanatic, General Pirzio Birolli attacked. By evening, the encircling maneuver was complete and the Second Battle of Tembien was over.

These faithful defenders of civilization have given their lives for our new Empire. Now, thanks to the Fascist regime, the dead of Adowa have at last been revenged.

Zeri knew that the few thousand Ethiopians who were trapped had put up a desperate resistance earning even Badoglio's admiration. But they could do nothing to change the course of the battle. Some eight thousand Ethiopians were killed. The Italian forces lost less than six hundred, most of them the Eritrean native Askaris. Steep odds, Zeri calculated. At this rate, we will exterminate the entire population.

The news of victory at Tembien was received in Italy with the same frenzy that had characterized the news that Adowa had been taken. Zeri knew that the timing of these victories was not exactly unexpected. Il Duce had told Badoglio that he would replace him with General Rudolfo Graziani, commander in Italian Somaliland, unless he achieved some glittering coup.

Badoglio had pulled off the victory and he was elated. He summed it up saying: "The curtain has fallen on the second act, gentlemen. Now we must think of the third. The enemy has suffered such a shattering defeat that for the first time in its history, it has lost all desire to continue."

Zeri consulted the rest of his notes. He knew that as the retreating Ethiopians straggled back along the only road they were bombed repeatedly. For people who had never seen an aircraft, the effect was devastating, and the rocky ravine where they were to cross the river became a mortal bottleneck.

To the Italian aviators, the solid mass of defeated Ethiopians was a bomber's dream. For the next few days, every pilot on the northern front took part in the bombing of the hapless fugitives, including Mussolini's own two sons.

Zeri was certain that this was the sort of battle that was best suited to Badoglio's taste: a modern industrial nation's war of annihilation. He was using clubs to kill fleas.

The Ethiopian armies were disintegrating and Haile Sellassie was well aware of the gravity of the situation. He had become a desperate man, a man who had held out for five months against an enemy infinitely more powerful still hoping that the League of Nations would come to his aid.

From his headquarters in Dessie, he was vainly trying to coordinate the actions of his four armies on the northern front. He studied the map spread out on his desk. The main aim of the Ethiopians' plan was to cut the Italian army in two and isolate Makalle. The Minister of War, Mulugeta now found himself in a vulnerable position.

"It's Mulugeta," Yifru said, handing Haile Sellassie the bulky radiophone.

The Negus listened while Mulugeta described his position. The emperor put his pen down on the spot that Mulugeta was indicating.

"We will send a telegram to Ras Kassa ordering him to go to your aid," he said, indicating to Yifru that this be done. Yifru knew that although there was not a great deal of jealousy among rases, one was usually loath to ask another for assistance. The fact that Mulugeta had done so only confirmed the urgency of his situation.

"What's happening?" Ceseli asked Yifru later that day.

"Mulugeta is surrounded. He has asked for help."

"What about the emperor?"

"He is planning one last battle. We are moving up to the Agumberta Pass. It is the decisive battle. At times like this I can see only blackness. I wish I had more faith," he said, lowering his eyes.

"It's not always a question of faith. There is such a thing as reality."

"But we will go to Maytchaw. Perhaps our luck will change," he said, unconvinced. "Now I must return to the emperor."

It was not for several days that the emperor learned that his faithful and courageous Minister of War, Ras Mulugeta, and his son had been killed during his retreat by the strafing of the Royal Italian Air Force. His other leaders, Ras Kassa and Ras Seyoum, were in full retreat.

CHAPTER 43

Ceseli looked out over the valley noting the spectacular beauty of what would be the last battlefield. It was a pleasant, almost smiling countryside with lush green plains watered by thermal springs and the Mekan torrent. It was March 23rd.

It was hard to believe that the fate of the emperor and of his empire would be decided here at Maytchaw. Yet, contrary to his own better judgment and that of his foreign advisers, the Negus had bowed to the power of his chiefs. He would lead his army for one great daylong battle.

Haile Sellassie, from his cave on Mount Aia, looked through his field glasses across the lush green valley. Before him, across the endless expanse some forty thousand Italians and Eritreans were dug in. The emperor knew that behind them another forty thousand were distributed between the neighboring Belago and Alagi passes.

Haile Sellassie had come to Maytchaw with the finest of his troops. His army of thirty-one thousand included the yet untried Imperial Guard, of which Yohannes was a part. The guards were solid units, trained to European standards of high moral and aggressive spirit. With them were also the survivors of the armies of Ras Kassa and Ras Seyoum.

Two days before, the emperor had sent his Russian military advisor, Colonel Konovaloff, through the Italian lines to reconnoiter. Yohannes went with him. When he reported to the emperor the next day, Konovaloff noted that the Italian defenses were flimsy and that there was only a thin veil of Eritrean Askaris on the left flank. The colonel was adamant in his advice: Attack at once while the Italians are still unprepared.

The Negus decided instead to launch his offensive on March 24, believing that by then the local population would be in full revolt against the Italians.

Again the battle was postponed. It was now March 27. Yifru turned to listen to his nephew.

"I know they are high dignitaries, but these generals are not trained in the military tradition. Ras Kassa and Ras Seyoum have already suffered crushing defeats. We have officers trained at St. Cyr. Surely, the emperor will listen to them."

"Yohannes, the emperor understands what you are saying. But tradition compels him to lead the army himself. He thinks that if we wait a bit, the Azebu Galla tribe will destroy the left flank. He's been giving them thousands of Austrian Thalers. All will go well. Have faith."

"But you know the Galla hate the Shoans. I would not trust them to do anything. I bet they are being paid by the Italians as well."

But even as he consoled his nephew, Yifru was growing desperate. The emperor seemed unable to make decisions. Yifru was upset, but not surprised, when the attack was put off again and again and again.

"I don't understand the delay, Yifru," Ceseli finally asked in exasperation. "What's happening?"

"There are many different war plans being discussed."

"I need to know what medical help we are going to get. Where is the nearest Red Cross Unit?"

"I think it's up there," he said, turning to point at a hilltop out to the left. "If I am not totally wrong, that is where your Italian doctor friend might be."

"On the top of that plateau?" she questioned, following his finger. Marco was right over there. It wasn't very far at all and she was upset that she was only hearing this now. *Doesn't Yifru know what Marco means to me,* she thought. "We should warn them. If the doctors are going to be of any help, they should be ready."

Yifru looked at Ceseli knowing it was sound advice. It was not far and it was not dangerous if she traveled after the bombers left for the day.

"Go ahead. But make sure you're back by eight in the morning. The Italian bombers don't fly before that."

Ceseli turned, and walked back to the makeshift dispensary and started to arrange the medicine the doctors would need for the following day. Marco was right over there. Damn what a waste these four days had been. If she had only known before. *Don't worry about what I didn't know,* she thought, *concentrate on what I can do now.*

CHAPTER 44

"THIS IS THE LAST person for today. Go home, Fikerte. See you in the morning." Marco turned to the Ethiopian nurse working beside him. She was young and pretty, and just as tired. It was difficult working surrounded by so much death. Both of them deserved a rest.

The girl smiled, her eyes meeting his over the cloth she wore over her mouth.

Marco was exhausted. He couldn't remember when he had last really slept. He had already seen so much death he had ceased to count. He had lived with the dead and now wondered whether he could ever be a civilian again. He remembered his conversation with Ceseli on whether you grow immune to death. There was something sure: he hadn't.

He walked outside looking at the people who were waiting for his help. He could see the horrible suppurating burns on their feet and on their emaciated limbs. They looked at him with begging eyes and raised their plight-filled voices. The sound was a low, moaning wave of misery –*Abeit! Abeit! Abeit!* Mercy! Mercy! Mercy!

He saw that a brown mule was coming up along the winding path. The rider was shrouded by a dark gray burnoose. The animal drew abreast and stopped.

"Ceseli!" he almost yelled. "Ceseli!"

"Marco!"

He didn't need to know why she had come. It was sufficient that she was here and with a smile only for her, he helped her down from the saddle and into his arms. Their eyes met and held for a long time. She had come a long way for him and now in the middle of a battlefield, hidden from anyone who knew them, they realized they were there for each other, for as long as it was possible, for as long as they had.

He kissed her warmly and then turned holding her tightly. The coarse wool of the burnoose was so different from the soft skin of her arms. "I thought you were in Addis? Or home," he said, looking into her eyes. "I thought you were safe."

"I know. I got your letters. No, I'm with the doctors attached to the emperor."

"I guess it's stupid for me to tell you that you're in great danger."

"It was something I needed to do. You of all people can understand that."

He continued to look at her, his voice muted, but not the expression in his eyes. "The Italians are going to attack. And they will win. You know that."

"That's why we came to Maytchaw. For one great battle. As custom demands, the emperor will lead it himself. But for the last week there have been nothing but delays. Yifru is very worried. He's convinced that these delays are killing the emperor's chances. That the Italians have had more time to dig in."

"He's right," he said, taking her hand and leading her to the only small tree on the plateau. He took her saddlebags off the mule. "I'll get him some water."

"He's afraid of the bombs, but I'm sure he'd like some water."

"How did you find me?"

"Yifru told me he thought you were here."

Ceseli took off the heavy burnoose and sat down. While she waited she took her camera from the satchel. She looked out across the peaceful valley. It was almost twilight, but in the far distance she could just see the emperor's campfires. They seemed so far away.

She looked around at the men who were waiting patiently on the other side of the tent. They were almost lifeless automatons in their acceptance of life and death. It reminded her of a recurring nightmare of battle where the severed limbs started a grotesque dance. She remembered the childhood verse that had been going through her mind for weeks. "*Early in the morning in the middle of the night, two dead boys got up to fight. Back to back they faced each other, drew their swords and shot each other.*" She shuddered.

After a bit, Marco returned. "I've put him down near the spring. There's a pretty deep cave. It could hide a whole herd of animals. He'll be fine there."

"It's the mustard gas, isn't it?" she said, pointing to the white splotches on the dark skins.

"The planes come every day. These are peasants from the area. There's no food. The crops are poisoned. The livestock are dead." Marco touched her hair caressing it and forming little curls with his fingers. "There's not much to eat here."

"I wasn't expecting a feast," she smiled.

"Good, because you're not going to get one," he grinned. "No special pasta. But we can have some soup. And the villagers bring me injera. That's their way of thanking me."

"You know I didn't come for the food," she said. "It's funny how our concept of food changes. There is food and Yifru looks after me. And while we were at Dessie, there was a little boy named Habtu. He brought me eggs and other treasures one takes for granted. I showed him the mirror of my compact. I don't think he'd ever seen himself before. He was smiling and moving his head from side to side. It reminded me of when I would sit at my grandmother's dressing table and try out her powders and rouge." Ceseli smiled. "I didn't know you were so close. I thought the Red Cross hospital was all the way on the other side of the valley."

"That's the British one. How did you find out?"

"I needed to warn the doctors to expect a great many wounded tomorrow. Yifru showed me where you were. But I had to promise I'd be back by early morning. He doesn't want me to be bombed along the way."

"You're safe here. See that," he said, pointing to the huge Red Cross on the top of the tent. It was a large square American army tent. The camp was marked by five Red Cross flags: three on the tent and two more, ten to twelve feet wide ground covers.

"We were bombed in Dessie, almost immediately after the emperor arrived. I was really afraid. It's something so completely out of one's control."

"You learn to live with it. The planes come here every day. They don't bomb. They're just trying to intimidate us. You'll get used to it."

"I don't want to get used to it," Ceseli smiled. "Have you heard anything from your family?"

"Not in a long time. When you think of it, we'd need those famous messenger pigeons you were joking about."

"On the train. I remember. It seems like another lifetime."

"So will this one day."

"I hope you're right."

"Zeri's here you know. With Badoglio. He came to see me the other day. He left me a pack of his Tuscan cigars."

"That you don't smoke."

"It was a gesture. He's a thoughtful person. Those cigars are precious to him. He took a letter that I had written to my family. It isn't hard for him to get it mailed. He has a secret reef of papers. Musical sheets. He told me he'd tell me about it when this is over. He's not very fond of Badoglio. I asked him why he didn't leave."

"And?"

"Said he needed to watch him."

"Badoglio?"

"Yes. Says he made a pact with the devil."

Later that evening, she sat leaning back against him. She had taken pictures of the men with their white scarring burns and a few of Marco, pantomiming in front of the hospital tent. A timed one of the two of them. She hoped that they'd come out.

The soup was good and so was the injera. The night was very still now. Below, across the valley, the bonfires were covered by the mist, but the stars were gleaming overhead. The crickets were vibrant in their chatter.

"Funny," Marco said. "I was just thinking about a badly injured Muslim soldier. He was just sitting and waiting for me. There was a green parrot overhead in the tree and he was studying it. He said, 'You know that we have a belief in our religion, that all of us who are killed in battle for our faith go at once to heaven.'

"But, you're not fighting for your faith in Ethiopia," I told him.

"I'm cheating just a little," he smiled. "Our belief is that until the Day of Judgment, the souls of the faithful go into the crops of green birds, which eat the fruits of paradise and drink from its rivers. Look at that beautiful green bird," he said. "I wonder if it will please Allah that I shall be killed and my soul take its flight to paradise in its crop."

"What happened to him?" Ceseli asked.

"He didn't die."

"I'm glad. Green is a sacred color for the Muslims. It's the green of grass and fertility." She turned to study him. "You know, you're like that warrior."

Marco studied her quietly. "You, too." They looked at each other, not needing words. Marco took the chain from around his neck. "Now that you've come all this way, I want you to have this. I think you need it more than I do."

"I can't take it," she said, fingering the delicate gold chain with its small medal.

"Of course you can. It's the patron saint of Florence. I want you to keep it. I'll come and retrieve it."

"On loan then. That's a promise, and I'd like to give you this," she said, undoing the dog tag she wore around her neck and handing it to him. "It was my father's."

"I would be honored to wear it," he said, kissing her lightly, then more tenderly as she moved into his embrace. They kissed urgently both understanding what little time they had to be together. From deep within, from her soul and her heart, she felt she knew everything about him.

"Shhh," he said, covering her mouth with a finger, and then without another word, he lay down next to her and took her in his arms. As they lay in each other's arms, her kisses were as passionate as his. And there was something very sweet about the way they felt about each other physically and emotionally. It was at the same time romantic and old fashioned.

Early the next morning, a summer fog cast a lacy mantel and the grass lay like a white bed of clouds. Birds floated on the wind sunning themselves, or alighted on the wet limbs that looked like a gigantic spider's web casting knitted shadows on the ground. As she sat looking out over the valley, minute crystals of moisture hung to her hair like seed pearls.

"Good morning," she whispered as he sat down next to her.

"You look like some kind of fairy," Marco said, putting his hands on her shoulders. "You should make a wish."

"I have. I can't tell you what it is because otherwise it won't come true. Will this ever end?" she asked, continuing to stare out over the valley.

"It will end. You must go, now. It's getting late." He continued to hold her to him. "Yifru will get worried."

"I know. It's just . . ." her voice trailed off. "I know."

"And I must begin my work. By the time I have tried to help these people there will be many more. I don't mind. I just wish there were more of us. But it won't be for long."

Ceseli clung to him as if to a raft in a stormy sea. She didn't want to leave him, but she had made a promise to Yifru and she needed to keep it. She hoped Marco couldn't see the tears that were beginning to sting behind her eyes. Then he pulled away from her and Ceseli watched as he went back into the Red Cross tent. He returned with her canteen bottle. "I'll just be a minute. I'll get you fresh water from the spring."

Returning from the spring, he saw the first white Caproni bombers flying in formation, approaching along the rim of the valley. It was very early. He watched fascinated as they neared, their silver bodies glistening like a polished sword. He continued to watch mesmerized like a deer at night with a light flashed into its eyes.

Marco turned to make sure the large Red Cross lettering on the tent was clearly visible. Relieved, he ran back up the steep incline looking around him. The planes were approaching now. Ceseli was standing near the tent her camera bag next to her and ready to start back.

"I should have brought the mule," Marco said, as she turned to look at him. The menacing planes were approaching. Suddenly, Marco realized that the planes were headed directly for the tent. The tent was the target. They were the target. He could do nothing. Even as he looked around for cover, Marco knew there was none.

He ran to her, grabbing her and then instinctively crushing her headlong to the ground beneath him, holding her to him. His body was hard on top of her, like a protective shield, covering her. "I'm here. It's okay."

She held his hands feeling him on top of her, holding on to him for dear life. "Pretend it's a beautiful display of fireworks," Marco whispered. "Remember the emperor's party."

"I'll try."

He could feel her relax under him. Then he lifted his head to watch as the first of the planes began dipping toward the tent, letting loose its deadly load of bombs. Around him the men started to wail.

Abeit!

Abeit!

Abeit!

"This one is blue. Do you remember?"

"Yes. It was beautiful."

The next three planes were releasing the spray of gas.

"The next is green. It's beautiful, too."

"Yes."

"We're missing only the yellow and the red?"

Ceseli was hardly breathing.

"Everything will be over in a minute."

She could hear the planes going over them very low. Bombs were dropping all around them. The noise was crescendoing. The bombs like firecrackers, ptut, ptut, ptut. The smell of the gas was nauseating. Then they were past. Both the yellow, and the red. Thank God. She could hear the planes leaving. She waited a moment, needing to control her breathing. "Marco?"

She moved her hand in front of her looking out from her clasped hands. The tent was a shambles, the iron bars bent like matchsticks. The tarpaulin was smoldering. From under him she could see the bodies of the men like sacks of feathers. She could feel his dead weight on her. She struggled to free herself. "Marco. It's okay. They've gone."

The silence was louder than the pounding in her heart. She struggled out from under him. Then she looked at him as her hair suffocated her scream. Up his back, against the white of his shirt, was a little red picket fence. Blood burst from the back of his head where the curls of the Renaissance angel had once been.

CHAPTER 45

On the night before the battle, while Ceseli and Marco slept together and made plans for the future, Yifru accompanied the emperor to meet with his generals and inspect the forward positions. Haile Sellassie gave his rases orders for the positions of the artillery and mortars.

As the soldiers prepared for what might be their last battle, priests passed along the lines with their hand crosses hearing confession from these very religious people, granting absolutions and offering blessings.

By four the next morning, the thirty thousand Ethiopian soldiers were formed into three columns. Under cover of darkness, the columns moved within a few hundred yards of the enemy trenches, set up their machine guns and waited for the signal to attack. It came at dawn. A Mausser fired twice and two red rockets soared into the still dark sky.

In time with the thudding war drums, wave after wave of Ethiopians fell on the enemy trenches with that fanatical courage described in the Italian troop manuals. The sound of battle became unearthly: blood curdling yells and the low booming of the war drums. The sky was stagnated by the yells that seemed to rebound off the enemy as if waves were piling up along some rugged shore.

Crouched down with others of the imperial guard, Yohannes took the silver filigree cross which hung around his neck and polished it nervously with his fingers. To his right, he could see endless waves of amber and white, like so many puppets jerked and faltering on twisted cords. The men were running, falling, being replaced, and continuing to run as they headed for the storm.

The Italian artillery fire intensified. The sound of the machine guns was interrupted by the crack of snipers and the barrage in front of them.

Haile Sellassie's men kept up a furious onslaught supported by the fire of a few machine guns. Then the Ethiopians switched their attack to the Mekan Pass and the left flank of the Italian army where they were hoping for less stubborn resistance from the Eritreans troops.

Pitter patter, pitter patter.

Yohannes now saw the squadrons of the Italian Royal Air Force overhead. Having earlier bombed all the Red Cross units, the same Caproni bombers had refueled and were once more on the attack. The emperor, with his only Oerilikon antiaircraft, shot into the air.

By noon, the sun was scorching. There were no clouds to hide it. No wind, not even a breeze to bring relief. Yohannes felt his tongue engorged by thirst and his khaki uniform was wet with sweat. If only night would come.

Still waiting for the guards to be called, Yohannes saw the pitted land where lumps of bodies were now obstacles. He could see the suicidal scruffy lines still struggling forward only to be driven by some divine purpose into the death-dealing guns. To his left, a man fell and a companion stopped to help him. As he watched, the man was hit again and his head opened up like a sword slashing open a melon.

At this point, Haile Sellassie ordered the Imperial Guard to attack the Italian left flank. As he ran forward, Yohannes's whole being was now controlled by some automatic determination.

For three hours, the guard struggled to roll back the Italian flank. But despite their gallantry, the accuracy of their fire, and the fury of their onslaught, the Ethiopians were unable to break through. By 4 p.m., it was apparent that the guard was not going to capture its objective.

Although the emperor now knew that his chances of success were poor, he ordered his troops to attack along the full front. The sky was ominously overcast and it had started to rain when the three main columns stood up and surged forward one last time to attack the trenches held by the crack Italian Alpine troops.

Pitter patter, pitter patter.

Once more, the ragged suicidal line raced toward the guns. Death meant nothing as Yohannes ran on and on across the plain into the cocoon of death.

Soon night did come. As the guns grew quiet, Haile Sellassie ordered his army to fall back. It was not an orderly retreat. The soldiers were tired and demoralized. Discipline had broken down in many of the units in which the commanders had been killed.

Close to exhaustion, Yohannes staggered to the water he had craved since noon. He put his rifle on the shore and started to wade into the water. By the light of the full moon, he could see the floating corpses of animals that had come to drink from the contaminated water. He fell to his knees. For what seemed to him an eternity, he knelt there, neither praying nor thinking, letting the tiredness wash over him. Finally, he rose and started to walk back, as if sleepwalking, to the emperor's cave on the mountainside. All around him the earth began to move. Bent and crippled, the wounded crawled back to the other side of the valley.

After the defeat, the emperor retreated to the cave at Mount Aia. An officer approached the cave and not recognizing the man, Yifru went to intercede.

"I've come from the Red Cross Hospital," he said, turning to speak to the emperor. "The field hospitals have all been bombed. The doctors and all their staff are dead."

The emperor looked at him with tired brooding eyes. "Bombed? The Red Cross?" he asked. "The League must hear of this," the emperor said, shaking his head as he retreated into the protection of his cave.

"There was one Italian doctor," Yifru interrupted. "Over there," he said, pointing up to the hill where he had sent Ceseli.

"All of the hospitals were bombed early this morning. There is nobody left alive."

"There was a white woman," Yifru interrupted.

"I just came from there. There is no white woman," the officer said. "There was one doctor who was burned on a pyre, but he was already dead."

Yifru stared at him. No, he wanted to say. It can't be, but somehow he knew in his heart that it was. He lowered his head to hide the pain. Where was Ceseli? Was she too dead?

When the emperor withdrew for the night, Yifru looked out over the vast valley. The plight of the wounded was pitiful. Thousands were crying out to their emperor. "*Abeit! Abeit! Abeit!*"

The women who moved with the army to cook and care for their men, were keening. The low wailing sound of their ululations filled the night with grief. From the mountaintop cave, Yifru could see the tiny glimmer of the torches that seemed like fireflies as the women tried to rescue the wounded. According to the direction of the Coptic priests, the dead were burned.

As soon as he knew that the emperor was sleeping, Yifru left the cave and went in search of his nephew. He had a very urgent assignment for him.

CHAPTER 46

AT FIRST THE CARRION birds were just specks against the sky. Then, in circles, they lay on the imperceptible currents of air. They approached in the same orderly way, as had the Italian bombers. They turned circling on their wide wings and then descended. There was no one left to beat them back.

Bruno Zeri, following the vultures, looked around, the enormity of what he saw registering slowly in his mind. There were bodies in various stages of decomposition everywhere around the tent. The vultures had torn open some of the bodies and their feathers were red from the blood and meat they ripped away.

On the right side of the plateau, were the remnants of Marco's Red Cross tent, its metal structure twisted and burned and the canvas charred and blackened. Zeri took his camera and began to photograph.

He walked toward the tent. The body of the Ethiopian nurse he had seen three days before lay on the ground. Her dark face had huge patches of whitish-yellow and her eyes were wide in horror. Zeri knelt beside her and closed her eyes. He found a bloodied sheet and covered her.

He hurried through the sea of bodies, hoping to find someone alive. Finally, he found the white skin he did not want to find. He walked to the body, knelt down and said a prayer. Then he unfastened the dog tag from around Marco's neck and turned it over in his hand. H. Larson. He squeezed it and put it in his pocket. *Ceseli Larson,* he thought. Where was Marco's gold chain? Had someone already stolen it?

Zeri looked for something to cover the body. Working quickly he dragged a branch over and heaped it on the body. He found two wooden chairs, already in pieces, and some small tree branches. He went back into the tent. With a precious bottle of alcohol in his hand, he approached the body and doused the wood. Then with the tip of his Tuscan cigar he lit the funeral pyre. Zeri watched until he was sure that it would burn.

Turning back to the remnants of the tent, he noticed the papers strewn about. From the charred papers, he rescued the well-worn sepia photograph. The eyes of the Afar girl seemed to have changed from mirth to profound sadness. Next to what had been a makeshift table, he found Marco's diary.

Outside, his eye caught the metal canteen with a bullet through the side. He picked it up noticing that it was smeared with blood. *Whose blood*, he wondered? Looking at the ground, he saw a consistent trickle of blood that led down the hill. *The well*, he thought.

Zeri drew his pistol and followed the blood. There was more of it on the ground in front of the trickle of water that came over the lip of the rocks. He turned and looked warily around him. In front of him was what looked like the entrance to a large cave. Pistol in hand, he slid along the wall of rock, inching forward. The rock felt hard against his back. As he turned to peer into the cave, a mule came bolting toward him. Instinctively, he grabbed for it and caught onto the stirrup. He was dragged along with the frightened animal, almost falling before he could regain his balance. His pistol fell to the ground clattering across the rocks.

He grabbed the leg of the rider pinning it against his side and blocking the path of the mule. He grabbed the reins and weighted them against him halting the scared animal. In the dim light, he could see the rider stiffen. He pulled and the rider fell off against him. Bruno was too astonished to speak immediately. "Miss Larson!"

Ceseli looked at him, her eyes large in terror. Then she started to cry. Great heaving spasms of sound that were strangely erupting as from a wounded animal.

"Please," Bruno Zeri said as he held her to him. It was a long time before the heaving gradually subsided. "Are you all right?" he asked with apprehension.

"I feel very dizzy. My arm hurts a lot."

"Let me look," he said, easing the burnoose off her shoulder. The arm was red and badly swollen, but he was sure there was no bullet inside. He noticed the thin gold chain around her neck. "You were there when they bombed?"

Ceseli Larson hesitated only for a moment. Then she threw back her tear stained face defiantly. "You bombed the Red Cross tent. That's against every League of Nation dictate. Marco saved my life. He wouldn't be dead except for you. He shouldn't be dead," she repeated, fighting back the spasms of tears that were now like a dry retching noise.

Zeri waited, holding her while her breathing returned slowly to normal. "Miss Larson," he said, pausing. "I agree with you. Nor should thousands of others. I'm truly, truly sorry."

Ceseli looked up into his troubled eyes. Eyes so black she almost could not see the color. Kind eyes, despite everything.

"I ask your forgiveness. I despise this war. I can't tell you how sorry I am about Marco. But remember him as the hero he was. He would have saved you again, if need be."

Ceseli looked again into those eyes. She nodded, imperceptibly. "What are you going to do?" she asked.

"I'm not sure," he said, taking the reins as he led the mule back into the cave and tied it securely. "I have a jeep down on the other side of the hill. I'll need to take it back to the Italian headquarters. I don't want to arouse any suspicion. But I need to get you to safety before they come up here."

"Safety? Where could that be? Marco told me you came to see him. Brought him your cigars. He doesn't smoke," she added, forlornly.

She's speaking in the present tense, he thought. He stopped and looked at her more closely. "I need to get my jeep back to camp, then I'll come back to get you." Zeri looked at Ceseli. "I promise you, Miss Larson. I'll be back."

"Then what?" she asked, trying to regain her composure.

"I'm going to take you somewhere where you'll be safe. You're just going to have to trust me."

Ceseli looked up at him. "Whatever."

"Now take care of the mule. We're going to need it. It's dark at around six, I should be back here soon after. Do you have a gun?"

"Yes. And I know how to use it."

"Good. Try to rest. I'll be back."

"Won't they miss you?"

"I'm a journalist, not a soldier. They won't miss me."

"If you say so. It's not that I'm going to go anywhere else."

"Miss Larson, please trust me. Don't go off on your own. Promise?"

The silence was disconcerting. But it didn't last long. "I promise."

When Zeri had gone, Ceseli looked out at the well before sneaking out to get some water. Should she trust him, she wondered. Or should she take her chances and try to get back to Yifru. One thing she was sure of, although Zeri had not mentioned it, if they had bombed the Red Cross, what was her life worth? *He could turn me in*, she thought, *but if he were going to do that, he would have taken me now*. She filled a small terracotta cup with water and went back into the cave.

She curled up in the corner near the mule and thought about Marco. It seemed like a horrible nightmare. Through her tears she looked around her. She was hiccupping with sobs and tears. Marco was dead and there were dead people all around her. There was a deep wound just above her elbow. She was briefly mesmerized at the sight of her own blood dripping down her arm. She needed to staunch its flow. She thought of the train ride. She needed a tourniquet.

In the distance she saw the planes banking and then returning. She struggled to her feet. She looked around her as if the planes were chasing her. She ran headlong down the path to the well. Looking around her frantically she noticed the entrance to the cave. She was barely inside when the planes were back. She slid to the ground in a huddle and held her head in her arms trying to keep the hum and blasts from penetrating her brain.

They were flying overhead and dropping more bombs. If anyone were still alive, these planes would destroy him. She was terrified that the planes would find her. She was praying and sobbing at the same time as tears rolled uncontrollably down her cheeks. But they couldn't see her here. Rationally she knew that. *Marco. Marco. Marco.*

CHAPTER 47

It was just after six when Zeri reentered the cave. He could smell the mule, but in the dark he couldn't see Ceseli.

"You're back?"

"I promised you that I would be. But you weren't sure, is that it?"

"You're right."

"I don't know what I have to do to gain your confidence, Miss Larson. Save your life? Will that do?"

She smiled. "If you're thinking of doing that, perhaps you should call me Ceseli."

"All right, Ceseli. Can you get on the mule or should I help you?"

"I can do it."

But he helped her anyhow. "Are they at least comfortable, these wacky wooden saddles?" he asked, trying to give some levity to the moment.

"You get used to it."

"You get used to almost everything," he said. "I brought you a hunk of bread. Can you eat while we walk?"

"Yes."

"Good."

They started down the hill in silence and at the bottom made a sharp turn away from the human destruction in the valley of Maytchaw. As they walked, Zeri could not help thinking about Marco. What if Marco had not come to the Tigre? A few thousand Ethiopians would never have been treated for their wounds, but would have died, like hordes of others, on the well-worn caravan tracks at the edge of the plateau, without water, or medicine of any kind, poisoned, emaciated, gangrened, sun struck, and eaten with worms. Was that reason enough to die? He wondered if he would have had that courage.

"Where are we going?"

"We're going to visit a Falasha monk. There's a village not too far away and it's the only place I think you might be safe. I was over there the other day and we can get to it quite easily."

"So your Falasha research did amount to something," she smiled into the dark. "Why a Falasha monk?"

"Because I trust him. And he lives in a pretty secluded place just outside the village. There won't be anyone to see you."

"Well, at this point I guess you're the boss."

They had been walking without speaking for more than an hour when Zeri suddenly stopped and drew his gun. "What's wrong?" Ceseli whispered, alarmed.

"I think there's someone following us."

The two of them saw him at the same time because the light of the moon glinted off the barrel of his gun. "Stop!"

Zeri didn't move.

"Ceselí!" the man called out. Then repeated, "Ceselí!"

"Yohannes!" she cried out thankfully, starting to sob with joy.

"Who is this man?" Yohannes asked, coming up to them, his pistol still pointed in their direction.

"He's an Italian journalist. He's not trying to harm me. He's trying to take me to safety. To a village of Falasha Jews. Don't hurt him," Ceseli said.

"No, Ceselí. I have specific orders to bring you to my uncle," Yohannes said.

"We are going to Dessie. The crown prince has gone there to raise an army."

Ceseli looked from Yohannes to Bruno Zeri. "I think maybe he's right, Zeri. And you won't be in any trouble over this."

"All right," Zeri said, hesitating as he turned to Yohannes. "Please protect her with your life and get her to the Americans. Italy and the United States are not at war. I will return to some unfinished business with Badoglio."

"Thank you, Bruno," she smiled into the dark. "And if I get to Rome, I'll look you up. That's a promise."

Bruno Zeri took her hand and kissed the back of it. "I want you to have something," he said, taking her father's dog tag and handing it to her. "And these are some songs I've been composing for my harmonica. Guard them with your life. And here is my Afar girl," he said, giving her the worn photo. Ceseli knew where he had found it. "Take care, Ceseli. Goodbye for now."

"Thank you for everything," she smiled down at him before turning to follow Yohannes.

CHAPTER 48

"It shouldn't take us very long. I'm probably as fast as your mule," Yohannes said as they stopped for a moment of rest. "But it's been a hard day."

"Has Yifru heard about the bombings against the Red Cross?"

"Yes, and he also knows that Marco is dead. He thought you were too. That's why he sent me to find out."

"Marco died saving my life," Ceseli said as she started to choke up.

"Let's talk later, Ceselí. I can't talk and run."

In the distance Ceseli could hear the howling of the hyenas. She thought of the compound garden. Strange, she had never heard the hyenas. She wondered if they were just a bad joke. But tonight, hearing their howls, she knew this was no joke. "I didn't mean for you to have to take me to safety."

"Yifru certainly does. Remember on the ride north?"

"You wondered why he ever let me go."

"But he thought it necessary. I cannot second guess my uncle."

Ceseli looked at him smiling to herself. There had been a time when she had said almost the same thing about Bruno Zeri. She wondered where he was as she pulled her burnoose tighter. It was very late when they reached the emperor's cave.

Yifru came out immediately. "Thank you. She's okay?"

"She's alive," Yohannes answered. "I'm not saying she's okay."

Yifru helped her off the mule holding her tightly in his embrace and letting her dissolve into dry heaves of sobbing. "Go ahead and cry. It's good for you," Yifru said, taking a large white handkerchief from his uniform's pocket. It was a long time before she regained her composure. "Now you need to rest. We'll be moving at daybreak. You can ride, can't you?"

"Yes, of course."

"I'll ask Yohannes to watch out for you."

"Please don't do that. I can take care of myself and Yohannes has already done enough," she smiled. "And I need to get back to my job."

"We need your help, Ceseli."

The next day, the twenty thousand survivors of Haile Sellassie's once proud army were straggling toward Lake Ashangi carrying the wounded on crude litters made from tree branches. When they stopped to rest, Ceseli had time to change the dressings on those she expected to survive. "I don't have enough supplies to help everyone," she lamented.

"Do what you can. Anything is better than what we had without your help," Yifru said, encouraging her. Yifru knew that although the emperor might have overcome his immediate post-battle shock, he was so isolated from the reality of his situation that he could delude himself about organizing a new army when he reached Dessie.

Haile Sellassie met with his surviving rases arguing about the possibility of another attack. Yifru, listening, looked around him, realizing what a small group it now was. Statistics of how many men had been lost meant little to the Ethiopians. They could easily see that their numbers had been woefully depleted, ammunition was virtually exhausted, and their morale was dismally low.

Yet, despite the tragedy of the moment, it was a glorious morning. The graduated terraces that sloped down to the basin and the lake were festive with green corn waving as if in greeting. The approaches to the lake had no cover or protection as the long column of men approached the open plain. They were trying to put as many miles as possible between themselves and the Italians.

Yifru held open the car door as the emperor got out. He donned a khaki cloak and allowed his anxious chiefs to press a steel helmet on his head. Standing at his side, Yifru thought of the moment when he was crowned, the moment when he was at the zenith of his power and seemed invincible. Now five years and six months later, his soldiers stumbled along the difficult mountain tracks, like automata.

Suddenly they heard the roar of engines coming in from their right. Then the Caproni bombers were directly overhead. The deadly bombs began to explode among the dense mass of fugitives who bent double and clapped their hands over their ears as if they had been caught in a heavy hailstorm. Men and animals alike were blown to bits or fatally burned. The survivors of the imperial guard, who had fought so valiantly at Maytchaw, died in the cornfields, the easy targets of an enemy that had lost all sense of decency.

Yet there was no time for emotion. Soon after the survivors had resumed the march toward the town of Quoram, a messenger brought news that the Eritrean Askaris were already there. So they turned right for Dessie, where ammunition and supplies had already arrived.

CHAPTER 49

"AND SUCH A WASTE of lives. I wonder if the League will even believe us. We don't have any real proof."

Ceseli was quiet for several moments weighing what she would say. "Yifru. We do have proof."

"What proof?"

She drew in her breath and began in a just audible voice. "After the planes left, I waited for them to return and they didn't. I realized then that my cameras were up on the plateau. I needed to get them. So I walked quickly back up to where they were. Just in front of the tent. When I got there I looked around. I was scared, distraught, heartbroken, but when I looked around me what I saw drove me to a feeling of incredible anger. It was right then that I decided to avenge Marco. And Ethiopia. But I said to myself just that. I need proof. So I took first one camera and then the other and I photographed everything on the plateau. The charred canvas of the tent. The twisted poles and the big tarpaulin Red Cross markers, the dead. All of them and several of them singly." She stopped. "Marco as well."

"Ceseli, I'm so sorry. He was such a courageous young man."

"But let's transform the waste into something positive. If my photos can prove what Italy has done, let's use them."

"What can I do?"

"Help me get the film back to Addis where I hope I have enough developer."

He paused obviously considering different options. "I see two possibilities. You stay with the emperor and his entourage. It'll take longer, but you are safer in the end. Or I can have Yohannes take you to Dessie and have Standish meet you there. Faster. Riskier from here to Dessie, but safe once the Americans can get to you. You can sleep on it, if you want."

"I don't need that. I'll go to Dessie."

"We will move only at night," Yohannes said as they stopped for a moment of rest. "It will take longer, but we can't risk the planes."

Several days later was the Coptic Easter Saturday, and Ceseli and Yohannes had reached a small mountain town a few miles north of Mugia. They met with the village chief and joined him in his small and humble tukul, eating the traditional raw meat and drinking tej to celebrate the Resurrection. Although Ceseli had never eaten raw meat excepting beef tartare, she devoured it realizing how hungry she was.

On Easter Day, Yohannes made an extraordinary decision. Though he was sure the Italians must be traveling south with all possible speed, he decided to stop at the holy city of Lalibela where they could find safety. Traveling all of the night, they reached the holy church, Medhane Alam, the Savior of the World. It was the largest and noblest of the churches hewn from the mountain, and probably copied from the Church of St. Mary of Zion at Axum.

Inside they were safe to rest and to sleep. The next morning, the light glanced on the graceful lines of the many columns and arches sending strange patterns of light through the arched doors and interstices of the pierced stonework. The church was safe. The priests and monks would protect them. It was somewhere where Ceseli could rest. "Sweet dreams, Yohannes."

"And you too, Ceselí." Before he slept, Yohannes's thoughts turned to his uncle. He was devoted to him as would be any young man whose father Yifru had replaced from an early age. His uncle had never married, and not for lack of possibilities. When he had asked him, he had said he had only one heart to break. But that was a long time ago and now he wondered whether Yifru was in love with Ceseli. Or whether he knew he was in love with her. What would happen if he weren't able to get her to safety?

The next morning, Ceseli and Yohannes climbed through the narrow alleys to reach the St. Giorgi Church. Excavated in the form of a Greek cross, it was the last of the rock-hewn churches and was dug twelve meters down into the red rock.

It was difficult descending and Yohannes gave her his hand. Once inside, he walked to the altar to pray while Ceseli looked around her. As her eyes adjusted, she studied the dark ceiling and damp walls. It was quite by accident that she saw the cross high up on the wall. It was a Templar cross. She knew that she must live to tell Yifru that yes, there was a Templar cross in this most famous of the Lalibela churches.

CHAPTER 50

"Marco's dead," Standish announced, walking into Warren Rutherford's office and finding him sitting at his desk. "Yifru just called."

"Oh, my God! I'm so sorry. He was such a fine young man. Ceseli must be devastated. Where is she?" he asked.

"She was going to see Marco on the condition that she'd be back early in the morning. The Italians never fly until at least eight. He didn't want her bombed."

"He hasn't learned anything," Warren said, taking his pipe. "Ceseli doesn't believe in conditions."

"You know Warren, I don't think that's fair."

Warren Rutherford shrugged. "Maybe you're right, I'm just uptight and worried. Damn it, Forsythe, I never should have permitted this."

"A runner came to tell the emperor that all the Red Cross hospitals had been bombed. Direct targets. That's how he knows Marco is dead."

"Repeat that! The Red Cross hospital units were all bombed? That's against the Geneva Convention. I'm sure the Italians know that."

"I can't imagine them bombing without orders."

"No. You're right, of course."

"Where is Yifru?"

"With the emperor."

"Even I know that!" Rutherford snapped. "I knew this was a lousy idea. I was afraid it might end like this!" He filled his pipe, lit it, and then turned back to Standish.

"Did he say where?"

"He's retreating with the emperor, but he wouldn't say where he was. He thinks the Italians are intercepting their messages."

"Which is probably true."

"It has to be somewhere near Maytchaw. That's where they fought the other day. His army was badly defeated."

"How far north is that?"

"Above Dessie. But I'm not sure how far above. Ceseli is alive. Yifru has sent her with his nephew, Yohannes, to Dessie. He said it might take them awhile to get there because they're only traveling at night. He wants me to meet her there."

"Will you go to Dessie?"

"Yes, of course, but we'll wait two days. I'm taking Daniele."

"Of course." Rutherford walked over to Standish. He put his arms on both his shoulders. "Please take care of yourself, my boy. Enough with the dead."

"Thank you, Warren. And I will bring her back."

"I know you will, Standish. Good luck."

CHAPTER 51

"CESELI, CAN YOU HEAR me?" Standish asked, kneeling next to the inert form on the goatskin rugs. "Ceseli?"

The form moved and the burnoose lowered. She nodded her head. "Standish?" She took his hand and smiled. "How did you find me?"

"Yifru called to say you and Yohannes were going to Dessie and that I should come up and then bring you back to Addis. Daniele and I drove up and then we looked for Habtu. Can we leave tomorrow? Warren is anxious that we get back. The Italians are here now, but they won't hurt us. The emperor is no longer coming."

"You heard about Marco?"

"Let's talk about that when you feel better. Try to rest now."

As he left the cave, Standish thought about the emperor who was now in danger of losing his life, as well as his empire. As important as it was for Badoglio to destroy the Ethiopian army, he now faced another equally important task: the capture of Haile Sellassie. If he failed, and the emperor could succeed in his flight south to Addis Ababa, he could escape the Italians and reach the safety of some hospitable country where he could tell his side of the story. He might be an embarrassment and a nuisance to Italy for many years to come.

Yohannes was waiting for him just outside the cave. The two shook hands.

"Will you come with us to Addis, Yohannes? The car has diplomatic immunity."

"If it won't be a problem."

"I assure you it won't," Standish said. "And thank you for all you've done."

"Then I gladly accept," Yohannes said, shaking his hand.

They noticed the young boy standing behind Yohannes. "It's Habtu," Standish said. "Do you want to talk with Ceseli?" he asked, in his faltering Amharic.

The boy nodded and Yohannes took his hand. "Come then."

Yohannes and Habtu walked to Ceseli. "I've a very good friend who wants to say goodbye."

Ceseli straightened up. "Of course. Habtu, you must thank your mother for her kindness. And I need to thank you for all your help," she said, reaching into her satchel. "I'd like you to have this," she said as she fished out her compact. "Now you can see yourself as you grow, and remember me." The young boy's eyes gleamed with appreciation. "And the next time we see each other, you'll be a young man like Yohannes."

That's going to take a very long time, Yohannes thought.

CHAPTER 52

It was late in the afternoon of the second day when Standish and his precious party finally reached Addis. Rutherford threw his arms around Ceseli and held her to him. "You're safe now."

"I know," she said, not making any movement just standing there and letting him hold her.

"Everything is going to be okay. You must be starving. We'll eat in a little while," he said. "I'll have Hilina bring you some hot water."

"That would be wonderful," she smiled.

Five minutes later, Ceseli opened the door to the tukul. Standish stood by her as an emotional support. "I don't think you'll find any change," he said.

"Thanks." She looked at him over her shoulder and smiled wanly. *If you only knew*, she thought tiredly.

There was still plenty of light inside the tukul so that she didn't need a candle. On her little table was a stack of letters. Sotzy. Oh dear, thank god for Sotzy. She took the one highest up on the pile and opened it. It was postmarked March 31, from New York. Maytchaw she thought.

Ceseli Dearest,

I know letter writing has never been your forte, but after almost four months of hearing nothing I would like to know whether you still abode in this heaven on earth or have flown off to a more ethereal habitat. I have heard from Warren though, so I know you are still alive.

I liked your description of your young doctor. I would have no problems with his being Italian. As to being a Fascist, that's a mute question because everyone in Italy is one. I hope he doesn't believe in Mussolini, but the very fact that he has volunteered with the Ethiopian Red Cross is clear indication that he does not.

I agree that humor is one of the most important parts of a good relationship. Looking like an angel doesn't hurt either. I think it might be great fun to be one of his patients. I love Florence. I stayed there with my mother when I was about five. I'm sure he will find the cure for malaria. Please give him my best.

Please contact me immediately. Consider yourself kissed.

Your loving grandmother,

Sotzy

P.S. All the bills in New York and Geneva have been paid. Don't worry about a thing.

Ceseli read and then reread the letter. She needed to answer immediately by telegram. The tapping on her door startled her. "It's me, Miss Larson. Hilina, with your hot water. Can I come in?"

"Of course, Hilina, and thank you," she said, opening the door.

Hilina put down the pail. "Thank you, Miss Larson. Thank you for all you did for my country. And I'm very hurt by Mr. Marco's death."

"Thank you," Ceseli said, hugging her as the tears rushed down her cheeks. "Thank you."

After Hilina left, Ceseli poured the water into the tub and got in and pampered herself with a long, leisurely bath. She needed to write Sotzy and tell her about Marco. But it didn't have to be tonight. Tonight she was too exhausted. It would be all she could do to get through dinner.

CHAPTER 53

"Convey my greetings to your President, and tell him that the fate of my country may serve as a warning that words are of no avail against a determined aggressor who will tear up any peace agreements when they no longer serve his purpose," Haile Sellassie said, holding out his hand to Rutherford.

It was the end of April, and the emperor had mercifully escaped the Italians and returned to Addis. They were shocked by his appearance. His face was haunted, his eyes deep and brooding.

Later that afternoon the emperor issued a short statement to the press: "Ethiopia is not defeated," he said. "It will carry on its fight to the last man. But Addis Ababa will continue to be an open city."

The foreigners were thankful that there would be no last stand in the city. They were less worried about the number of deaths that might cause, than that their property might be destroyed.

In the evening, Haile Sellassie summoned his councilors to his throne room. They were the country's most powerful and influential aristocrats. Conversation was subdued. Dutifully, they knelt and kissed his feet. His chartreuse uniformed servants passed silver trays with small glasses of white vermouth. He told them about his plans. He planned to move the seat of government into the western mountains, perhaps to Gore. A majority of them seemed interested.

Ras Kassa, the emperor's respected and loyal second cousin, the second most powerful voice in the empire, a Christian pacifist who had survived the battle at Maytchaw, was sick of the war and was adamantly against the plan from the beginning. He spoke passionately. "You must go to Europe. To Geneva. You must appeal to the League for help from those great nations that promised help under the Covenant of the League. These nations, despite what they have done so far, are our only hope for liberation."

After the long meeting ended, Haile Sellassie, by now tired and depressed, rode up to the Little Ghibbi, where, for the first time in many months, he was to see his wife.

A deeply religious woman, Empress Menen had surrounded herself with attentive clergymen, who held a strong influence over her. Among these was the Wooha-Boha, a Rasputin-type pagan priest. His dirty clothes hanging in rags, his crazed face and scrawny neck decorated with amulets and lion-claws, splinters of dried bones; the Wooha-Boha was to decide the fate of the empire. He had already conquered the ear of the Coptic Priests and through them the empress. Empress Menen agreed with these clergymen that the war was over: Ethiopia was defeated.

Plans had already been made for the empress and their children to leave on the railroad on Saturday for Djibouti where the British ship, *Enterprise,* was waiting to take them to safety. The empress argued vehemently that he should accompany them. She pleaded with him that his days might be better spent in a life of prayer in the Holy City of Jerusalem, rather than the mountains of Gore or the corridors of Geneva.

The next morning, May 1, 1936, Yifru entered the emperor's study holding a single sheet of paper. The emperor read it, then looked up. His eyes were hollow and tired.

"The Italians are only one hundred miles from here. Your majesty is in great danger."

Haile Sellassie sighed heavily. "Have the great drums of Menilek placed on the hillside in front of the Grand Ghibbi. I will address my people at noon."

The green, yellow, red Ethiopian flags with the great lion's mane in the middle were raised for the last time. Menilek's war drum sounded for an hour and a half. All of Addis heard it.

Yifru stood attentively behind him as the emperor faced his people. He was like a sundial measuring the feelings of his people. When the crowd grew quiet, the emperor decisively rejected the advice of his council. He issued an appeal for a last effort to keep the Italians from entering Addis Ababa. He asked every able-bodied man to take up whatever arms he possessed, supply themselves with enough food for five days, and march the next morning against the invader.

"We shall go!" they cried out. But they did not. Of all the men and the young military cadets ordered north, only a handful went. Yifru knew that the emperor was vacillating: part of him wanted to escape, to leave, to flee. He did realize that his only chance lay in convincing other League members to come to his aid. He must go to Geneva to plead his own cause. The fate of his people, his empire, depended on it.

Overhead they heard the engine of an Italian plane. Haile Sellassie knew there were no alternatives, and no more time. Alone the emperor walked out into his garden and went to see his Arab horses. Very few of them had returned from Dessie. They were thin, their bones protruding. He also visited his lions, petting them one last time.

CHAPTER 54

She knocked before opening the door. "Warren, can I talk with you?"

"Of course, my dear, come in," he said as he knocked the ash from his pipe into a small green ceramic bowl.

She looked around the room where she had spent so much time. "Warren, I'd like to go to Djibouti on the imperial train tomorrow."

"That's an excellent idea. I'll send Standish to arrange it."

"Warren, if you don't mind, I'd like to do this myself."

Warren studied the determined look in her eyes before nodding. "Of course, my dear. I'll give you the money to get to Geneva and what we call a *laissez-passer*. It testifies that you are part of my family and that you are not subject to searches."

"Will that mean I can go to Italy through Naples? I'd like to find out if I can still take my fellowship from the American Academy."

"I can't see any problems with that."

"And you, Warren?"

"My orders are to close down the mission, ship out papers we might need, burn the rest. Then I will go to Washington, and Standish to Geneva. At the end of the month."

"Warren, I'd like to ask you something. I've sat here in front of that painting," and she pointed to the one with the purple mountains, "I know your paintings have a theme. What is this one?"

"If you excuse my tone deafness, I'll sing it.

'O beautiful for spacious skies,

For amber waves of grain,

For purple mountain majesties

Above the fruited plain!'

Ceseli joined him in an equally tone deaf, but loud refrain.

America! America!

"Would you like it? I'm flattered. Take it as a birthday present."

"I'd love it. Thank you. But for me, these are the purple mountains of Ethiopia."

"I'm pleased you like it. Now go see Yifru."

That evening, Ceseli walked up the familiar staircase. Everything was in flux. There were no pet lions on the landing, nor any attentive barefoot guards. All day long the packing of important documents and personal belongings continued. Now instead of moving out of the city westward, the trucks carried their cargo to the railway station. Ceseli knocked softy on Yifru's door. Even here the packing continued.

"Ah, Ceseli," he said as she peeked inside.

"I've come to pack my papers and photos."

"Of course."

"I wish there were something I could do, or say. What about Yohannes?"

"He will go with the freedom fighters to Gore. He's leaving now."

"Yifru. I've come to ask you a favor," Ceseli said, awkwardly. "I would like to go to Djibouti on the imperial train. I don't need any special treatment. All my papers are in order. From Djibouti, I can go to Europe."

"The train may be bombed," Yifru said. "I can't guarantee your safety."

"Warren doesn't believe that Mussolini will bomb the train. He has too much to lose. And it doesn't matter where the emperor is as long as he's not in Ethiopia."

"Does he know you want to do this?"

"Warren? Yes. He thinks it's a good idea. There's nothing more I can do from here."

"How are you doing, Ceseli?"

"As well as can be expected I guess. I'm keeping busy. I feel just like I did when Daddy died. But life went on."

"Warren and Standish are staying?

"Yes. They have orders to close the mission. Warren will go to Washington. Standish to Geneva. You will tell me where you are?"

"We will go to Jerusalem. Their majesties want to pray at our church there. Then we go to London. We've been offered asylum. And of course, Geneva."

"I will catch up with you." Ceseli hugged him and then turned, closed the door, and left the little Ghibbi.

CHAPTER 55

Ceseli began packing the few things she would carry with her. The first thing was Zeri's music. He had told her to guard these pages with her life, and she would. She would catch up with him in Rome.

She picked up Marco's worn leather bible and opened it briefly. She planned to deliver it personally to his father in Florence as she traveled from Rome to Geneva. She thought of whether she should meet his family and decided that yes, it would be hurtful and difficult but it was a small thing in comparison to saving her life. Her own bible held no surprises as she tucked it into her satchel next to the cameras. The Afar Girl. She looked at the photo again now. The edges were frayed, but the eyes of the girl were haunting.

She took her photos of the war. She must succeed in getting them to Geneva without risking going through any customs point in Italy. Even with the laissez-passer, she was worried. She thought of her options and then went to find Daniele.

"How good are you at carpentry?"

"Is something broken?"

"No. I was hoping you could make a second bottom for my trunk."

"I'm pretty sure I can do that, Miss Larson."

And he had. The false bottom was perfectly concealed and now held her photographs. Now she had no doubt she could get these photos to whomever she could get to help. Later, she would vindicate Marco's death. She would one day prove to all those who believed in decency that the Italians had used mustard gas. Her precious photos must be protected as much as Zeri's music.

She looked around the small tukul then she sat down on the bed next to the candleholder. She rubbed her eyes trying to eliminate the thoughts that kept pushing themselves forward. So much energy had been used to get her to Axum and so much to get her back. Marco crept into her thoughts, and Yifru and Yohannes. The dreadful waste of the war: the smell of bodies, the burning of houses, and the breakdown of every social structure. She thought of total destruction and of its physical attributes: the arson, pillage, putrefaction that were all part of it. And then she thought of Habtu. What would become of the future generations of Ethiopians? What would become of him? She took her pen and wrote to Sotzy.

Dear Sotzy,

I know you have heard from Warren that I'm alive and well. Well, not as well as I might be, but dealing. I think Warren has also told you about Marco and the circumstances leading to his death.

Ceseli paused. Warren's telegrams were protected by diplomatic immunity, her letters were not and though she wanted to tell her grandmother about the Red Cross bombings, she didn't want to play her hand just yet. She also didn't want to jeopardize her fellowship at the American Academy in Rome.

I'm leaving tomorrow for Djibouti and from there I will catch a ship for Naples. Then to Geneva. I'll write you from there.

Thank you for paying the bills there. I'll repay you for that.

All love,

The light knocking on the door of her tukul surprised her. She walked over to the door and slowly opened it.

"Ceselí."

"Yohannes. What a pleasant surprise," she said, kissing him three times on the other cheek in the French style of greeting.

"Mr. Standish said you were here. I wanted to say goodbye. My uncle says you are leaving with him on the train."

"I need to go. I have work to do and a life to live. What about you, Yohannes? Where will you go?"

"I'm going with the Freedom Fighters to the mountains. We will wait for the Emperor to return."

That might take a lifetime, Ceseli thought, but would certainly not voice her misgivings.

"Ceselí, I must go, *à bientôt*," he said, again kissing her three times.

"*Bon chance*, Yohannes, and thank you again for all you did." She closed the door when he left. What would become of Yohannes, she wondered. She thought about the war. Italy had lost only three thousand men, most of them Eritrean Askaris. Ethiopia was broken. She had lost two hundred seventy-five thousand lives. Those are people, not numbers. They were human beings. People killed for utterly no reason. She closed her satchel and blew out the candle. If Yifru could smuggle German guns in piano crates, she could smuggle her photos in her Louis Vuitton trunk. She was ready. She would do it.

CHAPTER 56

By 2 A.M. ON that May 2, 1936, Haile Sellassie, bowing finally to the pressure of his wife, his chiefs, and his religious advisers, was ready to leave his home and his empire. As he strolled through his palace office, the cuckoo clock struck. He heard his pet parrot answer, "The emperor, Haile Sellassie!" He wondered if he would ever hear his title again.

He walked to the gilded cage, opened it and took out the bird. Carrying it carefully, he opened the window and then helped it lift into flight. Out the window, following the flight of the bird, he looked for the last time at the vast expanse of his mud and wattle capital, where even at this hour, tiny fires like fireflies illuminated the sides of the steep valley. Then he shut and locked the window and walked out of his still unfinished Ghibbi Palace.

It was hauntingly empty inside the railroad station, like a theatre before the audience arrives. Several extra wagons had been added to the train to haul the documents and Austrian silver Maria Teresa *Thalers* the emperor would need in exile. A few passenger cars had been added for those who would share exile with him.

Ceseli and Standish stood over to the side waiting. Ceseli felt like crying, but she kept back the tears. "I know it's time for me to go, it's just . . ." she paused. "I don't know. This has become my home. I would like to stay on and help," she said, looking up at him.

"It's time to go. It's different for us. We need to close down the mission. There will no longer be a Minister to Ethiopia. Ethiopia is now Italian."

And then the play began. The imperial party entered the station and walked to the train that would change their lives. The emperor, Empress Menen, who was wearing a heavy mourning veil, and their six children climbed into their special railroad car with its white leather cushions. The high court dignitaries, who intended to share their exile, climbed aboard.

"We are ready, Ceseli," Yifru said. "If you want to come, it has to be now."

She nodded and stooped down to pick up her satchel containing her precious cargo and some food. The trunk was already loaded.

At 4:20 a.m., the imperial train, slowly, sadly, without any whistles, pulled out of the station in the direction of Djibouti. The emperor was not deserting his country, although many had deserted him.

It was already late in the morning of May 4, 1936, when the train reached the safety of Djibouti. Ceseli hung out the window as the train pulled up along the same track where she had first seen Marco. She sat remembering the renaissance angel running up to the train, and into her life. It seemed like a century ago. Nervously, she fondled the thin gold cross Marco had given her and felt it next to her father's dog tag. It had protected her.

The French soldiers, in dress uniforms, fired a royal salute as the emperor stepped down from the train followed by his family. Ceseli cried at the sight of Haile Sellassie, King of Kings, Conquering Lion of Judah. He was bareheaded and looked travel-stained, weary, haggard and dejected. The rows of ribbons seemed to decorate a cave not a chest.

The French Governor General escorted the royal family to his executive mansion for an official luncheon. Meanwhile, Yifru took Ceseli to the American consulate.

"Thank you for everything," she said, choking with emotion.

"I am very sorry about Marco. He was a fine young man. But I've said that."

"Thank you, Yifru. That's very kind of you."

"You shouldn't have any trouble now. The Americans will help you get home."

"Yes, I'm sure they will," she said, thinking that if I only she knew where that was. "And I'm grateful. But first I have an appointment in Geneva."

"Then we shall see each other in Geneva," he said, taking her hand. "The emperor asked me to give you these," he said, taking a small pouch from his pocket. "He always meant to pay you."

"The coins," she said, recognizing the pouch.

"He is sure they will be safer with you, and perhaps you can do the necessary research on them," he said, smiling at her. "These will keep you tied to Ethiopia."

Ceseli smiled up at him, hardly able to breathe.

"There's a French ship leaving this evening. I have asked that you be favored and your trunk will be loaded shortly. It stops in Naples, if you don't mind going to Italy. Otherwise you can get off in Marseilles and from there you can catch a train to Geneva."

"Thank you, Yifru, you don't know how much that means to me. But I feel confident I can go to Rome and then Geneva." He held her hands and bent down to kiss her. He held her to him.

"You have to have faith in Ethiopia, Ceseli. It might not be tomorrow. But in the end, this is my country, my whole life, and I will come back."

"I hope that happens." Ceseli smiled up at him. "Yifru," she began. "There's something important I have to tell you," she smiled, realizing how trivial this all would sound. "There's a Templar cross at Lalibela."

He held her to him hard cradling her head under his chin. "Perhaps one day you'll show me," he said, still holding her.

"I'd like that," she said, leaning back from him and turning her head so he could not see the tears forming in her eyes.

"And I will keep my promise about the Ark. I'm a good promiser, remember that. I will come back."

Ceseli smiled. "If that happens, I'll come as well." He kissed her gently on the forehead. Yifru, she realized, was everything his name implied. '*Let them be afraid of him*'. Yet she had not been afraid of him. She had come to love and admire him. And she would miss him, dreadfully.

At 4:15 in the afternoon of May 4th, Haile Sellassie boarded the British cruiser *Enterprise* sent to carry him to safety rather than face the last humiliation of capture by his conquerors. They would go to the British mandate territory of Palestine and to Jerusalem, where they would pray.

As the ship left the harbor, the French gave a farewell cannon volley and an aircraft flew by. The cruiser was escorted at a discreet distance by five British torpedo boats.

Two days after his arrival in Jerusalem, the emperor had Yifru send a cable to the League of Nations: "We have decided to bring to an end the most unequal, most unjust, most barbarous war of our age, and have chosen to take the road to exile in order that our people shall not be exterminated, and to consecrate ourselves wholly and in peace to the preservation of our empire's independence. We now demand that the League of Nations should continue its efforts to secure respect for the Covenant, and that it should decide not to recognize territorial extensions, or the exercise of an assumed sovereignty resulting from an illegal recourse to armed force and from numerous other violations of international agreements."

The hope of gaining the sympathy and support of the world by appearing in person at the rostrum of the League of Nations was all the Negus now had.

CHAPTER 57

ALL AFTERNOON AND EVENING, in the torrential rain, the tanks, trucks, and armored cars rolled forward. Some three thousand vehicles were strung out along the only road to the city of the King of Kings. Finally, on the afternoon of May 5, 1936, seven months and two days after the start of the war, the "March of the Iron Will" reached its destination.

General Pietro Badoglio, at the head of his victorious columns, made a spectacular entrance into the capital. The pouring rain did nothing to dampen spirits. With him rode the Italian journalists. Bruno looked out at the Ethiopian people lining the roadway. Some were waving white flags, some held up their arms in the Fascist salute.

Behind him were the Eritrean Askaris: tall, handsome, and fast running, wearing their red fezzes and waving curved swords. Yet, Bruno knew that for nationalistic reasons, they would not be the first to enter the city. That glory was reserved for the white Italian troops: tired, dirty and hungry, but undaunted by this test of endurance under the tropical sun.

At 5:45 that afternoon, while several Italian R.O.-37 pursuit planes flew in an aerobatic display, the red, white and green tricolor flag was raised above the Italian Embassy. There were three cheers for the King and three for Caesar. Ethiopia was finally Italian.

Bruno sat down on the nearby stump of a Eucalyptus tree and began scribbling in his notebook. He didn't want to miss this historic moment. He watched attentively as Badoglio turned to Air Marshal Magliocco, whose face was wet with rain or tears. Suddenly, the two older soldiers embraced, kissing each other Italian style on both cheeks.

"We've done it! We've won!"

The Emperor did not see his beloved city burning. In the absence of authority, pillaging, rioting, and violence ruled for three and a half days after his departure. Even ex-soldiers joined in the destruction to vent their frustration over a war that could never have been won. Most of the foreigners, fearing the carnage, had taken refuge at the British compound that was well protected by Indian Sikh troops.

Warren Rutherford and Standish Forsythe stayed put for those three days. The U.S. Legation, unlike most of the others, was not sieged. Daniele had warned his countrymen that he would stand for no such defacement.

They had not gone to see the Italian forces enter the city, but a few days later, Standish Forsythe was surprised by a visitor. Daniele showed him in. "Zeri."

"Forsythe. I'm glad to see you again."

"I heard it was a spectacular occasion. Sorry we didn't put it on our agenda."

"You weren't missed. Badoglio was looking for divine guidance," he smiled, taking the seat in front of Standish.

"You're well, I see."

"Oh yes. And ready to start home."

"You're leaving then?"

"With Badoglio. He has asked to be relieved. He wants to enjoy his fame in his beloved motherland. I can't blame him, although it will be hard on the Ethiopians. I brought you something you might like to see. More propaganda." Zeri lit his cigar. "You know, Forsythe, I really can't tell you how much I love propaganda. It's so floral. Beautiful adjectives. The Fascist ones that are fashionable today. It may change tomorrow, mind you, but today! The soldiers are always brave, the speeches of their leaders are vibrant and Italy, of course, is great and powerful and noble. Adjective diplomacy."

"You have to follow those directives?"

"Oh, no. You can do whatever you want. The piece just won't get published." Bruno seemed as if he were about to laugh, but he caught himself. "Sorry. It's not funny."

Standish looked at him carefully. *It's not as funny as he's making out*, he thought, *perhaps that's the weight of the war*. "Just as long as you don't get too much of it," Standish added.

"Oh, you can never get too much of it. That's why it's propaganda. This one, however, has been more of a sporting event than a page of military history." Zeri smiled as he fished something out of his pocket. "Here, you should see this."

"What is it?"

"Mussolini's latest orders to Badoglio. His formula for restoring law and order to the ravished capital."

"Can I read it?"

"Of course. That's why I brought it."

"When Addis Ababa is occupied," Il Duce had written, "Your Excellency will give orders that all those in the city, or its surroundings, who are caught with arms in hand will be summarily shot. All of the so-called Young Ethiopians, cruel and pretentious barbarians, and the moral authors of the sacking of the city be shot summarily."

Standish paused thinking of Yohannes and glad that he was out of the city. He and most of the other Young Ethiopians were already at Bulga with the Freedom Fighters.

"Anyone who participated in violence, sacking, or fires, be shot; all those who within twenty-four hours have not given up their arms and munitions, be summarily shot. I await word which will confirm that these orders will be, as always, carried out."

Standish looked at Bruno as he put down the paper. "This is not going to bring them garlands of roses."

"No. It's not meant to. One wonders how he kept silent so long," Zeri smiled. "Can you imagine what pre-verbal Mussolini must have been like?"

"Pre-verbal? I don't understand."

"He never talked for the first three years of his life."

"You're sure of that?"

"Absolutely."

"He has certainly made up for it."

"And Miss Larson?" Zeri asked, as he puffed on his cigar.

"She's gone back."

"I'm glad she's out of here. Has she gone home?"

"She is going to Geneva. We got a telegram from Rome. That's all I know."

"If you see her, please give her my best."

"I will, and thank you for saving her life."

"Saving her life? Please, not so dramatic. That sounds like more propaganda. Helped her in a minute of need."

"As you want. Modesty does not become you, Zeri."

"Oh really? Well, until the next time. Take care of yourself, Forsythe."

CHAPTER 58

The night was warm for May. Rome's huge scenographic Piazza Venezia was already splitting at its seams. Jubilant crowds overflowed with great excitement into the Via dei Fori Imperiali and surged into other neighboring streets. More people climbed over the huge white marble monument to Victor Emmanuel II, while the fascist youth groups crowded its marble steps and perched on balconies and rooftops. It was 10 p.m. on May 9, 1936.

Rome was decked out like a beautiful woman going to a masquerade ball. The multicolored lights harmonized with the red, white, and green flags flying from all the flagpoles. The squares and ancient monuments were as light as day. The huge umbrella pines stood as sentinels above the lighted ruins of the ancient Roman Forum. Even the trickling water of the fountains seemed transformed into cascades of pure crystal.

All over the city, sirens and church bells vied with the braying of horns and rejoicing voices. A human avalanche of more than four hundred thousand people, massed in murmuring suspense as a tidal wave of pink faces, looked up to the balcony.

A militiaman, as motionless as a statue, raised his long trumpet and sounded three loud blasts. In the square, the noise ended. Caesar was ready. A spotlight from across the square trapped him like a poacher would a dear. Silver trumpets burst forth and an ear-splitting roar, a twenty-one gun salute, erupted on the waiting swell of people.

Mussolini placed his square hands on the marble balustrade, his massive face was expressionless as he leaned forward in the harsh glare of the floodlights. Then with the help of the amplifiers, he exhorted them, his voice rich and vibrant.

"Officers! Noncommissioned officers! Soldiers of all the armed forces of the state in Africa and Italy! Blackshirts of the Revolution! Italians in the Fatherland and in the world! Listen!

"With the decisions that in a few moments you will learn a great event is accomplished. Today, May 9, of the fourteenth year of the Fascist era, the fate of Ethiopia is sealed.

"All the knots were cut by our shining sword, and the African victory stands in the history of our Fatherland, whole and pure, as the fallen legionnaires and those who survived dreamed it and wanted it.

"At last Italy has her empire! A Fascist empire, because it bears the indestructible signs of the will and might of the Roman lector. Because this is the goal toward which for fourteen years the disciplined energies of the young and lusty Italians were driven.

"An empire at peace, because Italy wants peace for herself, and for everyone, and resorts to war only when compelled by the imperious, ineluctable necessities of life. A civilizing empire, humanitarian toward all the peoples of Ethiopia.

"This is in the tradition of Rome, who, after winning, allowed the defeated people to share her destiny.

"Italians, here is the law that closes one period of our history and opens another, like an immense passageway to all future possibilities. The territories and the peoples that belonged to the Ethiopian Empire are placed under the full and whole sovereignty of the Kingdom of Italy. The title of Emperor of Ethiopia is assumed by the King of Italy, for himself and his successors.

"Officers! Noncommissioned officers! Soldiers of all the armed forces of the state in Africa, and Italy! Blackshirts! Italians!

"The Italian people have created the empire with its blood. It will fecundate it with its work and defend it against anyone with its arms.

"Legionnaires! In this supreme certitude raise high your insignia, your weapons, and your hearts to salute, after fifteen centuries, the reappearance of the empire on the fated hills of Rome. Will you be worthy of it?"

Below the pink sea of moving faces burst forth in one resounding "Si! Si! Si!"

"Your cry is a sacred oath that binds you before God and men, for life and death!"

As soon as Mussolini finished speaking, the crowd broke out in an unparalleled ovation. Ten times the cheering masses clamored for his return while the fascist youths on the war memorial burst into the newly composed "*Hymn to the Empire.*" The Governor of Rome, Prince Pietro Colonna, breasted the human mass to reach the raised traffic rostrum in the Piazza Venezia and with the policeman's white baton, directed the screaming mass of people. The pink waves were totally with him. In the loud rejoicing, only one word could be distinguished: "Duce! Duce! Duce!"

It was Mussolini's crowning moment.

CHAPTER 59

It was now mid-May and Ceseli was making her way to Geneva. The trip from Djibouti had been easy. The train ride from Naples to Rome was equally uneventful.

It seemed important to her to maintain some continuity with her previous plans. So in Rome, she climbed up to the Janiculum Hill to find the American Academy.

At Penn she had learned that the academy grew out of the inspiration of several American architects, painters and sculptures who had been asked to plan the fine arts exhibition of the 1893 World Columbian Exposition. These farsighted men wanted an American school in Europe where American artists and scholars could study and further their skills. Ceseli's father had been a handsome contributor to the academy. Ceseli had applied for, and won, the coveted Rome Prize that would give her a place to live and a stipend for her to conduct her research. Ceseli's father had been keen on this solution because she would be close enough to Geneva that they could visit often.

Now with the certainty that she could begin her studies in September, she was free to go to Geneva. She wanted to get there in time to hear the Emperor address the League of Nations.

She had thought about finding Bruno Zeri in Rome in the ghetto just at the foot of the Janiculum Hill where the American Academy was, but she knew it was premature. She had made him a promise that she meant to keep. But that would have to wait until her return to the Academy in the fall. *Would he be back from Ethiopia*, she wondered.

On her trip from Rome to Florence, she was very nervous. She wondered if she should be doing this at all: going to see Marco's family, rather than just sending his book by mail. She decided that it was something she should do personally.

Out of the fast moving train window, she saw the Tuscan hills stretched out on each side of the train, with their symmetrical neat rows of vineyards as far as she could see. *This is such fertile land*, she thought, comparing it with the Ethiopian high plateau. The land the Italians were by now beginning to farm. The land that Mussolini seized. Ceseli decided not to think any more of the war. It was over. Italy had won.

The train pulled into Florence's St. Maria Novella train station. As she pulled her satchel down off the rack, she noticed that many of the passengers were unloading suitcases through the train's open windows. *So it isn't only Marco who likes windows better than doors,* she thought. She left her trunk in the baggage deposit at the station and looked around her.

"*His office is right next to the church.*"

She walked out of the crowded railroad station and looked across the square. The façade of the *basilica* of the fourteenth century Santa Maria Novella Church, with its inlaid black and white marble squares was imposing. She had the fleeting thought that she had seen it before, perhaps on her visit here with her father. There was a small building on the left of the church.

She dodged the oncoming bicycles and crossed the square. Inside, she found immediately the buzzer for Dr. Antonio Antinori. She rang the bell and waited for the buzzer. After it came, she shoved the heavy door open and walked up the two flights to his office.

"*Avanti, la porta é aperto.*"

Ceseli opened the door, as instructed, and walked inside. To her left was a tall mahogany bookcase full of leather bound books. There was a dazzling print by contemporary painter Giorgio Di Chirico on the opposite wall, and a soft red and blue Persian carpet. There was nobody in the waiting room.

An older lady, dressed in a black dress and black woolen shawl despite the warmth of the evening nodded pleasantly to her.

"You have an appointment, signorina?"

"No, but I was hoping I could see Dr. Antinori." *But pamper me. Should anything happen. Send the book to my father in Florence.* "I have brought him something from his son, Marco."

"Just a moment. Please be seated," the lady said as she opened the door to the left and disappeared. Ceseli put her satchel on the ground and sat down nervously. She wondered what Dr. Antinori would be like. *He's an expert on Renaissance gardens. He knows where every plant and tree come from, and what they can be used for.*

The door opened immediately and Dr. Antonio Antinori came toward her, his hand outstretched in greeting. *He looks remarkably like Marco*, she thought as she stood and took his warm handshake. He was wearing a brown corduroy jacket with a green braided wool tie. His eyes were the same color as Marco's were.

"I'm Ceseli Larson," she began.

"I know who you are, my dear," he interrupted. "I'm so pleased to meet you. I know how much my son cared for you. Please come in."

She followed him into his office, where a large oak refectory table dominated the room and was heavily loaded with books and files. On it was a bronze candlestick lamp that cast deep shadows over the table. Ceseli took the seat in front of him.

"I'm so glad to meet you," he smiled. "But then, I just said that."

"I've brought you this," Ceseli said, taking Marco's brown leather book from her satchel. "I promised him that if anything were to happen to him that I would send it to you. I decided to come in person."

"I'm so glad you did. Marco wrote us about you before he left Addis. Then we had a letter from his hospital unit."

"He told me that Zeri had helped him send that letter. Bruno Zeri is a journalist with *Corriere della Sera*. He knew Marco, and of course liked him. Everybody did."

"Mr. Zeri was here. About a week ago."

Oh, thought Ceseli, *that was nice of him*.

"He told us he had burned his body on a pyre so that it would not be mutilated. My wife was thankful for that. May I call my wife and tell her you're here? She would so like to meet you."

"I don't know," Ceseli began, looking at her watch. It was 5:30. "I was planning on taking that night train to Geneva. My father died last year and I haven't even been there yet."

"Won't you consider staying with us tonight and leaving tomorrow? We would appreciate it so much."

"All right then, if you're sure I won't be a bother."

"It won't be any kind of bother, I assure you."

"Then I'd like that very much."

"If there's any tree you associate with the hills of Tuscany, it's the cypress," the doctor said an hour later as they drove the small FIAT up the winding hillside the eight kilometers to Fiesole. "But they're actually from Persia or Syria. Some say the Etruscan brought them here, but I think it was the Romans."

"You see them in the background of so many Italian paintings," Ceseli ventured, noticing the tall cylindrical trees that stood vigil over the lush land and intermingled with the white and pink oleanders.

"Do you know Florence?" Dr. Antinori asked as he changed gears on the small car.

"I was here with my father when I was twelve. It was for a conference on art."

"In 1923 there was a week-long symposium on Tuscan art and archaeology."

"That may have been it, but I'm not sure."

"It drew experts from around the world."

"My father was an expert on stolen art, particularly archaeology. That's where my interest came from. He and I were going to Ethiopia together, but then he died and I went alone."

"I see. Fiesole is older than Florence, you know," he continued as they drove up into the hills above the city. "It was an Etruscan town. We like it because we have a wonderful view of the city and enough land to grow all our own food. It's more like a small farm."

Ceseli looked at the narrow tightly curving road with its stonewalls on each side. Finally, they turned into a long driveway that led sharply up the hill toward a villa of stone and plaster painted the color of soft ochre.

As Dr. Antinori swung around to park, the heavy oak door opened and his wife came shyly forward. Ceseli wondered what to say, but Mrs. Antinori, who came to her kissing her warmly on both cheeks, quickly dispelled her apprehension. "Thank you for coming. It means so much to me to meet you," she said warmly, standing back to look at Ceseli more closely.

Ceseli liked her immediately as she noticed the warmth in her hazel eyes. She had her Titian red hair pulled back into a chignon setting off the high cheekbones and light skin. She was tall and slender, and very friendly. "I don't want to be a bother . . ." Ceseli began.

"You could never be a bother. Marco wrote that you were a very special young lady. We had a letter from him just before the accident. He hadn't seen you or heard from you in months. But he was determined that he would find you after the war, even if it meant going to New York. He said that he might really like that. Something about eating Chinese food."

Ceseli smiled, remembering their first discussion at the Italian compound. "There was no mail up there in Tigre. If I had known that he was so close that last week, I would have gone to see him earlier," she said, realizing what a feeble excuse it must sound like. "The Emperor was preparing for a final battle, but it kept getting postponed."

"Please, come in, or would you prefer to have some tea in the garden?"

"Whatever is best for you."

"Then first come inside. Paolo and Chiara will want to meet you. She's just finishing her homework and Paolo is most likely kicking his soccer ball near the barn. I'll call him."

She turned, and Ceseli and Dr. Antinori followed her into the large entranceway with its terracotta tiles and startling white walls. They walked through the formal living room to a large kitchen in the rear. The door to the garden was open and she could see the olive trees with their gnarled trunks just on the other side of the bricked garden.

A long-legged shy thirteen-year-old came to her, holding out her hand. Ceseli took it as she studied Marco's sister. She was very slight, with her massive curly red hair held back behind her head, and penetrating blue eyes from among light lashed eyes and freckles.

"I'm very pleased to meet you," Chiara said in English, shyly.

"And I'm pleased to meet you too. You go to the British School?" Ceseli asked, holding her hand. "Your English is so good."

"Yes. Marco went there too, you know."

"Yes. He told me that when we first met on the train to Addis."

"Was it scary being in Ethiopia all alone?" Chiara asked, quietly.

"No, not really. Of course it's very different than being in Florence, but all the people there are very kind, and very gentle. And Marco took care of me. And there was a friend of my fathers who is the American Minister there. I lived in the American compound with tortoises as big as this," she said, holding out her arms to give the young girl an idea of their size.

"Really that big?" Paolo interrupted, smiling. Ceseli noticed the same mischievous eyes. "You're joking aren't you?"

"No, really." Ceseli thought about mentioning the hyenas, but decided not to.

"Marco said he'd invite me when the war was over. He liked it very much." Paolo smiled, and as she looked at him she was surprised at the family resemblance.

"Yes, he did. And the people liked him tremendously," she smiled, keeping the young boy's eyes. "You would have liked it too."

"Perhaps we should have some tea," Mrs. Antinori said, inviting them into the garden.

"That would be lovely, thank you," Ceseli added, following them. Their talk continued through tea, and through a delicious dinner that was preceded by small Tuscan crostini made from olive paste and mashed chicken livers.

"Marco told me you were a wonderful cook," Ceseli said as they finished. "That the key to your success was that all the ingredients were fresh."

"Marco was a wonderful flatterer," his mother smiled. "He was a good cook too."

"Yes, he certainly was."

"Ceseli," Dr. Antinori began gently, "Mr. Zeri told us that Marco died in a bombing raid by our own Air Force against the Red Cross unit where he was serving. Is that true? It seems hard to believe, even of the Fascists."

"But that is exactly what happened. I was there when it happened. Did Bruno Zeri tell you that Marco saved my life?"

"He did."

"Marco was protecting my body with his. He took the bullets I would have taken. Marco said the planes flew over every day. But that morning they must have had different orders. The tent was the direct target. The planes banked and came back. They were making sure nobody survived. After I knew Marco was dead, I ran down the hill and hid in a cave. Even if I had survived because of Marco, I would be dead if I were still on that plateau," she said as tears began to slowly crawl out of her lids. "I'm sorry," she said, wiping them away. "I wouldn't have lived if he hadn't done that."

Ceseli reached to her neck and released the thin gold chain with its medal of St. Mary of the Flowers. She handed it across the table to Mrs. Antinori. "I have brought this to you. He wore it every day. He gave it to me, as a loan, the night before he died."

"We gave it to him for his First Communion," she said, fingering the medal. "It's the patron saint of Florence. Even then he wanted to be a doctor. It was meant to keep him safe," she smiled wistfully. "You must keep it, Ceseli," she said, handing it back across the table. "I'm sure that is what our son would have wanted." Mrs. Antinori kissed it softly and handed the chain back to Ceseli.

"Then I would be honored to have it. I'll wear it next to my father's dog tag. I loved them both very much."

CHAPTER 60

CESELI TURNED THE KEY in the lock and quietly pushed the door open. She knew she was not prepared for the flood of emotions that poured out as she walked into her father's Geneva apartment.

She went to the large French window and pulled open the doors. Outside, the Jura Mountains were green with their white peaks. *It looks like the photo in some calendar of Swiss vacations*, she thought looking out across the lake. Walking out onto the wide balcony, she looked below her at the bustling Quai des Bergue and down the broad avenue to the illuminated Palais des Nations, the headquarters of the League of Nations.

Slowly, she retraced her steps coming back into the living room. All the furniture was clothed in white cotton sheets. She removed them. She took the key and stopped to wind the grandfather clock. Next to the fireplace was the huge brown leather stuffed pig she remembered buying with her father in London. *How many years ago*, she thought. Slowly she walked around the room, touching the mantelpiece, rearranging the small Etruscan statuettes they had bought at Cerveteri in Italy. *There's certainly a lot of dust, a year's dust,* she thought rubbing her hand over the mantel. She must ask Madame Sorell to come and clean.

She dragged her trunk down the hall to her bedroom. She opened the window to get rid of the smell of must. Not being able to settle down, she walked back to the living room to her father's favorite blue leather chair next to the fireplace. A fire was set, but it wasn't cold enough to need it. Next to the chair on a small piecrust table was a copy of Dicken's *Tale of Two Cities,* under it was the *Hounds of the Baskervilles. How ironic*, she thought, briefly remembering the conversation with Bruno Zeri. *I wonder what has happened to him*, she thought, putting her head back against the leather chair and closing her eyes.

A loud ringing of the doorbell drew her back to reality. She went to the door peeping through the little hole. She opened it, flinging it wide. "Standish? How did you find me?"

"Surprisingly easy. How are you?" he said, coming in. Ceseli noticed there was someone else on the stairwell.

"Zeri?"

"Can I come in?" the journalist asked politely, with his unlit Toscani dangling from the side of his mouth.

"Yes. Of course."

The two men followed her into the living room and took seats in front of her.

"Is there something wrong?" she asked, looking from one to the other.

"There is plenty wrong," Zeri said quietly. He was silent for a minute watching the curling smoke rise from his cigar.

"I thought you were in Ethiopia?"

"I was, but when Badoglio returned to Italy I came with him. He was already tired of being the viceroy of Ethiopia. He wanted to relish in his glory in Italy. Anyhow, my assignment was over. The war was over."

"Who replaced him?"

"Graziani? I'm sorry for the Ethiopians. He's a butcher."

Ceseli looked at him quizzically. "You went to see Marco's family. That was very nice of you."

"I felt it was my duty. I liked and respected Marco. I wish there were more like him. I'm afraid there won't be for a very long time. You have my music don't you?"

"You said to guard them with my life."

"Those little ditties document how the Italians used mustard gas and just how much of it, and when."

"You did it. You took sides."

Zeri shrugged. "Did you take pictures all through the war?"

Ceseli hesitated, looking at him more carefully. "Yes."

"Did they come out well?"

"Yes. Of course!"

"May I see them?"

"Could you tell me what this is all about?"

"You'll have to trust me. You don't like that, but you trusted me once."

"You saved my life."

"Several people contributed. Do you still think of me as the enemy?"

Ceseli shook her head.

"That's good, because this time, I'm going to have to trust you," Bruno said, putting his hand into his inner jacket pocket and taking out some more sheets of music.

"Look here," he said, opening one of the pages and handing it to her. "I'm glad I lived to do this. It took twenty-three thousand shells and four hundred tons of high explosives to defeat Mulugeta at Amba Aradam. Some seventy-three tons of high explosives at Lake Ashangi. That doesn't mention the mustard gas. If your photos are as good as they should be, I think we have proof of these atrocities."

"You've documented this?" Ceseli looked at him, finally understanding.

"You were right. It is Zeus or Hera," he smiled, cynically. "But these facts would be useless without your photos."

Ceseli got up and walked into the bedroom returning with several large envelopes. "The first are from Dessie. The first bombing. December 6, 1935. They're all numbered and cataloged," she said, handing the envelope to Bruno.

Standish looked across Zeri's shoulder as he went slowly through the photographs. He put a few aside. Most of them were of horribly disfigured people. In all the months he had been with Badoglio's forces, he had none like these. That was because Ceseli had been on the receiving end of the bombs and poisonous gases.

"Ceseli," Standish interrupted. "How did you bring out all these photos? I know you had a few in your satchel, but there are so many of them."

Ceseli hesitated for a moment. "I had Daniele construct a false bottom for my trunk."

Standish studied her for a moment. "I'm not saying I don't approve that you got them out. But have you heard about diplomatic immunity? You were traveling as if you were Warren's family." He paused, shaking his head. "Thankfully you didn't get caught. It could have been quite an incident."

"I guess that was of such a secondary consequence I didn't give it much thought. My first and foremost thought was to get these photos out. My trunk never left my side."

"Any of civilians?" Zeri asked.

"Plenty," she answered, returning with another larger envelope full of other photos. The obelisk. The boy on the obelisk. The lioness frieze she planned to use for her dissertation. She handed them to Zeri and sat down.

"It will be dangerous for you, won't it?" Standish asked.

"I thrive on danger. But this is a war we can win. It may take a long time, but we can win."

"I'll do anything I can to help you," Ceseli said, vehemently.

The three of them nodded in commitment.

CHAPTER 61

What seemed like half the population of Geneva was gathered around the white marble League of Nations building. It was just before 5 p.m. on June 30, 1936.

In 1771, Marquis Masson de Pezay warned his countrymen not to complain of mountains and rocks. The olive tree would flourish perennially. He expressed his hope that a "society of nations" would assemble within its frontiers. Some one hundred fifty years later his prophesy was realized when the League of Nations chose Geneva for its headquarters. Now, Geneva was to play its most dismal moment in history to date.

Ceseli looked across the wide glimmering waters of Lake Geneva. The emperor's boat-taxi was approaching. The cheering for the tiny monarch reached a crescendo as he stepped off the boat-taxi, carefully dressed in a voluminous black cloak over a white tunic. Standing on tiptoes, Ceseli was just able to see Yifru as he followed Haile Sellassie into the building.

Ceseli fought her way through the crowd and hurried up the staircase to the visitor's gallery. Many of the emperor's in-exile government were already there. Taking her assigned seat, she looked down noticing that by the time the emperor was led into the large general assembly hall, the Eighteenth Plenary Session of the Assembly had already started. Britain's Anthony Eden, the temporary chairman of the League, was making preliminary announcements.

The early minutes of the session were devoted to a long statement from Italy's newly appointed foreign minister, Count Galeazzo Ciano, Mussolini's son-in-law. The letter had been written with the intention of preempting any charges that the Emperor Haile Sellassie might make in his speech.

"May I sit here?" Bruno Zeri asked.

"You're not sitting in the press section?" Ceseli asked as he struggled to get through the narrow aisle.

"I'm here unofficially."

Ceseli noticed now that none of the delegates applauded as the emperor took his seat with the Ethiopian delegation. Yifru took the seat directly in back of the emperor. Next to him sat the Ethiopian delegate, Takla Hawariate. Yifru turned and nodded to Standish sitting in the observer section reserved for the United States.

Both Standish and Yifru knew that Italy, and several other countries, had tried to prevent the emperor from speaking. Britain and France, though no more eager to hear him than any of the other members, had nevertheless pointed out that it would be even worse to try to silence him. The emperor's request to speak had therefore been accepted, and the embarrassed League delegates would now have to listen to what he said.

The President of the Assembly, van Zeeland, of Belgium, turned to the day's important, if unpleasant, business. Tacitly acknowledging Italy's claim that its own King, Victor Emmanuel III, was now Emperor of Ethiopia, van Zeeland introduced Haile Sellassie as "His Majesty, the Negus, Haile Sellassie, first delegate of Ethiopia."

Haile Sellassie walked to the rostrum. As he unfolded the pages of his address, there was no pink silk veil to protect him from the blaring spotlights.

Suddenly a great jeering racket arose from the Italian section of the press gallery. About a dozen correspondents leaped to their feet, shouting and shrieking in the direction of the rostrum. They shook their fists and hissed. Ceseli looked at the names of the important Italian newspapers. Given the notorious obedience of Italian newsmen to Mussolini, it seemed unlikely that they would have staged such a scene without his authorization.

Several of the other journalists tried to shut them up, but the bedlam continued. The guards, it seemed to Ceseli, were very slow to take control. There weren't any in the press gallery, although there were many in the spectators' gallery where the danger of a demonstration must have seemed greater. Standish looked up and their eyes met.

After what seemed forever, she could see the guards grabbing the men and hustling them out. Ceseli looked at Zeri who sat unperturbed by her side. "*Ingra subucala induti vos novi rerum ordinis auctores*," he said under his breath. "The Blackshirts of the Revolution," he smiled at her. "Latin. He gets all his speeches translated into Latin. Part of the Julius Caesar act," he said, shrugging his shoulders.

Ceseli smiled at this and looked back to the rostrum where the emperor, who had waited impassively for the noise to stop, now began to speak in Amharic. Ceseli took her earphones and moved the knob on her chair to the English language channel. The voice she recognized immediately was Yifru's. She listened as he translated his emperor's speech.

"I, Haile Sellassie the First, Emperor of Ethiopia, am here today to claim that justice that is due to my people, and the assistance promised to it eight months ago by fifty-two nations who asserted that an act of aggression had been committed in violation of international treaties.

"There is perhaps no precedent for a head of state himself speaking in this assembly. But there is also certainly no precedent for a people being the victim of such wrongs and being threatened with abandonment to its aggressor. It is to defend a people struggling for their age-old independence that the head of the Ethiopian empire has come to Geneva to fulfill this supreme duty, after having himself fought at the head of his armies.

"I pray Almighty God that He may spare nations the terrible sufferings that have just been inflicted on my people, and of which the chiefs, who have accompanied me here, have been the horrified witnesses.

"It is my duty to inform the governments assembled in Geneva, responsible as they are for the lives of millions of men, women, and children, of the deadly peril which threatens them, by describing to them the fate which has been suffered by Ethiopia.

"It is not only upon warriors that the Italian government has made war. It has, above all, attacked populations far removed from hostilities in order to terrorize and exterminate them."

Ceseli's thoughts wandered to that docile peaceful people she knew from Addis and had met on her trip to Axum. She could feel tears welling up for the innocent children she had played with in the streets of Dessie. In her pocket, she felt the gold Ethiopian coin that was her lucky piece. She forced herself to return to the emperor's words.

"At the outset, toward the end of 1935, Italian aircraft hurled bombs of tear gas upon my armies. They had but slight effect. The soldiers learned to scatter, waiting until the wind had rapidly dispersed the poisonous gases.

"The Italian aircraft then resorted to mustard gas. Barrels of liquid were hurled upon armed groups. But this means too was ineffective. The liquid affected only a few soldiers, and the barrels upon the ground themselves gave warning of the danger to the troops and to the population.

"It was at the time when the operations for the encirclement of Makalle were taking place that the Italian command, fearing a rout, applied the procedure which it is now my duty to denounce to the world.

"Sprayers were installed on board aircraft so that they could vaporize over vast areas of territory a fine, death-dealing rain. Groups of nine, fifteen, eighteen aircraft followed one another so that the fog issuing from them formed a continuous sheet. It was thus that, from the end of January 1936, soldiers, women, children, cattle, rivers, lakes, and fields were constantly drenched with the deadly rain. That was its chief method of warfare.

"These fearful tactics succeeded," the emperor said, pausing for effect. "Men and animals succumbed. The deadly rain that fell from the aircraft made all those whom it touched fly, shrieking with pain."

I remember Marco's first letter, she thought as she fought to get her concentration back to the speech.

"All who drank the poisoned water or ate the infected food succumbed too, in dreadful suffering. In tens of thousands, the victims of the Italian mustard gas fell. None other than myself and my gallant companions in arms could bring the League of Nations undeniable proof. That is why I decided to come myself to testify against the crime perpetrated against my people and to give Europe warning of the doom that awaits it, if it bows before the accomplished fact."

After outlining the events that led to the war, he reminded the delegates again of their solemn commitment.

"In October 1935, the fifty-two nations who are listening to me today gave me an assurance that the aggressor would not triumph. I ask the fifty-two nations not to forget today, the policy upon which they embarked eight months ago, and on the faith of which I directed the resistance of my people against the aggressor. I thought it impossible that fifty-two nations, including the most powerful in the world, could be successfully held in check by a single aggressor. Relying on the faith due to treaties, I made no preparation for war and that is the case with a number of small countries in Europe. When the danger became more urgent, conscious of my responsibilities toward my people, I tried, during the first six months of 1935, to acquire armaments. Many governments proclaimed an embargo to prevent my doing so, whereas the Italian government, through the Suez Canal, was given all facilities for transporting, without cessation and without protest, troops, arms and munitions."

"*Gra. Gra. Gra. Ken Gra,*" Ceseli thought of the barefooted soldiers drilling outside her office window. How many of them had died? How many had survived?

"The Ethiopian government never expected other governments to shed their soldier's blood to defend the covenant when their own immediate personal interests were not at stake. Ethiopian warriors asked only for means to defend themselves. On many occasions, I asked for financial assistance for the purchase of arms. That assistance was constantly denied me. What then, in practice, is the meaning of Article Sixteen of the Covenant and of "collective security?"

"I assert that the issue before the assembly today is a question of "collective security"; of the very existence of the League; of the trust placed by states in international treaties; of the value of promises made to all states, that their integrity and their independence shall be respected and assured. It is a choice between the principle of the equality of States and the imposition upon small powers of the bonds of vassalage. In a word, it is international morality that is at stake."

Beneath her on the floor of the assembly hall, she could see Standish struggling with his own emotions. He looked up at her briefly. Next to her, she could sense that Zeri was moved by the emperor's words. *What is he thinking*, Ceseli wondered of the man who had saved her life?

"In the presence of the numerous violations by the Italian government of all international treaties prohibiting resort to arms and recourse to barbarous methods of warfare, the initiative has today been taken. It is with pain that I record the fact of raising sanctions. What does this initiative mean in practice, but the abandonment of Ethiopia to the aggressor? Is that the guidance that the League of Nations and each of the State Members are entitled to expect from the great powers when they assert their right and their duty to guide the action of the League?

"On behalf of the Ethiopian people," he paused, "a member of the League of Nations, I ask the assembly to take all measures proper to secure respect for the Covenant. I declare before the whole world that the emperor, the government and the people of Ethiopia will not bow before force, that they uphold their claims, that they will use all means in their power to the triumph of right and respect for the Covenant."

Ceseli started to sob thinking of the bombing of the Red Cross and of Marco. Beside her, Zeri took her hand and held it tightly.

"I ask the great powers, who have promised the guarantee of collective security to small States over whom hangs the threat that they must one day suffer the fate of Ethiopia: What measures do they intend to take?"

There was no sign of approval. The diplomats did not applaud. There were some who were obviously embarrassed. Others stared straight ahead, unmoved.

"Representatives of the world," Haile Sellassie paused. "I have come to Geneva to discharge in your midst the most painful of the duties of a head of a state. What answer am I to take back to my people?"

As he stepped down from the rostrum, Haile Sellassie knew that he might have moved his listeners, but that he had failed to galvanize their decisions. He murmured then the words he was to use publicly later: "It is us today. It will be you tomorrow."

Ceseli looked at her emperor. There were tears in her eyes and she did not care as they began rolling down her face. She was crying. She made no effort to hide it. The whole world should be crying. If only. If only what? If only Marco. The "if onlys" were so many. Too many.

ADDIS ABABA—JULY 10, 1941

CESELI LARSON CLIMBED THE steps to the little Ghibbi Palace noticing that it was now finished. Water spewed from the circular fountain and looking up she could see what had been her office window. Addis was no longer a mud and wattle city. In keeping with being the propaganda capital of Italian East Africa, the palace was now covered by stucco and painted a dazzling white, and the front door was now an Italian green. *Only the red of the Italian tri-color flag is missing,* she thought.

She hitched her camera bag higher on her shoulder recognizing how nervous she was by how much she was nibbling at her lower lip. She could almost hear Sotzy telling her not to. Ceseli looked quickly around her. Five years ago she had been used to walking up these steps to the little Ghibbi, greeting the guards and then walking through the hallway and climbing the stairs to her office. Now, she noticed that all the guards had new uniforms, a pistol in their holsters, and wore sandals. None of them knew her.

"*Ezi yemetahute yifrune lemayet new,*" she told the young soldier standing in back of a large desk.

"*Yifru betam sera yebezabet sew new. Anchin yawkeshal?*"

"I know he is busy, and yes. He does know me."

"*Arefe bey,*" he said, pleasantly.

Ceseli looked around for the seat he had asked her to find. She noticed that the yellow halls were now white and some of the floor to ceiling mirrors had been replaced by mural paintings of Roman ruins, including the Arch of Titus.

She felt lucky she had brought a good book with her and dressed for the heat. Now she was increasingly nervous. *Well,* she thought, *I have every reason to be this time.* She straightened the blue linen skirt she was wearing and tugged at the blue and white striped man's shirt that was belted at the waste. Her hair was in a ponytail and she knew that it was neat because she had checked it in the first mirror.

"Ceselí! Ceselí!" Ceseli looked up to see Yohannes striding to her. "Ceselí! It's you! I can't believe it! What brings you back to Addis?" he asked while kissing her three times on the cheek in the French way.

"I've come to see Yifru," she said smiling at him. "You look well."

"I am well. The emperor has appointed me to lead the new military academy. I'm very excited."

"That's wonderful. I'm so happy for you."

"You will have to come to dinner and meet my wife," he said, showing her his gold wedding band. "She will be teaching at the new university. My grandfather is here too. The emperor has put him in charge of the entire school system. Not only in Addis. Oh, and I was in Dessie to fetch my grandfather and I went to find Habtu. He asked for you. He's a fine young man. Was very active with the patriots. They used him as a messenger. I told him that when he was old enough he should come to Addis to our military academy."

"Oh, Yohannes, that's so nice of you. I'm sure he'll be so pleased, and his parents as well. And yes, I'd love to meet your wife."

"I'll take you to Yifru," he said, "although you certainly know the way. Nothing here has changed," he smiled as she followed him up the stairs. *There is something I don't know,* he thought as he opened the door to Yifru's office allowing her to enter and then closing it discreetly behind her.

"Ceseli!"

"I said I would come. You didn't believe me?" she questioned, looking at Yifru.

"Let me look at you," he said, smiling with a twinkle in his eyes. Then he held out his arms and Ceseli moved to him, crooking her head under his chin. As they embraced, Ceseli began to cry. "I'm sorry. It's just that I wondered if this would ever happen."

"It's okay, Ceseli. Cry as much as you want."

"I'm crying because I'm happy."

"I certainly hope so," he said, smiling again.

Ceseli drew back, fishing in her shoulder bag before withdrawing the silk pouch.

"The coins? Did they keep you connected to Ethiopia?" he asked.

"Of course."

"And you've come to see the Ark? I promised you that."

"Yes."

"But not only, I hope."

"No. Not only," she teased.

"I'm thankful for that. Where are you staying?"

"With Daniele at the old U.S. mission. The house was used as the residence of the president of the Banca d'Italia. He left in May. So Daniele said it was empty and that he and his wife would love something to do."

"That house belonged to the Minister of War, Mulugeta. He rented it to the U.S. He and his son were killed. You remember?"

"Yes, of course."

"How long are you staying?"

"I'm not sure," she answered as he held her close. "Sotzy, my grandmother, is here too. She wouldn't hear of letting me come alone. Yifru," she said as she drew back so she could study his eyes. "I need you to meet someone."

"Sotzy?"

"Also. When can you come?"

"As soon as you want."

"Then come for tea. At four."

"I'll be there. Now let me get someone to see you home."

"Daniele is here, but thank you."

The last five years had transformed Addis, she saw as Daniele drove her back to the mission. Wide paved avenues had replaced the mud ones and there were new buildings everywhere, and real street signs. *Daniele is no longer worth his weight in gold*, she thought wondering how her own life had been transformed in these years. In September 1936, she had gone to Rome to start her studies at the American Academy and the time seemed to fly out of her control. She had looked up Bruno Zeri only to find he was covering the civil war in Spain.

Throughout these years, she and Yifru wrote to each other on a frequent basis. She wondered if he waited for her letters with the same intensity that she waited for his. She knew he had been living in exile in Bath, England with the emperor and his family, and she knew under what difficult circumstances.

In the spring of 1940, having completed her dissertation and receiving her degree, Ceseli decided it was now time to go home. She reached New York only days before Italy entered the war, declaring war against England and France, and weeks before Germany invaded France. Soon after she got an encouraging letter from Yifru.

Dearest Ceseli,

We too are going home. I told you eventually we would go home and we are all excited, but very uncertain of how and when. Our position has changed radically since Italy entered the war. We have met several times with

Mr. Churchill who thinks we can invade and recapture Ethiopia. But how? With what troops? In any case we are leaving England tomorrow. You will be able to follow our progress from press accounts.

His last letter had come in March and bore a postmark of Washington, D.C. The diplomatic pouch, she thought as she tore it open. It was dated January 10, 1941

Dearest Ceseli,

I hope this finds you well. We are leaving Khartoum to enter Ethiopia from the village of Um Iddla. Our "army" is terribly small. We have only 100 Britishers, but a remarkable leader. His name is Orde Wingate. He's a Scot. He's betting that Ethiopians have been so badly treated by the Italians that they will join us in a revolt. Another British army will attack Eritrea and more British forces are on the way from Kenya. We have 15,000 camels loaded with arms and ammunition. Many more camels than men I'm afraid.

Take care of yourself.

Yifru

She had reread that letter until it was fraying apart. She had followed his movements until May 5, when Emperor Haile Sellassie reentered Addis on the fifth anniversary of when he had been forced to flee. He restarted his rule.

As Ceseli walked down the wide staircase from her bedroom to the entranceway at exactly four that afternoon, the knocker hit the door.

"I'll answer the door, Daniele," she called towards the kitchen as she opened the door. She smiled at Yifru as he entered holding a bundle of red roses. "They're beautiful, Yifru. Thank you," she said, smelling them.

"They come from the emperor's rose garden, and he sends with them his best wishes and can't wait to see you about the university."

"I'm glad you could come. I'm touched by the emperor's greetings. Let's sit on the verandah." Ceseli said, leading him into the dining room on the way to the terrace.

Yifru stopped. "That's very nice," he said, indicating the painting above the sideboard on the dining room wall.

"My Uncle Warren did it. It is good, isn't it? He painted it in Wyoming, but I've always thought those were the purple mountains of Ethiopia. It always travels with me."

Opening the French doors, Ceseli lead him outside to the veranda where the table was set for tea. "You must be very used to high tea by now," she laughed.

"Actually, no. Every spare dollar, or pound as you will, went to buying arms. Not tea and crumpets." He paused looking out at the garden. "I've never been here before. To Standish's office and the minister's, but not inside the actual residence."

"It's very sparsely furnished, as you can see," she frowned, looking around her. "Not at all as it was with Uncle Warren. He's in London, you know, and Standish is still in Geneva. Sotzy will be here in a moment. She's having a little difficulty with the altitude."

"I wish Warren Rutherford had been in London when we needed him. Probably nothing would have changed, but hope springs eternal," he sighed.

Ceseli sat down smoothing her long shantung silk skirt over her knees. "I almost didn't recognize the city. All these new buildings, the wide streets and avenues. The Italians have done themselves proud. And the parks."

"To build them, they bulldozed all the tukuls that were in the way."

"Yes, I saw that. It's a typical Fascist technique. When Mussolini complained he couldn't see the coliseum from his office window in Piazza Venezia, they bulldozed the entire neighborhood around the coliseum and built a long wide avenue that passed the forum and named it the Imperial Way." Ceseli paused feeling increasingly nervous. "You know they brought my obelisk to Rome. Zeri and I went to see the unveiling. You remember Bruno Zeri? The Italian journalist? It was on the fifteenth anniversary of the Fascist March on Rome. Mussolini was in full dictator form."

A few more minutes passed before tall and erect Frances Sheraton walked out to the verandah dressed in a long, flowery skirt with a white silk tunic. Her white hair was pulled into a neat chignon that framed her face, accentuating her piercing blue eyes.

"I'm Ceseli's grandmother," she said, shaking his hand warmly. "And you must be Yifru. She calls me Sotzy, and I hope you will too."

"Thank you," he said, smiling at her. "My grandmother had eyes like yours. She was British."

"As was mine. You see, we have something in common other than Ceseli."

Then Yifru saw the small child clinging to Sotzy's hand. She was blond, with curly angelic hair floating around her face and wore a light cornflower blue flowered dress that matched her eyes.

Yifru turned to Ceseli. "You never told me?"

Ceseli audibly drew in her breath. "I didn't think it was something I could put in a letter," she explained. "Then it seemed like it was too late."

"What's your name sweetheart?" Yifru asked, smiling at her as he squatted down to be at her level.

"Marca."

"Marca?"

Ceseli smiled. "The feminine of Marco. If my father can create names, why can't I?" Smiling, she added proudly, "And Marca speaks Amharic."

Yifru looked surprised. "Do you?" he asked Marca.

"Awo Amaregna enageralehu, Yifru," she said, timidly rocking from side to side.

"You know my name? Do you know what my name means?"

"Sort of," she answered shyly, now twisting her finger in her hair.

Yifru looked up at Ceseli and smiled at her before continuing. "Marca, I promise you that you will never be afraid of me," he said, taking her hands into his. "But I will call you Meklit," he said, smiling at her. "Do you know what that means?"

"What does Meklit mean?" Ceseli and Sotzy asked at the same time.

"God's gift. She truly is a gift from God."

Yifru rose and went to Ceseli. "You thought she would make a difference to me?"

"I truthfully didn't know," Ceseli said, wiping away a tear, "but hoped she wouldn't."

"Sotzy, does Meklit look like Ceseli did at the same age?" he asked, pleasantly.

"Oh, yes, she certainly does," Sotzy replied, encouragingly. "Very much so. And she has her mother's temperament as well. Beware."

"Warning heard and understood," Yifru smiled openly. "My grandmother used to say a word to the wise is sufficient."

"Mine used the same phrase," Sotzy laughed easily.

"Yifru hugged Ceseli, then held her away from him. "But I assure all three of you that I wouldn't have you any other way. I'll love all three of my ladies," Yifru smiled broadly, holding Ceseli to him. Then he laughed as Ceseli had not seen him do in a long time and nodded his head "Well, indeed, we are going to need those schools, my love, and a very big house. It's good that I am a good promiser."

ACKNOWLEDGMENTS

I AM DEEPLY GRATEFUL to the many people who helped me to get this book published: For my agent, Peter Riva, and his team, for having confidence in this book.

Yohannes Mengesha and Ketema Yifru, my Ethiopian colleagues at the U.N./FAO World Food Programme in Rome, Italy, who in 1985, introduced me to their country for the first time.

Professor Richard and Rita Pankhurst in Addis Ababa, for taking me under their wings and personally taking me to all the places I would have to describe.

Romia Bull Kimball, who helped me devise the harmonica code for Zeri's music on the amount of mustard gas being used to win the war.

Meklit Menkir in New York, who helped me find the right Ethiopian names for my characters.

For my family, children and grandchildren, and the many friends who absorbed with good humor the many numerous changes that went into this final version—some offering advice and others offering good ideas in differing degrees of attachment.